Alexis has that special something about her that Seth can't fathom. His friend Mirabelle's new employee is even prettier than the merchandise she sells. Too bad she's distantly polite when he tries talking to her.

Alexis is attracted to Seth, but she's in hiding from her past and her mistakes. Getting involved with the one person she's attracted to could blow her cover.

When they're forced to work together, their libidos ignite. Alexis is terrified to open up and give in to her feelings for Seth. If he remembers that night five years ago, he'll never speak to her again.

It becomes a question of whether Seth will expose her and force her to keep running, or if he'll help her face her past.

Under Your Scars
Copyright © 2020 V.J. Allison
ISBN: 978-1-4874-2848-8
Cover art by Martine Jardin

Published by eXtasy Books Inc or
Devine Destinies, an imprint of eXtasy Books Inc

Look for us online at:
www.eXtasybooks.com or www.devinedestinies.com

UNDER YOUR SCARS
TRI-TOWN SERIES, BOOK TWO

BY

V.J. ALLISON

DEDICATION

In loving memory of Noreen Frances Hirtle, aka Nanny.
September 20, 1931 – September 17, 2010.

For my husband Aaron, who reminded me to open my mouth for
once instead of keeping it shut.

For my dear friend Maggie Blackbird, who yanked me out of my
shell.

For Denise, Dawn (D.S.), Angie (Taryn), Gabby, Cameron, Curt,
Cheryl, Amy, Jo, Lynn, our beloved owner Tina H., and the rest of
my fellow authors at eXtasy Books and Devine Destinies. Without
all of you, this book and Away to Me would never be.
Thank you all so much for all of your love, support, and advice
since I came out of my shell.

Lastly, for our amazing editors, Trish, Nicki, Jay, and Bri, who
have taught me more with one book than I had learned in ten years.

Tons of love to all of you. ~V.J.

Chapter One

Seth hated taking sleep aids, but he was getting desperate. It had been weeks since he had a decent night's sleep, and today, he needed to concentrate. They were getting measurements for the wall between Mirabelle's shop and the unit next door to expand her store.

He opened the glass and steel door and realized he didn't feel any cool air. *That's right. The air conditioning is turned off so it won't blow around the sawdust. Great. This is going to suck moose balls.* Working in humid conditions wasn't new to him—he worked outside in 30 Celsius plus weather sometimes, with a heat index pushing 40. Working in it when he wasn't at one hundred percent was going to be horrible.

Alexis Graves, Mirabelle's newest employee and friend, sat behind the counter. She was staring at some papers in front of her, and her brow was furrowed as she scribbled something down on a yellow notepad.

Seth had never gotten a good look at her despite meeting her once or twice in the last week. It was time to take more than a fleeting glance or two. Her long dark brown braid curled around her neck and dangled between her small breasts. She leaned her chin on her right hand and tapped the pencil on the pad with her left. Her flowing blouse was a soft lavender, and she wore glasses with subtle gold frames. She shook her head, and a soft tinkle emitted from her silver chandelier earrings before she let out a soft sigh and erased something on the page. His gaze travelled down to her left hand. All but the ring finger were decorated in silver rings of various stones.

She pursed her lips, lifted her head, and blinked in surprise when her gaze met his. Alexis's eyes were a soft brown, the colour of milk chocolate, and they were framed with thick, dark lashes.

Sweat started to form under his arms, his eyes slammed shut, and his mouth went dry as the image of another pair of brown eyes blinking at him overlaid his vision. She looked almost identical to the girl that had been plaguing his dreams. That was why he wasn't sleeping. *Shit.* The bitter taste of bile hit his tongue. He felt his body going left, then right.

"Seth? Are you okay?" A cool hand touched his bare forearm. A soft tingle flowed from her fingers into his skin. It felt odd, and although soothing, added a bit of confusion to his already addled brain. His eyes opened. Alexis was staring at him with wide eyes and her lips parted slightly.

"Yeah," he mumbled and cricked his neck as he moved his gaze from hers. He took a deep calming breath and felt the dizziness start to ease. He could see her staring at him out of the corner of his eye.

"Do you want some water?" she asked. "It's hot out there, and it's going to be worse next door." They were propping open the shop's main door, but not the door to the next-door unit, due to curious passerby. If they were moving something in or out of the unit—equipment or drywall, for example—the door would be open then. No air circulation meant it was going to be a long, hot day. *Fucking meow.*

"I'm fine, thanks. I'll get some later," he replied, and he tried not to smile. Alexis was normally somewhat prickly. The offer wasn't like her. *Maybe she's overcome by my charm?*

She shrugged and pointed to another stool behind the counter. "Blaine may be talking to Mirabelle for a while, so you may as well sit while you can." Blaine was Mirabelle's husband, as well as Seth's best friend. The men were like brothers, and therefore Mirabelle was like Seth's sister. She was also overprotective of Seth and would freak out on him if she saw him out of sorts.

Seth shakily sat down next to Alexis with a nod of thanks.

She gave him a small smile in reply. His gaze was drawn to the soft pink fullness of her mouth. She turned her attention back to the pad in front of her and started doodling again.

After several minutes of waiting, he stretched his neck and tried to hold back a yawn. *At least I'm productive on the nights I can't sleep. I hope Mirrie loves the trim I'm designing for the archway.* Seth wanted this expansion to be perfect for Mirabelle. She loved the thrill of a sale, purchasing unusual merchandise, and chatting with her customers. He'd never tell her, but he was highly uncomfortable in her shop on his best days. It was filled with too many frilly and glass things for his taste. A yawn escaped his mouth without warning.

Alexis glanced at him and turned back to her doodling.

A few minutes later, he let out another one, this one a bit louder than the last. A trickle of sweat ran down his cheek. He wiped it away. *Shit, I'm more tired than I thought. If anyone suggests getting some iced coffee, I'm game.*

Alexis stopped doodling, raised her head, and shot him a dirty look before she started drawing again.

He smiled internally. *She's kind of cute.* Covering his mouth with his hand, Seth yawned for the third time.

Alexis turned her head and gave him a blank look over the top rims of her glasses.

He sheepishly grinned in reply. There was a weird flutter in his gut when she smiled back.

"You didn't sleep well last night, did you?" she asked.

"It's been so damn hot." It was typical July weather for

Nova Scotia. Temps hovered around 28 Celsius with a heat index of 35. The weather wouldn't break for another month. It always started cooling off around mid-August most summers unless there was a hurricane coming up the coast. Seth hoped it would cool down soon. *Maybe then the damn dream would stop harassing me.*

The pencil in her hand made a soft scraping noise as Alexis glided it across the paper. "There's a pot of fresh coffee out back, unless you want something cold to drink."

He grinned. "Are you offering to get me something?"

"Nope." There was a light note in her voice, almost teasing.

He snickered. "I tried."

"Hmm, it was a good one," she replied with a soft giggle.

He didn't miss how she tried hiding her smile by ducking her head. *She is adorable.* His gaze drifted downward, following the line of her thick braid to her arm and hand. Her fingers efficiently guided the pencil in a flowing pattern, like she was creating flowers on the page. He could make out something that resembled leaves. "What are you drawing?"

"Not much, it's an idea I have." Her tone was dismissive.

He stood up to peer at it over her shoulder and caught a whiff of something soft, flowery and feminine when he got close to her. *Damn, she smells as pretty as she looks.* He saw a glimpse of a fairy a second before she quickly flipped the pad over and stared up at him with a filthy look.

"I don't like it when people look over my shoulder," she said defensively with narrowed eyes.

Seth gave her one of his most charming grins. "I can see it from the other stool, and it looks great. Will you please show me?"

Alexis glared at him. "I'd rather not."

"Why not?"

"It's not finished yet." She turned her back to him and leaned her right arm across the pad.

Taken aback that she was able to resist that smile — his best, according to Mirabelle—Seth narrowed his eyes and tried to come up with alternatives. He wanted to see that damn picture, and if he had his way, Alexis would be showing him before Blaine and Mirabelle were done talking. "Are you sure? I always like to get critiques on my work before I finalize it." He added a soft plea to his words.

She glanced at him over her shoulder, and her eyes rolled skyward. "Using the *we're creative pals, so you have to share your work with me* line doesn't work, Seth."

It seemed like she wasn't going to budge after all. Seth should have left it at that. It would have been the smart thing to do. *On the other hand, I would like to see what she's drawing.* He tentatively reached for the notebook. He blamed his actions on the heat and humidity. Or was it the lack of sleep? It could have been her perfume.

The instant his fingers brushed her arm, he knew it was a dumb move. She grabbed the pad, jumped off the stool, and whipped around to face him. Her glare could have melted concrete. It was that nasty. "Mind your own fucking business, Seth Mitchell!" she yelled and shoved his chest, hard, with her left hand.

A voice saying something similar echoed in his mind, and he grimaced as he tried to shake it away. The image of the girl, wearing a black hoodie, covered the canvas of his mind. What in the hell was happening to him, and why did the visions of the girl in the dream keep bothering him that day? It had been her voice he heard, not Alexis's. Bile rose in his throat. *Oh fuck. Don't let me be sick!* He squeezed his eyes shut, weaved in place, and grabbed the counter in hopes of remaining standing. Crashing onto the floor in a faint wasn't his idea of fun.

The subtle perfume hit his senses again, stronger, and he felt a hand on his upper arm as his hands visibly started to shake. "Seth, are you okay?"

Alexis. "I'm not sure." His t-shirt was stuck to his back. *It's not even nine AM, and I'm soaked in sweat. Great.* He took a few shaking breaths to balance himself and wiped his cheek with the back of his wrist.

Her hand, cool and soothing, pressed against his hot forehead. "You're awfully warm."

"I may have gotten overheated. I'll be fine in a minute." For some reason, he was reluctant to admit how her defensiveness and prickly attitude had affected him. He opened his eyes to meet her gaze. Her forehead was wrinkled in what he hoped was concern, and her soft brown eyes peered up at him for a long moment. Her cool fingers brushed his chin and forehead before she briefly cupped his cheek in her hand.

Seth relaxed and resisted the sudden urge to lean into the caress. *She's six inches shorter than I am.* He was six-foot-one, meaning Alexis was closer to five-foot-seven inches. She was the perfect height for a man his size to kiss. *Where the fuck did that come from?* He shook it off and smiled, his way of conveying he was fine without words.

She smiled back, although the furrow between her brows didn't disappear. "Stay here." She walked to the back area and went into the doorway.

He swallowed hard a few times, and the fog started to lift. The nausea started abating, too. *Thank fuck. I thought I was going to throw up on her shoes.*

Alexis returned a scant moment later, a bottle of water in her hand that was covered in condensation. He took it with a nod of thanks and cracked it open. A shot of icy goodness slid down his throat as he took a long gulp.

"Is that better?" Alexis asked.

"Yeah, thanks," he replied and took another swig.

She gave him a quick, shy smile and nodded.

Mirabelle flew into the main area with Blaine on her heels. "Seth Mitchell, you get back into my office and lie down!" she snapped.

"Mirrie, I'm fine, I—"

"Now!" She pointed toward the staff area, located in the back.

"What about the—"

"Shut up and listen to me, damn you!" she hissed. A few tendrils of her curly blonde hair stuck to her sweaty face.

He nodded sheepishly and got up. It took a lot of effort to walk to the employee's area without falling on his face. Somehow he kept the shaking under control, and although he allowed one yawn during the trek, he didn't waver. The last thing he needed was another bawling out from Mirabelle, and she would really give it to him if he didn't pretend he was fine.

Mirabelle muttered, "That man hasn't taken good care of himself ever since Janie left."

He flipped her the finger over his shoulder.

Seth shifted to his other side on the short, uncomfortable sofa in Mirabelle's office and sighed when a spring poked him in the ribs. *I hope she gets a new one when we're done with the renovations. I feel like I'm lying on a bed of rocks.* He propped an arm under his head and wiped the sweat from his brow. *Fuck, it's hot back here.* At least he wasn't out front, where the sun hit the windows. Someone could easily get heatstroke if they were out front for too long without the shades pulled down.

Seth glanced at the clock hanging above the office door. He had been back there for over an hour. *It feels more like three hours in this humidity, and lying on this piece of garbage makes it feel even longer.* He grunted and grimaced as he shifted to a less painful position.

Alexis poked her head into the office.

He greeted her with a pained grin.

"You scared her." Alexis leaned her shoulder on the door jamb and hooked her thumbs into the front pockets of her faded blue jeans. They were almost skin-tight, and they moulded to her slim, almost boyish shaped legs perfectly.

Mentioning his best friend's wife was the perfect way to distract him from Alexis's appealing body. "Mirrie worries too damn much," he muttered and sat up with a groan.

Alexis snorted. "Be glad you can't hear her. She's spouting off how a man needs someone to take care of him, and a lot of other shit. Blaine's getting an earful."

"Better him than me," Seth grumbled around a snicker.

Alexis giggled, and her eyes lit up behind her glasses. "Are you feeling better?"

He loved to hear her laugh. "I am, thanks. Am I allowed to get up? I'm here to work, not lie on this stupid couch." *Please let me get up, Mirrie. I feel like I've run twenty marathons.*

"I think she'll let you up once she sees you're fine. It's cooler back here than it is out front. I have to come back here for a few minutes between customers, so I don't get sick."

"I can see why," he mumbled and stretched his neck. *Ouch, that fucking hurts. Fuck it. I'm buying Mirabelle a brand new couch when the renovations are done, one that turns into a bed. That way, if anything like this happens again, I won't feel like I've been stoned half to death. Christ!*

The chime above the door jingled, and Alexis let out a sigh. "I'd better go see who that is."

She disappeared, and Seth suddenly felt odd without her there. With a shake of his head, Seth realized he liked her a lot. *Being standoffish makes her even more adorable.* His gaze lingered on the door. His reaction to her was a mystery.

Late that afternoon, Seth held a measuring tape along a piece of wood he was prepping for carving when something blocked the light from the doorway.

His gaze moved upwards to meet Alexis's. The noise from Cody's work on the table-saw made it too hard to talk. Seth nodded and waved to her, tossing in one of his most charming grins.

Alexis smiled back, not as widely, and returned the wave.

Good. She sees I'm okay, and I've put in a lot of work. Maybe with a little luck, I won't have any more episodes like I had this morning. Their gazes locked for a moment before she turned and walked away. Her perfume hit his nostrils over the scent of sawdust and lingered long after she disappeared from view.

Friday morning
Seth's Bedroom, Wileville, Nova Scotia

"Jesus Christ!" The pillows flew off the bed as Seth's body shot upwards, a crushing sensation on his chest and his scream echoing in the room.

The image of the young woman, sitting in the corner of the grey room, stabbed his mind and lingered despite blinking several times and shaking his head. Sweat dripped into his eyes, which burned his corneas, and it soaked the sheet beneath him. His throat felt like it was full of concrete. It was so hard to breathe. Nausea rumbled in his throat. He swallowed several times to keep it at bay, grateful he hadn't eaten anything strongly flavoured for supper. *Barfing up something like lobster isn't my idea of fun.*

He grunted a few times and tried to get out of bed. The top sheet was tangled around his legs, which made him stumble. Finally he was able to untangle himself and chuck the damn thing in the corner, away from the bed. He let out a long sigh and stared at the green numbers on the clock. 2:47 AM. Anyone in their right minds would be asleep this early in the morning. He wiped more sweat away from his eyes as he tried to make sense of everything. *What the fuck is going on? Who is that girl? Why do I keep dreaming about her? She's not real. Or is she?*

Something tingled at the back of his mind. He tried catching it, but it eluded him. With a shrug, Seth stood up and started stripping the bottom sheet off the bed. *I may as well wash them. I won't be sleeping anymore tonight — fucking dream.*

Later that morning, he and Blaine arrived at the store early. Like Thursday, Alexis was sitting on a stool behind the counter with her drawing pad in front of her and a pencil in her hand. She glanced up with a smile and a nod in greeting and turned back to her work. Blaine went toward the back again, and Seth made sure he stayed away from the front part of the store.

Seth let his gaze wander over Alexis while he waited. Yesterday's lavender blouse had looked amazing on her, but that soft blue t-shirt really caught his eye. One eyebrow went upwards in masculine appreciation as his gaze followed the line of her small breasts. The sudden twitch of admiration from other, sexual parts of his body came as a surprise. *Hey! She's not my type, don't go there! Focus on your work, dumbass. Jesus.*

Seth moved toward the side of the store that was cleared to let the men work as a way to keep his mind focused on his job. They were creating the archway halfway toward the back, on the opposite side from the checkout counter. *It looks great. I didn't realize they were clearing out the area while we were busy in the other part yesterday. Good.* He examined the wall to be sure they had the correct measurements. *Mirrie wants at least a foot between the top of the arch and the ceiling. We can do it.* His gaze followed the lay of the ceiling, looking for any uneven areas. *This old place was built in the 1950s, but it's good and sturdy. I don't see any flaws we have to watch out for.* He reached into his pocket for the stud finder, and with an inward sigh, he realized Blaine had it. So much for getting that out of the way. He dug his drawing pad out of a pocket on his carpentry apron, so he could work on the trim design while he waited.

A whiff of the same flowery scent he remembered from Thursday hit his nostrils. He wasn't expecting to talk to Alexis much that day due to the noise. Plus, he was expecting her to be busy with customers most of the day. "Morning, Alexis," he said without looking up from his pad.

"Hi. I thought you two had the measurements for here already," she replied.

He spared her a glance and shrugged. "We do, but Mirrie asked me if I could design some trim for the arch. I wanted to get a better look at it from this side. That way, I know what would look great and get a feel to make it look good for all parts of the store." He peered at the wall for a moment, made an adjustment in the drawing and stared at the wall again. Something was missing. What was it?

Alexis was quiet, and he could feel her watching him. "May I take a peek? I know what she has in mind. If you get it right the first time, it'll be less work for you."

"I'm not done yet," he replied and moved a foot away from her.

"Come on, don't be chicken. I promise I won't laugh." There was a coaxing note in her soft voice. It sounded like honey to Seth's ears.

Damn, I love her voice when she talks like that. But I can't give in, not after the way she acted on Thursday. She wants to look? Fine with me. Game on, girl! He snapped the pad shut and grinned evilly and dangled the notepad above his head. "Come and get it." He batted his eyelashes at her and backed up a step.

Her eyes narrowed, and there was a challenge in her dark irises. "Don't even try it," she muttered and tried to reach it.

He wanted to tease her a bit, to see if he could get her to open up more and to show her that messing with him wasn't a great idea. He backed up a couple more steps toward the main door and dangled it in front of his face. "You're not seeing it until I see what you were doing yesterday." He added a taunting note to emphasize his point.

She smirked. "Don't start something with me, Mitchell, because you won't win."

They stared at each other for several heartbeats, two opponents locked in mock combat. Alexis sprung at him again.

11

Seth barely had time to evade it. Her slim, firm body collided with his, and the image of the girl in his dream hit him, which made him a little woozy. *She's not the dream girl. Alexis is real. Focus on teasing her!* The vision disappeared, and with it, the dizziness. He backed up another step and felt the door behind his back. "Come and get it," he sneered jokingly and held it at arm's length as he physically prepared for another dive.

She smiled slyly a split second before she jumped at it. He yanked it out of her reach with a snicker.

"Prick." Behind the lenses of her glasses, her eyes twinkled with merriment.

"Be nice, or you won't see it at all," he said with a tone of mirth.

With a roll of her eyes, she shrugged, folded her arms across her chest, and turned away. "If that's the way you're going to be, fine. I can wait until it's done." She stuck her nose in the air and marched primly back to the counter.

Seth chuckled because he knew he had won that round.

"Show me yours, and I'll show you mine." She giggled and held up her closed notepad.

He sighed and grimaced. He was as curious about her drawing as she was of his, and he knew if he made a dive for her pad, she'd really let him have it.

They stared at each other across three feet of crowded space. She was grinning devilishly, her cheeks were flushed, and there was suppressed laughter in her stance, which made her more endearing. He tried to keep his mirth in check, but it was a losing battle. He could feel it in his chest, rising in his throat, about to explode.

At the same moment, their mutual amusement broke free in a joint round of laughter. Seth leaned back against the door and held his stomach as Alexis used the counter for support.

Her laugh was high-pitched, and it sounded sweet to his

ears. "Stalemate?" she gasped after a minute between giggles.

"Stalemate," he agreed with a snicker.

They exchanged a playful grin, and she flopped down on the stool behind the counter.

A moment later, Mirabelle and Blaine started walking toward the front of the store.

"See you two later," Seth called on his way out with a wave, following the bear-like Blaine.

"Yeah, later, Seth." Alexis still had a giggle in her voice.

Damn, what a great way to start off a day.

He exited, and with a mental snicker, he started wondering how much he could tease her before she really let him have it.

Later that morning, Blaine came into the store with an electric saw in his hand. "Sorry, but we're going to be invading your space for a bit," he said apologetically.

Alexis nodded and closed her notebook. She knew this part was coming, and although she didn't like the noise, she was relieved Blaine was doing it. She had seen way too much of Seth over the last two days. He was too friendly and way too sexy for her comfort. "It's a necessary evil. Let me know if you need me for anything."

"You can keep the customers out of our way." Blaine smiled at her. His reddish-brown beard and shaggy hair made him look like a cuddly bear when he smiled, even with the safety glasses and while wearing his carpentry belt, loose jeans and a stained grey t-shirt.

"Gotcha." She gave him a thumbs-up. The bell over the door tinkled again, and when she glanced at the newcomer, her insides did a tailspin. Despite his open, easy smile, her relaxed grin snapped into a coolly polite expression when she saw Seth. *Like I have enough distractions without adding him to the mix?*

"Hi, Alexis," Seth drawled with a smile.

Thankfully, she was spared returning his casual greeting when Mirabelle came out of the office. "Alexis, flip the sign to closed for the day and put a note on the door saying why. It's not like we're fighting off a crowd. Everyone is at the exhibition. I forgot to tell you to do that yesterday and to take the day off. My mind's been on other stuff." She turned to her husband. "Since Alexis is here, we're going to take inventory while you get the hole cut. Don't break anything!"

Alexis ran off to do her boss' bidding, grateful she wouldn't be tortured by having Seth in her line of vision the rest of the day. She grabbed her drawing pad and pencil on her way back to the small, cramped storage area. It was hotter back there, but cleaner. *An iced tea would hit the spot. Maybe I'll make a coffee run for everyone, just to get out of this heat.*

Mirabelle walked into the room and closed the door.

Alexis began to breathe easier. Good, now she wouldn't hear Seth talking.

Her boss handed her a clipboard with a long list fastened to it. "I'll search the boxes while you take notes," she said with a wink.

Alexis hated counting and math in general, and Mirabelle knew it. "Thanks," she replied with a grin. "We didn't sell any of the glass bowls yet? I thought they were gorgeous."

Mirabelle frowned. "Um, I think one of Seth's cousins bought one for a friend of hers that's getting married." She did a quick count. Her manicured fingernails sported pink roses on a yellow background this week, while last week's had been a green, blue, and gold plaid pattern. "Yes, one of them is gone."

Alexis vaguely remembered a blonde woman talking to Seth outside, and how he introduced her as his cousin. "His cousin's name is Gina, and I think it's her friend Neil that was getting married. He's a freelance writer."

Mirabelle glanced at Alexis over the top of her reading glasses. "Yes, that's it. Great memory. His girlfriend's name is

Kelsey. She's been in here a few times on her way home from taking his daughter to Art Happening. They're really nice."

The whine of a saw echoed through the door.

Alexis had a vision of Seth holding a saw above his head, with his muscles playing beautifully under his tight green t-shirt and his form-fitting jeans. She grimaced and blinked to dispel that image. *Not going there! He's the one guy in the area you cannot go around much. What if he remembers?*

Mirabelle glanced at the door. "It sounds like the men have started."

Alexis shrugged and hoped her boss hadn't noticed her frown a moment earlier. "I guess."

"How are you fitting in? Are you making any friends yet? That's twenty-five of the crystal dog ornaments." Mirabelle closed the box and opened another one.

Alexis scribbled the number down and sighed. *I know she means well, but good fucking grief.* Leave it to Mirabelle to start in on her about growing roots when she was unable to escape. Alexis resisted the urge to bang her head on the wall and shrugged.

"Well?" The large blue eyes twinkled behind Mirabelle's glasses.

Alexis rolled her eyes and mumbled, "I haven't had a lot of time for socializing." *There, I admitted it. Shut up, Mirrie!*

"Uh, huh," Mirabelle murmured, and her expression brightened after a moment. "A bunch of us are going to the exhibition this evening. Do you want to tag along? It's not all couples. There are a few single people that go, too."

Alexis's brow wrinkled as she thought about it. She wanted to check out the largest event of the year in Lunenburg County but hadn't because she didn't want to go alone. From what she'd heard from customers, it was a lot of fun, and there were a lot of interesting things at the fair. There were farm animals, a midway, lots of crafts on display, several competitions, lots of locally produced food, and even the International Ox Pull between teams from eastern Canada and the New England States. It sounded like it was a great spot to have fun and not be noticed in a crowd. She grinned at her boss. "Sure, count me in, thanks. When and where do we meet?"

"We're meeting inside the front gate, by the First Aid Station, at seven o'clock. Wear jeans and sneakers because it can be dirty, and you're going to be doing a lot of walking," Mirabelle replied airily.

Alexis nodded and turned back to taking notes. *This is going to be awesome!*

CHAPTER TWO

Friday Evening
South Shore Exhibition, aka The Big Ex
Top of Dufferin Hill, Bridgewater, Nova Scotia

The smell of animals, food, and other scents clashed as the throb of twenty different songs boomed together with human and animal chatter, and lights from the midway flashed and sparkled in the evening light. The sun was still high in the sky in its descent toward the west, and a soft, cooling breeze eased the blanket of heat and humidity that lay over the small riverside town.

In Alexis's opinion, Bridgewater was a gem on the gorgeous LaHave River. The exhibition grounds were at the top of Dufferin Hill, away from the river that the town straddled, and across the street from what locals called the West Side Plaza. The plaza was a familiar sight to Alexis, and she shopped at the chain department store on the far side of the plaza. There was also a home improvement store and a large-chain coffee shop on the other side of Dominion Street, which graced the other side of the plaza. The centre of the spacious parking lot, where no store could claim was for their customers only, was packed with cars. Alexis assumed it was people who didn't want to pay the fare for parking in the lot across from the grounds on Exhibition Drive, by the nursing home.

She let out a long sigh, grateful she'd worn comfortable sneakers as Mirabelle had suggested. It was a bit of a hike from the opposite end of the parking lot to the Main Entrance, all uphill. *I hope Mirrie doesn't mind sitting down for a coffee or iced drink after we go on some rides. That was quite a walk!* She paid her entrance fee and pushed her way through the gates. As she looked around, her gaze landed on Blaine almost right away.

Mirabelle saw her and waved. With a glance around, Alexis recognized Jerry and Norma Zink, along with Wayne and Kathy Nixon. With an inward groan, she saw Seth was the eighth person, and she wondered what had happened to Angie, Mirabelle's cousin who was supposed to be there, too.

"Brody is sick," Mirabelle explained. Brody was Angie's ten-year-old son and was always into mischief of some sort. "I guess he ate too much junk this afternoon and threw up all over his father's car."

Alexis cringed. "I was hoping to see her this evening." *Shit. Is that why Seth is here, too, or was he a part of the group from the start, and Mirrie kept her yap shut?* She kicked at the gravel beneath her feet — a touch annoyed that her boss hadn't mentioned Seth.

"You two can gossip and catch up later on when her kids aren't pulling off stunts like that. I think he did it deliberately so she couldn't go have a night of fun without him," Mirabelle replied.

They headed toward the Midway, the smells of hot dogs, hamburgers, and fries mingling with the scent of horses and other livestock drifting along the breeze that came from the more central parts of the grounds. The Midway itself was on the outer edge of the area, facing Dufferin Street, and a lot of the trailers banked the stainless-steel fence separating the grounds from the street.

It was crowded, noisy, and the smell of manure wafted through the air a few times, but Alexis was in heaven. Her gaze landed on a cotton-candy stand. *I am getting a bag or two to take home. I love cotton candy!* Other food trucks gave way to games, from Bingo to races, and shooting games. *This is awesome! I'm so glad I decided to tag along, even with Seth here.* She mentally kicked herself when her gaze flicked toward him, and she forcefully turned her head away. *Why does he have to look so damn sexy, even when he's covered in sawdust?* Her gaze was drawn back to him, a tall, lean figure in a brown leather jacket, black button-down shirt, hiking boots, and faded, form-fitting jeans that hugged his muscular ass and legs perfectly. His dark brown hair was ruffled from the breeze, and his deep blue eyes seemed almost navy in the fading light.

Ugh, why him? Why do I have to be attracted to the one guy in the area who will expose my past if he remembers? She let out a long sigh and switched her focus to the rest of the Midway. They passed the Merry-Go-Round blasting its country music, which made Alexis flinch. She hated the genre. She smiled when they passed the Orbiter and its modern rock music. *Much better.* More rides became visible, and excitement rose in Alexis's chest when she saw some of her favourite rides, like the Scrambler, the large Gondola-style Ferris wheel, and her favourite of all, the Zipper.

"You look like a kid in a candy store." Seth's deep, rich voice penetrated her senses.

Damn, he could woo the meanest of people when he talks like that. She grinned up at him, almost skipping in happiness. "I haven't been on some of these rides in years. I can't decide what I want to go on first."

They got in line for a bracelet, a one-time fee that let them go on as many rides as they wanted until closing at midnight, almost five hours away. With coupon prices being high, and a lot of the adult rides requiring at least three to four per time, it helped, a lot.

Alexis wondered if that was why they'd gone that night instead of Saturday, when it was a *toonie*—two dollars—per ride, even though that wasn't overly expensive in today's prices.

"Let's try that one first, just to get our feet wet," Mirabelle suggested.

Alexis followed Mirabelle's finger, which was pointing at a funhouse housed in a trailer. She saw a plexiglass maze at the bottom of it, and when she looked up at its second level, she saw a rope bridge, along with the tops of mirrors. The trailer shook as people walked around inside of it. Sounds of laughter, excited screaming, and the pump of loud electronic music surrounded them as they walked up the steps into the start of the maze.

Alexis was the last to enter it, right behind Seth. She smiled as she remembered the trick to get through the glass maze and kept her eyes on the floor. An opening was indicated by no reflections from the floor or her white and green sneakers on the plexiglass. She neatly stepped through and heard a thump followed by a grunt. She glanced around and didn't see anything unusual. There was a small group of teenagers behind her, but they were too busy laughing to pay attention to her.

A moment later, she heard a louder bang and an annoyed-sounding sigh. She looked up again and realized she couldn't see Mirabelle or the others through the various planes of clear plastic. Only Seth was ahead of her, and he was moving at a snail's pace. The temptation to push him so he'd move faster rose within her. *Why is he going so fucking slowly? The others are probably through the maze now and upstairs. They're not going to like waiting.*

Her urge to shove past him was quashed when she saw him take a step forward into an obvious panel of clear plastic. He hit it face first and pulled back with a shake of his head, then glared at it in disgust. Seth held up a hand and turned to his left. His hand hit a panel with a loud whack. He let out a long sigh, and his cheeks turned red.

She held back a giggle as he repeated the motions and almost cheered when he found the next opening. She followed him through, and when he hit another panel, she snickered.

He shot her a dirty look over his shoulder. "What are you laughing at?"

"Nothing," she replied airily. *Normally, I'd be annoyed, but this is really funny. I never thought Seth would be the kind of guy that walked into glass walls. He seems like the type that breezes through something like this because he's so put together.* It somehow made him seem more human to her and more likeable. *Damn, there I go again. Focus on helping him, and stop drooling on his boots.*

"If you're only staying with me to watch the fun, I'm going to turn around and get out of here," he muttered irritably and motioned for her to go ahead of him.

Seth turned around and walked into another wall. She winced in sympathy. He glared at it with fisted hands, and his face was a bright shade of crimson.

Maybe it's not so funny after all. He looks pissed. I guess I should help him. He has been sweet to me, and it's the least I can do. "I don't desert a friend in need," she said quietly. She linked her arm through his and tugged him toward the next opening. "If I leave you alone, you'll be in here all night and won't have any fun."

She felt him hang back, and a moment later, a tingle of pleasure ran up her arm as his fingers entwined with hers. She squeezed his hand and felt a strong and warm pressure in return. Holding his hand wasn't smart, but she relished the sensation of his calloused fingers caressing hers. A feeling of safety flooded her body, unlike anything she had felt in her life when she stood this close to a man. She forced the feelings aside and pointed to the floor with her free hand. "Look for reflections," she whispered, so the people behind them couldn't hear her. "See how there's no reflection in this spot? That's an opening." She stepped through, leading the way.

They came to another intersection. "Try it now." She stared up at him and smiled.

Their gazes locked, and another tingle zinged through her,

this time hitting her stomach. *God, he has such a gorgeous smile.* His full lips hinted a sensuality that made her insides shake with desire. *Shit. I can't think that way about him. He's helping his best friend renovate Mirabelle's store. We're colleagues at best.*

Seth looked down, and for the first time, he walked through the opening without hitting a piece of plexiglass.

Triumph surged in Alexis's gut. She tried pulling her hand out of his, but it wasn't happening. His fingers were tangled around hers, and he wasn't letting her move. It was a larger taste of the exquisite torture she was enduring at the store, having him nearby. She felt some sexual attraction toward him, but the more she was around Seth, the more she liked him as a person. *He's a friend! Remember that!* They exited the maze and headed up the steel stairway to the second level.

"Ha, look at this," Seth said and pointed to the crazy, warped mirrors to their right.

Alexis grinned. She tugged on Seth's hand to pull him closer to one and laughed when she saw her reflection stretched to a full seven-feet tall and less than six-inches wide. "This is awesome!"

He pulled her to the next one. "Oh god, this one makes us look fat!" Sure enough, their reflections made them look less than one-foot tall but four-feet wide.

The third and last one was the weirdest. It warped their faces and bodies into something unrecognizable. "I don't think it likes us," Seth murmured around a snicker.

Alexis narrowed her eyes and stared at the mirror. "I think you're right."

She felt his arm lean into hers for a moment before he tugged on her fingers. "Let's get going, so Mirrie doesn't send out a search party."

Alexis gave Seth the lead through the second half of the maze, plexiglass like the first part. He only hit three panels the entire trip. Alexis was proud of him for making great progress. The warmth of his grasp left hers as they exited the trailer and walked down the stairs to the midway grounds, which sent a shot of unwelcomed disappointment into her gut. *He's a pal, and he's grateful you helped him, nothing more.*

Blaine gave them an odd look when they approached the remainder of the group. "What took you two so long?"

Seth's cheekbones started to turn red.

Alexis realized his friend didn't know about his lack of navigation skills in a maze. "I couldn't find my way through, and Seth was helping me."

"Yeah, watching her go face-first into a few panels wasn't pretty," Seth muttered.

Alexis barely held back the urge to stomp on his foot.

"Let's get moving," Kathy suggested, and they started heading toward another ride.

Alexis hung back, willing to follow the rest of the group's lead. Seth fell into step beside her. "Thanks," he murmured when the group was a bit ahead of them.

"You can pay me back later." She slyly grinned at him.

His warm, mint-scented breath brushed her cheek as he whispered in her ear, "Damn straight, I will."

A shiver of pleasure shot up her spine, lodging in her core. *Shit, why does his voice turn me on so much?* A woman could orgasm listening to his smooth tones. Alexis had never heard such a soft sensuality in a man's voice before she met him.

Seth moved ahead of her, which gave her the perfect view of his backside. *He's going to be the death of me or my vibrator!*

Alexis's shoulders slumped as they got into line for her favourite ride, the Zipper. Everyone else had a partner but her, and Seth was hanging back. *Why isn't he going on it? Damn, I wish there was a ninth, so I had a partner.* Since it was recommended that two people go into one car together for safety reasons, she had to wait until the next round, when someone would be able to go on it with her. She kicked at the gravel beneath her sneakered foot and tried to hide her disappointment.

"What's wrong, Alexis?" Mirabelle asked.

She sighed. "I don't have a partner for this ride. It's my favourite."

Mirabelle frowned. "Seth, why don't you go on with Alexis, so she doesn't have to wait?"

Alexis glanced at Seth and smiled eagerly.

Seth's face paled. "Uh, Mirrie, I don't think—"

"If I say please, will you do it?" Alexis asked. When he smiled nauseatingly, she added a little more urgently, "Pretty please with a cherry on top?"

He stared down at her for a long moment and sighed. "All right," he muttered and took her elbow as he guided her into the lineup behind Kathy and Norma.

Alexis linked her arm through his and grinned triumphantly. As they got closer and closer to the start of the lineup, Seth became quiet.

She glanced up at him. "You okay?"

He nodded, his face a little pale. "I'm fine. Let's get this over with."

She shrugged and focused on the heavy metal music blaring from the speakers by the Zipper's entrance while they waited. Alexis hummed along to songs she recognized and tapped her foot to the beat of one she didn't know.

A few minutes later, she crawled into the blue mesh cage and was getting comfortable as Seth slowly got in beside her. The operator secured the door, and as the ride lurched forward, she grinned. They stopped as the next cages were filled, and as the ride rolled forward again, she heard a strange sound to her right. Puzzled, she glanced at Seth, and her grin faded as she took in his pale face, how his eyes were squeezed tightly shut, and that his fingers were tightly locked around a safety bar in front of them. "Are you okay?"

"I'm fine," he muttered between clenched teeth and winced as their cage wobbled.

I've never seen anyone turn bright green before. Concern for him shot up Alexis's spine. "Are you sure? I can yell out that you want to get off, and I can go on with Mirrie or Norma later." She felt his side stiffen as the ride started moving.

He shook his head, marginally. "I'm on the damn thing now, no point in bothering anyone. I can handle it for a few minutes."

"Yeah, right, and I'm the Queen of England," she shot back sarcastically as their car went into its first loop.

Seth let out a long, pained groan.

Alexis's worry increased. "You know, if you opened your eyes, you wouldn't mind it so much."

"I can't. I'll throw up if I do that." His jaw was tight, and his face was alternating between green and white.

"If this ride makes you sick, why did you come on it with me?" she asked.

"I owed you one for the maze," he ground out, and his knuckles turned white as their cage started swinging back and forth.

Alexis felt guilty that his stubborn male pride forced him to repay a favour and sighed softly. "You can win a huge teddy bear at a game for me later. Open your eyes, Seth. Keeping them closed will only make you feel worse. Trust me." Her hand covered his.

His eyes opened to thin slits and shot dark blue fire at her.

She kept her gaze locked on his and rubbed the back of his hand with her thumb. "How's that?"

Seth groaned miserably in reply.

"Open them a bit more, and don't look anywhere else but at me." *Jesus, he really hates heights. Poor man. Why did I drag him on this? I should've known something wasn't right when he didn't get into line with the rest of us right away.*

His eyes cracked a little more, just as their cage made another three-sixty. He shuddered so hard that Alexis could feel the cage shaking. She tightened her grip on his hand and pressed her arm and leg into his. She smiled when she felt some of the tension leave his body. "Better?"

"Yeah." He leaned into her more, and their foreheads touched. "Keep talking, Alexis."

"About what?"

"You. I want to know more about you." His voice was a bare whisper, soft against the evening.

A shiver of something travelled down her spine as his deep, rich voice and the subtle, spicy and purely male scent of his aftershave filled her senses. She snuggled closer to his side. "What do you want to know?"

"Whatever you want to tell me. I don't care if it's about your favourite hockey team or your cat, just keep talking to me." He let go of the bar and turned his hand. His fingers entwined with hers.

She squeezed his fingers as the ride rumbled to a stop and started moving in the other direction. "I don't have a cat, but I love them," she began and started to ramble about the cat she'd had when she was a child, just to keep him focused on positive things and not on the fact they were spinning around in a small cage held to the ride by only a short three-inch wide steel bar.

When they lurched to a stop at the top of the ride as other passengers were let off below them, his head fell to her shoulder. She rested her cheek on his dark, thick hair. Tension started to ooze out of his body, and he only stiffened as the ride started moving again.

"It's almost over," she murmured soothingly and touched his cheek with her free hand.

He sighed softly and rubbed his cheek along her shoulder.

She could feel the heat of his breath against her neck.

Goosebumps created a warm and happy tingle along her nerve pathways. *Jesus, he smells nice, and his hair is so soft, too.* She let out a long breath and fought the urge to hug him close. *I won't be dragging him on anything else, and I owe him for doing this. I'll do something for him, even if it means no more rides for me tonight.*

Seth didn't fully relax until he saw they were closer to the ground and were to be unloaded next. He lifted his head from Alexis's shoulder and smiled sheepishly. "I owe you one," he murmured and pressed his forehead to hers again.

"No, you don't. I shouldn't have dragged you on the ride, so I owe *you* one." The ride shook as passengers crawled into the cages below them. *He didn't flinch, that's good.*

"You made up for it by keeping me from making a fool out of myself."

"Call it a stalemate then, because I still think I owe you one."

He grinned. "Deal."

Their gazes locked for a long second. Alexis saw that his eyes were not a full navy. The right one had a few green specks in it, and the left had paler blue spokes. His lashes were thick, dark, and long.

He nuzzled his face against hers as the ride moved again. Alexis closed her eyes when she felt his breath against her lips.

The ride came to a shaky stop, and a few clanks echoed in her ears.

"Everyone out. Good to see no one puked in your car," the attendant quipped.

Oddly disappointed the ride had ended without a kiss, Alexis followed Seth out of the ride.

"Yeah, sure," Seth muttered. He looped an arm around Alexis's shoulders.

She slid an arm around his waist and led him away from the exit to wait for the rest of the group. It felt amazing to be in his arms, even for a moment.

"How are you now?" she asked after a minute.

He let out a long breath. "Better, now that I have both feet on the ground again."

"Good." She smiled up at him.

His lips brushed her ear, and his breath was warm against her cheek. "If you ever drag me on that damn thing again, I'll do something you won't like," he murmured.

A shiver of delight went up her spine. She grinned, feeling a dare coming on. "Like what?" she asked innocently.

"I'll throw up on your shoes."

She pulled back and stared up at him over the top of her glasses. "Just for that, I should tell Blaine about how you almost puked on the ride."

Seth rolled his eyes skyward. "If I try to win a big stuffed animal for you, will that shut you up?"

She grinned triumphantly. "It'll do."

Seth was grateful for Alexis's help during their walk through the Fun House, and especially more so after he almost fainted while they were on the Zipper. *I am so glad I didn't throw up on her. It would have been even more humiliating.*

He stuck close to Blaine and Mirabelle as much as he could, but sometimes it was just him and Alexis waiting for the others. She seemed to be taking everything in stride, and she didn't mention his previous embarrassments to their companions. After checking out the Scrambler and the Ferris Wheel, Blaine suggested they walk around the grounds and take a break from the Midway.

There were various vendors in the Main Building, close to Dufferin Street, and by the Midway — from clothing to insurance, belts and other leather accessories, and finally, the delectable choices of food booths in the large main building.

Alexis purchased one item — a pair of handmade bead and

porcupine quill earrings. Pink, of course. She wore that colour more than anything else.

Seth found a new belt buckle at a booth, while Mirabelle was fascinated with what a trinket vendor had for wares.

"Checking out the competition?" Blaine asked when they left the Main Building.

Mirabelle shrugged. "I was hoping to get a few names for contacts. The one selling the crystal ornaments had amazing stock. They may sell well during tourist season."

Seth chuckled and shook his head. Leave it to Mirabelle to try wheeling and dealing even on her time off. His feet were starting to hurt in his boots by the time they started the long trek back into the Midway, past a few food and ticket booths, the Bingo game and other versions of Midway fun.

They closed in on the Orbiter, a fast, stomach-churning ride, with six arms of three cars that spun from a central hub. As the cars spun, the arms extended, going up and down as it twirled, sometimes hitting speeds of 50 miles per hour or more, and only the bravest of souls dared to try it. Seth hung back. So did Blaine, Wayne, and Jerry.

"Blaine? You're not going on this one?" Mirabelle asked.

He shook his head. "I'm crazy, but I ain't stupid. The Zipper was bad enough. That thing is a fucking death trap," he said around a laugh and pointed to the ride.

Mirabelle rolled her eyes at her husband and muttered, "You're a bloody chicken. Fine. I'll go on it with Alexis. She knows how to have fun."

Alexis grinned. "That sounds great to me."

They got in line behind Kathy and Norma, and the four women started chatting, their voice unheard over the din. Seth saw their mouths moving and Mirabelle shaking in what he assumed was laughter from time to time.

Seth was relieved no one asked him to go on it. His stomach was still churning from his experience on the Zipper. *Like Blaine said, it's a fucking death trap. I'd puke for sure on that one.*

He hoped no one tried dragging him on another ride unless it was the Merry Go Round. He didn't think his guts could handle it. He didn't say much and listened to the other men chat about the price of gas while they waited for the women to have their fun.

"A dollar twenty-seven for a litre this week. At least it dropped," Wayne said with a shake of his head.

"Where do you get it?" Blaine asked.

"Over on High Street. The one with the little brunette who is now Assistant Manager."

"You mean Kelsey? Yeah, she's a sweet kid," Jerry said with a nod.

"I know her, she's a friend of my cousin Gina's," Seth replied with a grin as he recalled the petite woman, and how fast she fit into his cousin's group.

"Didn't she marry Neil Falcon?" Wayne asked.

Seth nodded. "They're getting married next week." Gina hadn't stopped talking about the upcoming wedding and how happy she was to see her long-time friend Neil finally marry the woman of his dreams.

"It's great to hear happy news," Jerry said with a nod.

Wayne nodded. "Sure is."

Seth made a non-committal noise and turned his attention to the ride. Mirabelle, Alexis, Kathy, and Norma were on this round, and it wasn't hard to tell they were having fun. *I bet they can hear Mirrie screaming three hours away, down in Yarmouth, with her big mouth.* He could just make them out as they flew by in a sideways whirl. He couldn't make out their expressions, but deep down, he'd bank on Alexis having the time of her life.

They got off the ride a few minutes later. Kathy's sleek bob easily slid back into place, while Mirabelle and Norma looked like they'd been in a hurricane. Both had their hair sticking every way but their regular styles. Mirabelle's white-blonde locks puffed around her face, and it made her look like a poodle. Seth bit his tongue hard. It was tough not to laugh.

"What are you laughing at?" Mirabelle asked him and lightly swiped his arm.

"Nothing," Seth replied with a snicker.

Behind her, Alexis looked the same as always, and only her bangs were a little out of place. That was fixed when she finger-combed them. She pulled her glasses out of her pocket and slid them into place.

Seth couldn't help staring at her long, delicate fingers, and saw she had her nails painted. They were a soft blue, almost the colour of the sky on a Nova Scotia day. They were pretty, and they suited her perfectly.

"What do you want to go on next?" Blaine asked.

Seth turned his attention back to his best friend.

"Something Seth will go on," Mirabelle said flatly. "He's been a bit of a spoilsport."

"I prefer to watch all of you have fun," Seth muttered in his defence. He felt a nudge in his side and glanced down at Alexis, who stood beside him. He shot her a sheepish smile. *Yeah, I know. I puke on anything other than the kids' rides.*

She tilted her head to the side. "What about the Bumper Cars?"

Seth grinned. It was like she had read his mind. They were on the ground, didn't do anything fancy, and best of all, he could control its movements. Perfect.

"One condition. If we can get separate cars, let's do so. I have a few things to pay back," Seth said and gave Mirabelle one of his best devilish grins.

Beside him, Alexis snorted. He wondered if she was holding back a laugh.

I owe you for this, Mirrie. Prepare to be rammed.

Near the end of the evening, the others went on the gondola-style Ferris wheel, which had large, circular carriages instead of the regular car-style seats. Alexis hung back with Seth as the rest of the group piled onto the pastel green carriage. Although he was pleased, he said, "You don't have to keep me company. Go on if you want."

Alexis shook her head, which made her silver earrings swing back and forth. "Mirrie's mouth is running too much for me. I need a break from her gossip."

He shrugged, and they moved to wait for the rest of the group not far from the exit. Since it was close to midnight, the crowd had thinned considerably, and they easily found a spot where they could watch the ride and have a little privacy.

The carriage with their friends rose another notch as more people were let on and off the ride. The lights twinkled in the darkness as the gondolas swung back and forth.

Seth sighed and gave Alexis an apologetic smile. "I'm sorry I didn't get you a stuffed toy."

"It's okay. You tried." She smiled up at him.

He grinned sheepishly and shoved his hands into his jean pockets. "Baseball was never my strong suit."

Alexis giggled, and the soft tones felt silky and warm to his ears. "Yeah, I could tell when the ball hit the opposite side of the booth and missed all of the bottles." When she stared up at him with a teasing grin, his gaze was drawn to her lips, and the odd tremor travelled down his gut again as he moved his gaze upward to see hers sparkling behind her glasses in the shadows. She shoved the spectacles higher on her nose with a finger, and his gaze moved to the rings on her slim, long fingers—an artist's hands.

"Why are you in construction if you can't stand heights? Don't you get sick if you're in an open area a couple of stories off the ground?" she asked.

Seth was grateful the shadows on the midway hid any evidence of the heat on his cheeks. "I don't go up that high if anything's open and I stay away from the edges. The other guys do a lot of the heavy-duty stuff, while I stick to the decorations and anything that can be done at ground level, or in the middle of a room."

"Like the trim you're designing for Mirrie," she said with a nod.

He smiled. "Exactly."

"I noticed you sawing some planks the other day, and you were helping Blaine put in something in the expansion. It's not all decorative stuff."

"I'm one of the bosses, so it's my prerogative whether to go into an open, high up space if I want to or not. I handle the business end of things, while Blaine is the planner and supervisor," he explained.

"He knows, huh?" Another shove of the spectacles higher on her nose.

"Yeah, and he doesn't care, as long as I'm doing stuff I can do on the ground, like measuring and other stuff in between designing trim and other things." He shifted a little, his feet still hurting despite a rest an hour ago. "What were you doing before you weaselled Mirrie into hiring you?"

Alexis shrugged. "Oh, a little of this and a little of that. Not much." There was a distant note to her voice.

"Like what?" Sure, he was curious. She knew a few of his secrets, why not have her share one of hers with him?

"Seth, it's boring. You really don't want to know." She waved it off with a hand.

Why did it feel like she was distancing herself from him? Her reluctance to share much about herself piqued his curiosity. He moved half a step closer to her. "Honestly, I would like to know."

She stared up at him warily. "Why?"

He gave her one of his most charming grins. "I like you, and I find you interesting."

33

She blinked. "Me? Interesting? Since when?"

Damn, she was adorable when she looked confused. "You're a woman who likes cats, loves to draw, and can scream my ear off when you're having fun. I think that's enough to appeal to anyone."

Alexis turned away for a moment and turned back to stare up at him. "That's not enough for now?"

Aw shit. I didn't piss her off, did I? "Not for me, it isn't."

"Okay, what do you want to know?"

He relaxed. *Good, she isn't mad about it.* Normally, he would have backed off at the first sign of a woman being prickly, but for some reason, Alexis's backing away only made him more determined to get to know her. She was an enigma, and her distance was a challenge he could not resist. "What else do you like, other than cats, drawing, and the scarier rides?"

"I like swimming, watching hockey, playing pool, and just hanging out with a bunch of good friends on the weekend." She shrugged again.

Seth liked billiards, too. It was one of his favourite pastimes. "Blaine and I play, maybe you and Mirrie can join us one of these nights."

Her eyebrows shot upwards. "Did you just ask me out on a date?"

He shook his head. "Nope."

"Then what do you mean by that?" she asked warily.

The thought of dating anyone, even someone as kind and gorgeous as Alexis, made him feel smothered, all thanks to his ex-wife. "I'm only asking you to complete a foursome so we can play partners sometimes. Mirrie likes playing, too, but we haven't had a fourth in a while. It'll be a group of friends hanging out on a Friday night at the tavern, nothing more."

Alexis grinned. "That sounds like fun. Sure, I'll go. I will warn you, I'm pretty good. You and Blaine don't stand a chance."

His gaze dropped to her lips again, and an odd, primal surge to kiss her shot up his spine. Someone on another ride screamed, and Seth felt woozy as the feeling disappeared. *Where did that come from?* He raised his gaze to hers. "Game on," he said with an evil grin.

Chapter Three

Monday morning arrived, and the store was closed to customers again while the construction crew cleared the area around the newly made archway.

Alexis coughed as the sawdust and other things flew around the main shop area. She glanced around on her way back to the storage room to make sure everything was protected with sheets and plastic so that they wouldn't get covered in anything. She entered the back area and closed the door between it and the store itself with a grateful sigh.

Mirabelle was behind her desk, doing the books. "They're not done cleaning up yet?"

"Nope. Blaine said they should be done by the end of the day. I guess they ran into a few problems with the wiring. It wasn't done as it was shown in the records, and they're working around that." She snagged a seat on the sofa, wincing as something poked her in the ass.

Mirabelle let out a long sigh and shook her head. "Jesus, and then the town wonders why we small business owners go a little crazy when we want to do anything in our shops."

"Tell me about it," Alexis snorted and flipped open her drawing pad.

"How's the sign coming along?"

Alexis tapped the end of her pencil on the pad. "It's not quite up to what I want yet."

"Let me see it." The command was clear.

With a roll of her eyes, Alexis handed the notepad to her boss for her inspection.

Mirabelle stared at the drawing with a soft smile. "I don't see what's wrong with it. It's beautiful. You're being fussy again, aren't you?"

Stop ragging me about it, Mirrie. This is going to be the sign everyone sees. It has to be perfect. "I'm not being fussy."

Her boss handed the notebook back to her. "I think you are. It's perfect the way it is."

Mirabelle wasn't an artist, so she wouldn't get how wrong something would feel if it was missing anything. "It's almost there, but it's missing something."

"Like what?" A frown appeared between Mirabelle's eyebrows.

Alexis frowned as she thought about it. "I don't know."

Mirabelle tapped her pencil on the blotter in front of her. "Why don't you ask Seth? He has a good eye for design, and is an artist himself."

Alexis's stomach rolled. Seth was one of the last people she wanted to share her drawings with, especially since she had been taunting him all week with hers and closing the pad in his face before he could see anything. "Um, do I have to?"

"It's a suggestion, but a highly recommended one. He knows the store almost as well as you do and knows what would suit it. I'd also like to see the sign have something in common with the trim he's designing for the archway, to continue the theme inside as well as outside."

Alexis snapped the drawing pad closed and tried not to swear out loud. *Aw fuck, I'm going to be eating crow by the end of the day.* Seth wouldn't let her live this down, not after she had teased him with her closed notepad on several occasions. "I'll show him today."

"And while you're at it, he can show you the trim design. It's only fair after he's been joking around with you about that."

An evil grin spread across Alexis's face.

"Make sure he does it first, at my order." Mirabelle stared

at Alexis over the top rims of her reading glasses.

That big oaf will have to suck it up. "Oh, I will," Alexis murmured and cackled.

Mirabelle turned back to the papers on her desk. "You can help him paint the sign and the trim after it's finished."

Alexis's smile faded. Although she liked Seth a lot, spending time with him wasn't a great idea. He was too handsome and too easy-going for her peace of mind. *What if he remembers me?* She had to get out of that and fast. The only excuse she could think of was her regular duties. "What about the customers?"

"I can handle whatever traffic we get unless we're overrun. If that happens, you can help me, or I'll talk Blaine into working cash for a few minutes." Mirabelle made another note in her book and hit a few keys on her adding machine.

Alexis sighed and rolled her eyes heavenward, praying that her attraction to Seth wouldn't overrule her common sense.

Seth tried to hide a yawn behind his hand as he started drawing on a plank of pine in front of him. He hadn't slept at all after having the dream about the girl in the hoodie for the fifth time in three nights, and he wound up getting up for work two hours early. The image of the girl still haunted him in the daytime hours, especially after seeing something that shook him to the core. The girl in the dream had eyes identical to Alexis's.

It's not the same girl. Alexis is real, and the other one is a figment of my brain backfiring after too many sleepless nights. He shook his head and tried to clear the image out of his mind so he could focus on his task. Blaine and Cody were busy fixing any damage caused by the electricians the day before, while Ken and Larry were sawing any necessary planks to go under the decorative trim around the archway. Since he was so tired,

Seth opted to stay away from any dangerous machinery, and his only option was getting a jump start on the finishing touches for Mirabelle's expansion. He lightly traced the outline of a vine along the one edge and stopped to peer at it. The end of his pencil tapped against the wood as he stared at it. Why didn't it look right?

"Seth?"

He recognized Mirabelle's voice behind him and sighed inwardly. He didn't need her looking over his shoulder the entire time he was drawing and carving. "Yeah?"

"Do you have your sketchpad with you?"

Seth covered what little bit was drawn on the board with his free hand and glanced at Mirabelle over his shoulder. "I do. Why?"

"I want you to show it to Alexis. She's designing a new sign for the store, and I'd like it to match the archway."

Seth hid a triumphant grin. So that was what Alexis was working on. If they had to work together, that meant he'd have to see her drawing, as well as show her his notebook. Perfect. "Maybe she can help me figure out what's missing from the trim design, too."

"I'll send her your way when she's on the clock." Retreating footsteps indicated her departure.

Seth let the grin slide out and snickered. Maybe it wouldn't be a bad day after all.

Alexis wasn't happy she had to share her sketch with Seth, nor was she impressed that she had to work with him for long periods of time. She liked him, too much, and was scared that being in such close proximity to him for hours would drive her so crazy she'd give in to it. She didn't need to toss a rock into the still waters of the pond, especially with that particular man.

The sounds of saws, nails being battered into place, loud male chatter, and the scent of sawdust came to her before she saw any of the mess the renovations were causing. Her reminders evaporated when she came around the corner of a rack and saw him bending over to pick up his pencil. Her gaze was drawn to the outline of perfectly honed muscles beneath his tight, faded jeans, and a blast of appreciation for the male body shot up her spine. When he straightened, his t-shirt went tight against his back and showcased his broad shoulders and the slight bulge of his biceps.

She closed her eyes to dispel it and silently cursed when the image stayed burned into her brain. She clamped it down again and opened her eyes.

Seth turned, their gazes met, and he gave her one of his easy, relaxed smiles in greeting.

Her determination vanished, and her insides turned over oddly in that nanosecond. Why did he have to be so damn hot and so nice? Why couldn't he be an ugly asshole like her ex-boyfriend?

Seth motioned to her, and against her will, her legs started moving and didn't stop until she was beside him.

"I guess Mirrie wants us to make everything match," he said and tapped the eraser end of his pencil against the pine board in front of him.

"Uh, yeah, she does," Alexis replied and sheepishly held up her notebook.

He grinned and held his up, too. "I'll show you mine if you show me yours."

Their gazes locked, and a moment later, they laughed.

She held hers out. "I'll go first."

He replaced her sketch pad with his. "Nah, we'll do it together."

Alexis's heart flip-flopped and her pulse quickened. She nodded her assent, and in unison, they held the notebooks in front of them.

Seth winked at her and flipped to her drawings for the sign. At the same time, she opened his notepad, and her eyes widened. *He's good.* Her fingers traced the outline of vines climbing up the sides, with randomly placed flowers in the middle. It was coloured in with almost identical shades that she had in her design. *Correction, he's great. Mirrie was right. His design has exactly what's missing from mine.*

"Wow, Alexis, this is beautiful," Seth exclaimed, admiration deep in his voice.

The sign was of the store's name, *Mirabelle's* in gold, surrounded by a variety of flowers in various colours, and a faerie whose wand was touching the apostrophe in the name.

His design matched hers almost perfectly. "I have to make a few changes," she mumbled distractedly.

Seth frowned. "Why?"

She pointed to the flowers surrounding the name and said, "Those would look better if they were all one kind of flower, but in different colours, right?"

He contemplated their sketches for a moment and nodded. "Yeah, they would, just like using the ivy for the archway." His gaze rose to meet hers, and his grin broadened.

Alexis's awareness of him hummed loudly, and she hoped her smile wasn't too goofy as she returned it. "Mirrie was right, wasn't she?"

"As much as I hate to admit it, she was."

They traded sketchpads again, and she said, "I guess we'd better make the changes before she gets on our backs."

Seth nodded with a shrug, and they exchanged another grin before they picked up their respective pencils and got to work.

Alexis's flowery perfume remained in Seth's nostrils long after she left to help Mirabelle with designing the layout of the expansion, and his mind kept skipping back to the sight of her eyes twinkling behind her glasses each time she smiled at him.

His gaze had been drawn to her as she sashayed away. Masculine appreciation rose as he watched her, and the sight of her perfectly rounded backside made a strange tingle journey through his gut. Working with a pretty girl like Alexis was going to balance out having Mirabelle breathing down his neck during the rest of the renovations.

He softly whistled as he started outlining the ivy on the pine board.

Alexis finished sketching the elements of the sign on the plywood on Tuesday. The tulips they had included in her scheme fit perfectly, as did the type of ivy Seth had used in the trim. The outline of the large faerie was done to Alexis's satisfaction on Wednesday.

On Friday, Alexis saw Seth's notebook lying on the counter, open to the trim design. With delight, she saw he had added a few smaller faeries to his sketches. *Damn, I swear he reads my mind. I was going to ask him to add one on each side. He's good.*

Late Friday afternoon, Mirabelle took Alexis outside and pointed to the halfway point between both sides of the shop. "I think the new sign should go there."

Alexis stared at the spot and narrowed her eyes. "It's a little far away from the door, isn't it?"

"I think it would show the store is larger and it is more in the middle there. What are you doing tonight?" Mirabelle asked and pointed.

Taken aback by the abrupt change of subject, Alexis frowned. "Nothing. Why?"

"I was wondering if you'd like to go to the tavern with us," Mirabelle replied.

"Us?" Alexis wasn't sure if she liked the sound of that. Mirabelle had a habit of pulling stuff on her, like she did at the exhibition by not mentioning Seth would be there, too.

Mirabelle blinked at her. "Blaine, Seth, and I. He mentioned you like to play pool, and that you two have a bet."

Alexis rolled her eyes. Leave it to Seth to open his big mouth. "I don't remember that."

"He said that you bragged about being a pool shark, and the boys were dead meat. Or something like that," Mirabelle said with a snicker.

Alexis ducked her head to hide a grin. "I didn't say anything about a bet. I only warned him not to underestimate me when it comes to things like billiards."

"Well, he's convinced Blaine that there's a bet on, and you know Blaine and gambling," Mirabelle grumbled with a shrug.

"Yeah, I know." Blaine liked the slot machines, but he preferred to bet on crazy stuff with his friends, like who was going to throw up first on the rides at the exhibition.

"Do you want to do a small wager with them just to keep them happy?" Mirabelle asked.

Alexis shook her head. "Not this time, maybe the next one."

"Sounds good to me. How's about we meet you there at seven? We can have a couple of rounds, then have a bite to eat. Their wings are amazing." Mirabelle started walking toward the open door and motioned for Alexis to follow her inside.

Alexis complied and grinned. "That's perfect."

They entered the tavern via the front door promptly at seven that evening.

Alexis had never been inside the building before and

glanced around to get her bearings. The front part of the public house was a maze of wooden tables and chairs, and a dance floor seemed to be the divider between the front area and back. She quickly took in where the bar was, the ladies' bathroom, and the video gambling machines as she followed Blaine, Seth, and Mirabelle to the pool table area. Two tables were to the left of the dance floor, just between it and the bar. One was in use. Two younger men seemed to be in a battle of nine-ball, while some other men, who Alexis assumed were their friends, cheered them on from a table nearby. A couple of pitchers of draft beer, half full, were placed between almost empty platters of chicken wings and sauce.

Alexis decided to give them a wide berth. She didn't mind someone having a drink or two, but drunk men seemed to be drawn to trouble like a moth was drawn to a light. She was glad she'd decided to err on the side of caution and wear a men's style t-shirt with one of her favourite bands silk-screened across the front. The crew neck meant no one would be able to look down her top when she was bent over the table for a shot.

Blaine found a spot next to the empty pool table. Alexis dropped her purse on a wooden chair as Mirabelle did the same. Seth dropped a two-dollar coin into the required slot. The balls were released, and he started racking the balls for a game of eight-ball pool. When he bent over to scoop the triangle for setup out of its slot, it pulled his already tight jeans even tighter across his ass. *God, I wish he wouldn't do that in front of me. I feel like I'm ogling him each time he does it.* Alexis forced her gaze to fasten on the glass-covered tabletop in front of her.

"Flip for the break?" Blaine asked and held up a quarter.

"Heads!" Mirabelle called as he caught it.

"Tails," Blaine said and showed it to his wife.

Alexis chose a cue stick, coated the tip of it with chalk and waited her turn.

Seth broke without scoring, and Mirabelle took her turn. She sank the nine-ball in the corner pocket, indicating the ladies had the high numbers, while the men were going after the low ones. Her second shot, toward the thirteen-ball, missed.

Blaine scored three times for the men.

Alexis decided to take it easy and not show off her skills yet. Something told her to hold back and let Seth think she was exaggerating. *I'll let him have this one. He can eat crow later.* She sank the ten-ball on an easy mark but deliberately missed a slightly more difficult shot.

Seth's smug smile was an encouragement to keep her skills hidden in this game.

You wait. I'll get you, you jerk, and that adorable ass of yours, too.

Game one was a close match, and it went to the men when Seth sank the eight-ball in the side pocket. Although Seth seemed to take a few risks, he was accurate and had gotten most of the points for him and Blaine.

Game two started with Alexis sinking the two-ball on the break, and the five, one, six, and seven after it. She deliberately missed on the three-ball to give Seth a turn. He missed an easy shot at the ten-ball. "Son of a bitch," he muttered.

Alexis bit her tongue so she wouldn't rub his nose in his failure. "It happens to the best of us," she said with a shrug.

He glared at her in reply.

Mirabelle got the three-ball in the side pocket with ease, and she hit the four into the corner pocket on a rebound shot. Blaine got the twelve, fifteen, and nine balls, then had to use the bridge to sink the ten. He missed sinking the fourteen by half a millimetre.

Seth groaned when the ball lightly rolled away from the pocket.

"Well, shit," Blaine grumbled with a shake of his head.

Alexis bit the inside of her lip to hide a smirk. Blaine set her up to easily get the eight-ball without realizing it.

Seth must have seen the setup, because he glared at her.

Alexis flipped her braid over her shoulder and glanced around at the remaining balls on the table. It was time to put the sexy asshole in his place. She studied the table for a moment, calculated the angles with the diamonds on the side and headrails, and bent over the table. "Eight-ball, side pocket, rebound off the side, then head cushion," Alexis stated and pointed with her cue stick. She always called her eight-ball shot, so no one could call foul or fluke if she did a trick shot. She lined up her cue, took a moment to calculate the amount of power she needed, and hit the white cue ball perfectly. It smacked the eight-ball at the precise angle she needed. The black ball bounced off first the side, then the head cushion before softly rolling through the head string, and neatly easing into the side pocket.

"That was a beautiful shot," Mirabelle exclaimed and gave Alexis a high-five.

Alexis nodded in thanks and turned to the men with a grin.

Blaine was laughing and pointing to Seth, which made Alexis giggle, but it was the expression on Seth's face that sent her over the edge. He was staring at the green felt-covered table in shock, his blue eyes wide and his jaw hanging open.

"Close your mouth before you catch a few dozen flies in it, Mitchell." Alexis reached up and, with a finger, gently pushed Seth's jaw up into its normal position.

His glare latched on to her face. "What the ever-loving fuck?" he muttered.

Mirabelle started laughing.

"I think we've been had," Blaine choked out around his laughter. "How's about another round?"

Alexis smiled smugly. "Only if you want to be tromped again."

Mirabelle snickered and stood back as her husband started setting up for another game. "Your turn to break, Seth."

Seth broke and sank the nine-ball.

The men played a valiant game, but they lost when Alexis made a double rebound shot with the eight-ball.

Seth stared at the table in disbelief before he shifted his gaze to Alexis. "And I thought you were joking when you said you were good."

She batted her eyelashes at him and grinned. "Rule one of regular Eight-Ball pool—never underestimate your opponent."

Seth shook his head with a scoff and stared down at her. "Best three out of five?"

"Nah, I think you two have had your egos trampled enough for one night. I'm going to sit this one out," Alexis said with a fake yawn.

"Chicken." It wasn't hard to hear the taunt in Seth's tone.

"If you say so, loser," she replied and handed him her cue stick. "Be a darling and put this back for me, please."

He took it with a roll of his eyes and did as she asked.

Alexis and Mirabelle sat at their table and watched the men have a round. Blaine lost it when he sank the eight-ball while aiming for the ten-ball.

Mirabelle snickered behind her hand as Seth racked it up for another round with a shake of his head. To Alexis, she said, "This is fun. We haven't had a fourth in a while, and I missed having a good game with a decent player like you."

"Yeah, I'm having a great time, too. Doesn't Seth's girlfriend like to play?" Alexis asked. It was an innocent question. She hadn't noticed any girls hanging around, but Seth could have one on the sly that was either on the road working or didn't live in the area.

"Oh, Seth doesn't have a girlfriend right now. He's been

single since Janie left him a few years ago," Mirabelle replied.

"Janie?" Alexis gave Mirabelle a blank look.

"His wife. Well, former wife now."

Ex-wife? Alexis's eyebrows shot skyward. "He's divorced?"

"She left over three years ago, and it was finalized about two years ago," Mirabelle said with a layer of snark in her voice. It was obvious she didn't think much of Janie.

"I see." Alexis moved her gaze to the table and tried not to cringe. Why would any woman in her right mind leave a guy like him? He was sweet, funny, kind and easy-going, and gorgeous. However, his relaxed attitude could be his public front, and he might be a real jerk to live with. She didn't know him well even though they hung out and talked at the store and they'd gone on a few rides together at the exhibition. Plus she suddenly felt uncomfortable gossiping about the man, whether he was within earshot or fifty miles away.

Mirabelle sighed. "Blaine hated her guts, and I didn't like her much either."

Alexis turned her head to stare at her boss and friend. "Oh?"

Mirabelle nodded, her lips flat. "Yeah. He was so good to her, and in return, she treated him like dirt. I'm not sure exactly what all was going on the last while she was still here, but it wasn't good. Seth tried to hide it, but Blaine and I know him better than anyone else. He was hurting a lot, and when she finally left, he was devastated."

At least it was his ex-wife's fault, not his. Alexis shook her head. She shifted uncomfortably and mumbled, "He seems fine now."

"He wasn't for a while after Janie packed her bags, told him she couldn't take it anymore and left. Blaine had enough of watching him be depressed and had to kick Seth's ass to snap him out of it. If you ask me, Janie wasn't worth it. She was a little snob from the beginning and only went after Seth because she thought he was rich," Mirabelle muttered and took a sip of her draft beer. Her expression turned sour like Janie left a disgusting aftertaste in her mouth.

Alexis winced. *Shut up, Mirrie. You're a great friend and an amazing boss, but I would rather not hear all of this from you. I'd rather hear it from Seth if I heard it at all. This isn't my business!*

Both women smiled when Blaine gave Seth a good-natured shove after missing a shot.

Alexis nodded toward the men. "Speaking of Seth, I think he's kicking your husband's ass." *Hopefully, she takes the bait and stops yapping about Seth and his ex-wife. I'd rather eat nails than hear any more about it.*

Mirabelle glanced at the men, giggled and sighed. "That's nothing. Sometimes you can hear them cursing each other above the music."

That's better. Alexis snickered and turned her attention to Seth, and their gazes locked. He smiled and winked at her, and she smiled and felt her cheeks warm up. *He's so fucking cute. I wish he weren't the only person in town that could blow my cover.*

"Blaine and Seth got into a shoving match one night about a year ago. It was so bad. The bartender actually threatened to kick them out until she realized it was all in fun." Mirabelle took another sip of her beer and her smile faded. "Like I was saying about Janie, she was pissed when she found out the company wasn't worth millions. They were married by then, and I swear everything she did to him was punishment for not telling her before they tied the knot."

Alexis sighed inwardly. *Aw fuck. Mirabelle must be in a mood to gossip tonight. I'd better pretend I'm listening, or she'll think something is wrong.* She took a long gulp of her wine cooler and shook her head. "Janie sounds like a piece of work."

"Understatement, my dear. After she found out, she took

such a fit that she threw his shop vac through the front window of his house and told him he was useless." Mirabelle clicked her tongue, and her eyes narrowed.

That bitch. Hell with whapping her with Seth's hammer, I'd love to shove her on to the table saw while it's running. Alexis winced in sympathy for Seth. "Ouch."

"Mm-hmm." Mirabelle's grimace looked sinister in the shadows of the room. "Janie refused to clean anything, not even her own messes. Seth would come home and do all of it after a long day of work, while she sat on her ass in the living room, reading fashion magazines, in a silk robe or all dolled up like she was in a mansion. If she broke a nail or got a little lint or dust on her clothing, she'd have a fit and scream at Seth, even in public."

Whoa. Janie was the kind of girl Alexis used to beat up for something to do. "Yikes. I don't know a lot of guys that would put up with that," Alexis said.

Mirabelle nodded. "I'm surprised Seth did, for that long. He's easy-going until someone hits him for nothing. I guess he really loved her at one time, plus I had a feeling he was hoping she'd settle down after a while and start acting like a real wife. What I don't get is why that little bitch didn't see how good she had it. He's such a darling and wouldn't hurt a fly."

Seth moved into Alexis's line of vision. His dark hair and eyes seemed almost black in the low light, and his easy smile at Blaine sent a shiver of awareness through her. When he bent over to take a shot in front of her and Mirabelle, Alexis's gaze automatically moved downwards to the tight seat of his jeans, and she suddenly wished he wouldn't do that in front of her. It made her fingers tingle and made her wish for things that could never happen, like sex with him.

"He's got a nice tush, doesn't he?" Mirabelle asked with a sly grin.

Alexis jumped a foot off her chair. "What?"

"I said he has one of the best asses I've ever seen." Mirabelle turned her head to watch her husband and their best friend take pot-shots at each other across the pool table. "Jesus, to have a man built like that."

Alexis blinked. "You'd have sex with Seth? I thought you two were family." *Incest. Yuck.*

"It wouldn't work even if Blaine and I weren't married. We're too much alike. I'm just saying it would be fun to do it with a sexy guy like him, and you have to admit he is quite—"

"Dorky?" Alexis tossed in, with a hope Mirabelle would shut up. *Seth may be sexy as hell, and a doll to boot, but if he remembers how we really met, he'll never forgive me for not telling him.*

"Dorks can be sexy. I was going to say tempting or drop dead yummy. Don't you think so?" Mirabelle took a sip of her drink and winked.

Alexis shrugged. "Meh, he's okay." *He's almost perfect, in my opinion. If Mirrie knew the truth, she'd be planning the wedding before we started dating.*

"Only okay? I think he's right. You do need your glasses updated." Mirabelle looked confused.

"He's cute, but I've seen better." *Liar, liar, pants on fire.*

"Hey, don't lie. I've seen you looking at him from time to time."

"I don't—" Alexis sputtered.

"It's perfectly natural for anyone who likes men to stare at someone as gorgeous as Seth," Mirabelle reminded her with a pat on the arm.

Alexis didn't reply. She shifted uncomfortably in her chair as she fiddled with the salt shaker in front of her. Mirabelle was hitting the bull's-eye without knowing it. *Do not let her see how you think Seth is the perfect example of the male species!*

Mirabelle leaned in and said in Alexis's ear, "He watches you, too, you know."

Alexis gave her friend a blank stare over the top of her glasses. "Yeah, right."

"Sweetheart, you're a beautiful young woman, and anyone who doesn't look at you is out of their minds. Obviously, Seth thinks you're pretty and nice, or else he wouldn't talk to you so much."

"Mirrie, shut up. Please." *Yes, please shut your huge yap! I love you like a sister, but the last thing I want or need is to have Seth pushed on me.*

"I'm only stating facts," Mirabelle said and shrugged.

"Facts or not, I'd rather not go down that road." *Please do not go down that road.*

"Why? You're not fantasizing about sleeping with him? I bet he's—"

"Oh god, don't you dare say it, Mirrie. He's not doing that about me," Alexis blurted.

"I'm saying what I see, and I think if you gave him any idea that you'd be open to it, he'd probably be happy to oblige," Mirabelle stated with a wink.

Alexis's sexual awareness of the one man in Bridgewater she wanted to avoid went up by over 500 percent as her gaze latched on to him. He was looking right at her. Heat rose on her cheeks, and she gave him a nauseated smile when he grinned and held up his cue stick in acknowledgement. *I hope he doesn't find out what Mirrie and I were talking about. I'll never live that down!*

"Anyway, it's something to consider," Mirabelle said. "He needs a real woman, someone who would treat him right, love him for who he is, and make him happy in bed."

"I'm not her." *I can't be, even though it may be some of the best sex I've ever had. Seth hates secrets and women who lie, according to Mirrie. I'm a dead duck the instant he finds out.* Alexis flipped her braid over her shoulder and sighed. *I should tell him and get it over with.* She glanced at the men, saw they were laughing, and decided that waiting a few hours or until Monday wouldn't hurt. It would ruin their night, and it would give her time to think of the best way to tell him. *Plus, I'd prefer that we were alone so that he can scream at me without Mirrie in earshot.*

Mirabelle shrugged. "You may think that, but I see it differently. You two have a lot in common. He's artistic, sweet and kind, and you are, too. I think you guys would be a perfect match." She glanced up at the men and noted Blaine was racking up the balls again. "What do you say we show the men just who's boss, huh?"

With that, the subject was closed, and Alexis started to relax.

CHAPTER FOUR

Seth's Bedroom
Saturday Morning

"**T**hank you, Seth." The soft sound of the girl's voice kept echoing in his ears, hours after the dream woke him again.

This time, he could make out a silk-screened design on the sleeve of her sweatshirt, a band logo, although he wasn't sure which band or genre it was. He could also see her canvas sneakers, black with white trim and laces, pulled in against her bottom, as she pressed her face against her knees and pulled the hood down to shadow her face. He remembered how she put a pair of dark sunglasses on her nose and wondered why she was wearing them in a dimly lit area.

He closed his eyes and saw a few more elements. The walls of the room were a dull gray cement, and there were a few tinted windows. He could see sunshine and feel its warmth. There was a hum above him, the ventilation system, mixing in with her muffled sobs. No chairs. A desk behind a sliding window, with no one behind it. He could hear cars going by and almost smell the sterility of the area. There were a few bits of chatter mixed with static.

His eyes flew open.

He was familiar with that area, but where was it, and why had he been there? With a long sigh, Seth rolled onto his side and tried to get back to sleep.

Saturday Night, Mirabelle's Backyard

Crowds meant people, people meant curiosity, and in a small town like Bridgewater, that meant questions Alexis didn't want to answer. Going to the Exhibition was one thing. She was just another face in the crowd. At Mirabelle's barbecue, she was an item of interest. Alexis hated attention. She was an introvert at heart, despite working in Mirabelle's shop and how much she adored her job.

Alexis felt a migraine forming between her eyes as she allowed her boss to drag her from group to group in the large, noisy gathering in the Rogers' backyard. She loved Mirabelle, as a person and an employer, but hated how everyone's gaze was inquiringly fastened on her the entire day. *As soon as she's done showing me off, I am so out of here!* Once again, she regretted accepting her boss's invitation to the party. Mirabelle had described it as a few friends, a *little* party. *Small? It looks like the entire town is here!*

With an inward sigh, Alexis meekly followed Mirabelle toward another group and smiled, made small talk or nodded at everyone else while she inwardly plotted her escape.

Mirabelle was called away a few minutes later, and although Alexis had strict orders to mingle, she scooted to the sidelines to hide. She glanced around at the crowd from behind her sunglasses, and with a soft groan, she saw that Blaine was staring in her direction. There went her chance of escape. He'd alert his wife that her protégée had disappeared, and Mirabelle would come looking for her.

Her gaze moved to his right, toward Seth, then firmly toward the pool, where the Rogers' older children were swimming and horsing around with their friends. Seth crouched down so he could talk to the Rogers' youngest child, Mallory, at her level. She was small and dainty for eight years old, and Alexis could see the girl's appreciation for his thoughtfulness when Mallory beamed at him and threw her arms around his neck.

Alexis's gaze fastened on him again through her dark lenses, and a shiver of sexual awareness went up her spine when her gaze locked with his across twenty feet of grass and cement. He grinned at her and waved, and her stomach churned as she waved back.

She turned her head away from him again. *Shit.* The fact he liked kids and seemed to be comfortable interacting with them made him more appealing to her. Each new discovery about Seth was disconcerting to Alexis. *Ideal or not, he is not the right man for me. I have to tell him the truth, and soon. The longer I put it off, the angrier he's going to be when he finds out.* Her ex-boyfriend Brett's actions weren't her fault. Although she knew that, it still bothered her.

"He's not worth it. Tell him to take a hike, go home, and do something better with your life. You seem like a smart girl. Don't waste your life on someone that won't do anything other than cause trouble for you and others." The echo of the male wisdom and the feel of a warm, strong and calloused hand gripping hers resounded in her mind as her gaze was drawn to Seth again.

With a jolt, she realized he was walking toward her with a grin on his face.

Her eyelids closed behind her sunglasses. *Aw, motherfucker.*

Seth was glad to see Alexis at the Rogers' middle of summer barbecue that night. He was thinking of saying hi to her when Mallory jumped on him. His youngest godchild was small and made up for it with her enthusiasm and sunny temperament. He listened to her rattle on about summer camp while he kept glancing in Alexis's direction every few minutes.

Sympathy rose as he saw how uncomfortable she seemed in the crowd. She was obviously out of her element and looked like she was trying to make an escape. When Mallory ran off to join her friends and siblings in the pool, he made his move. He sauntered over to her side and gave her a bright grin. "Hey, Alexis. Having fun?" He could barely see her glance up at him through her dark lenses as she shrugged. "I take it that's a no."

"How do you know if I'm not having any fun?" she muttered with a dirty look.

He admired her soft pink blouse, faded, skinny jeans with holes in the knees, and how her ponytail curled around her neck, down between her delectable breasts. "At the exhibition, you were talking non-stop with all of us, and we couldn't keep up with you half the time. It was the same way when we were playing pool at the bar last week, or when we were getting things done up for the sign at the store. Tonight, you look like a deer caught in headlights."

Her jaw clicked, and she sighed. "Leave it to you to notice that."

"You're forgetting who you're talking to." He tossed in one of his brightest smiles for emphasis.

Alexis stared up at him over the top of her sunglasses. "I haven't."

Despite being surrounded by what felt like half the town, it was quiet in the shade of the big oak tree that dominated the north side of the Rogers' backyard, a private oasis. Seth was grateful no one was paying attention to them, especially Mirabelle. She would get the wrong idea.

I like Alexis a lot. She's a great friend, lots of fun, and really sweet. Her being so pretty is icing on the cake. What straight man doesn't like being with a beauty like her, even if it's only in friendship? A picture of his icy ex-wife rose in his mind. *I'm not ready to start dating yet or even have a friend with benefits. Sex with Alexis might be hotter than the sun, but Jesus, I'd rather not fuck things up with her. I'd rather keep her a mile away than ruin what we have now.*

Alexis groaned. "I thought this was only going to be a family thing. If I had known it was going to be the entire town, I would have told Mirrie to shove the invite up her ass."

The mental picture of Mirabelle doing that made Seth laugh. "She's pulled off the same stunt on me a few times. I'd get here, thinking it was just her, Blaine and the kids, and I'd see people here I don't know and don't care to meet. She thinks you're lonely."

Alexis sniffed primly. "I have enough friends, thank you."

"How many single men did she force you to meet today?"

She crossed her arms across her chest and growled.

Seth cringed in sympathy. "I see a lot of the single women she's tried to hook me up with, too, so it's not just you in her sights tonight." Although he was wearing looser jeans and a black t-shirt emblazed with a country music band on it, he was still getting admiring looks. *I wish they'd screw off. I hate desperate women. They always think you should marry them after the first date.*

Alexis gave him a sad smile. "You, too, huh?"

"Yup." He rolled his eyes and sighed.

"Shit. Next time, I should bring a date, so she buggers off and won't do this to me again," she muttered.

He held out his hand. "Deal."

Her head whipped around and stared at him over the top of her sunglasses. Seth felt an odd feeling in his gut. Bile started rising in his throat.

"Deal?"

Thankfully, Alexis's question drove away the nausea. He shook it off and focused on her. "Yeah, as in we come here and leave here together the next time Mirrie drags us to one of her parties," he said conspiratorially.

Her eyebrows shot up for a second, and the action made her spectacles slide down the bridge of her nose a little. Her nose wrinkled, which made Seth smile inwardly. *Damn, she is too cute for words. Too bad I'm not looking for a girlfriend. She'll be a perfect one for some lucky guy.* "It may make it easier to avoid her setting us up with people we're not compatible with," he reminded her.

Alexis nodded slowly. "I'd rather hang out with you because you know me and don't care if I'm quiet or not." With a soft smile, she stared up at him over her glasses. "Thank you, Seth," she murmured.

As his gaze locked with hers, the image from his recurring dream overlaid it, and a weird sweat broke out on his forehead. He shivered in the humidity, and his heart started racing. He lifted a trembling hand to his cheek as he closed his eyes and tried to shake it off. All he could see on the canvas of his eyelids was the girl in the corner of the gray room, the sunlight hitting her sneakers, with the smell of disinfectant burning his nostrils. He swallowed hard several times, hoping the nausea would disappear. Vertigo hit him like an eighteen-wheeler, and he almost fell face-first into the grass beside the massive oak tree they were standing alongside.

Someone said his name from a distance. His heart beat faster, and he felt like he was going to throw up. *Don't let me puke on her shoes! I'll never live it down, and she'll stop talking to me, for good reason.*

A soft touch on his arm and a light flowery scent in his nostrils helped bring back some of his equilibrium. He was still sweaty, his hands still shook, but his heart rate dropped noticeably, the queasiness started lifting, and his breathing evened out.

"Seth?"

He recognized concern in Alexis's voice, closer this time, and he swallowed hard to hold back the remaining nausea. He cleared his throat and opened his eyes marginally. Her perfume wafted around him again as a gentle hand touched his forehead.

"Were you out in the heat too much again? You're sweaty, and you're white as a sheet."

"Maybe," he mumbled in an effort to cover up the truth. Alexis would think he was insane if she knew about his recurring dream and how his subconscious was putting her in it.

"Mirrie's going to have a fit if you keep standing there and weaving like a tree in a hurricane. I'll take you inside, where it's cool, and she won't see you." She put her free hand on his arm, and the rest of the odd sensations went away.

He shook his head. "I'm okay now. It's gone."

Over her glasses, she peered up at him with concern. There was a softness in her dark eyes that he had never seen before, and it made him feel woozy again. *Oh shit. Please, don't let me faint on her. Alexis will not like it, and Mirrie will send me to the ER for observation.* He gave Alexis a reassuring smile, and without thinking, he put his hand on her hip. Jokingly, he leaned forward, so his forehead touched hers and winked at her.

"What are you doing?" Her nose wrinkled, and there was a confused note in her voice.

"I'm making sure you can see me. I know how blind you are without the glasses. Since you keep staring at me over the top of them, I thought I'd give you a better view." He grinned at her, and the last remnants of the sickening feelings went away. "I'm fine."

She whacked him on the arm and sighed. "Yeah, if you're picking on me about my eyesight, you're fine."

"Of course, having a pretty girl like you looking out for me helped a lot," he added and wagged his eyebrows at her.

He felt a hard shove on his shoulders and held firm.

"Go take a swim, Seth. It'll help more than I will." She tried pulling out of his embrace and gave him another shove.

He held her close, backed up another step, saw grass under his feet, and stopped. "I'd rather lean on you for a bit," he shot back and slid an arm around her waist. One more step back had concrete under his boots.

"God, you're an ass," she muttered and put her hands on

his chest.

He prepared for the inevitable and slid his other arm around her. "Ass or not, at least I'm not blind."

Just as she shoved him, he took three steps backward and held on to Alexis tightly.

Alexis shrieked in surprise, and Seth cackled as they fell into the pool together.

Monday morning
Mirabelle's Store

Seth yelped and dropped his chisel as a batch of icy water doused his head. "The fuck?" he exclaimed as the water soaked his shirt. With a frown, he wiped his face with a hand and whipped around to see who did it. He groaned, inwardly, when he saw Alexis, her back stiff as she marched into the main part of the store.

A few snickers behind him had him glaring at two of his contract workers, Ken and Cody, who must have watched the scene unfold. "What the hell are you two looking at?" Seth snapped.

"Not much other than our boss getting what was coming to him," Ken replied.

Cody coughed, but it was easy to tell he was covering up another snicker. "It's not hard to tell her panties are in a bunch, and for a good reason." Cody lived next door to Blaine and had been at the party Saturday night.

"You've made your point, now get back to work," Seth barked the order and bent over to pick up his fallen tools.

They evilly grinned before they went back to their tasks. Cody started hammering a nail into some gypsum board along the south wall, and Ken whistled while he sawed some planks into shelves for the east wall.

After his tools were back in their respective spots on top of his large toolbox, Seth went outside to dry off for a minute. Traffic along King Street was heavy that sunny morning, and there were a lot of pedestrians along the sidewalk, even with the tourist season starting to wind down. He crossed the street at the crosswalk beside Phoenix Street and went into the top part of Pijinuiskaq Park, on the west bank of the LaHave River, across from the mall, and not far from the Old Bridge. He sat down on a bench and sighed remorsefully. *Talk about a great way to make her hate me. I was trying to get her to loosen up.*

Obviously, she was still upset with him about pulling her into the pool at the Rogers' party, and Seth didn't blame her. Being contrite was easy. He felt rotten about it. Making it up to her wasn't as easy. He had to think about how to do it just right.

He glanced at the storefront and saw Alexis hanging something in the front windows. Her willowy body stretched as she reached upwards, and the soft curves of her silhouette made a weird shudder journey through his body, to lodge itself in his gut. She was one of the prettiest women he had seen in a long time, even better than his ex-wife. Janie was beautiful, in a cool, detached way. His gaze narrowed as he wondered why Alexis's looks appealed to him so much, and why he thought she was prettier than his ex-wife, who was now a model for some of the top designers in the world.

Through the window, he saw Alexis grin at Mirabelle, and a small smile formed on his face as it hit him.

Alexis didn't possess Janie's cold indifference. She was fun, caring, and artistic, and her spunk combined with her kindness to him and others shone through her wary facade. Another odd jolt told him he missed joking around with her, even though it was less than thirty-six hours since he'd pulled her into the pool.

How could he make it up to her in a way she'd accept?

An image came to his mind, and with a grin, he knew exactly how to get Alexis smiling at him again.

Alexis's Apartment Building
Near the Desbrisay Museum, Bridgewater

Alexis was shocked to see Seth at her door, and even more so when he handed her a bouquet of flowers. "What are these for?"

Seth rolled his shoulders. "They're, um, to say I'm sorry." His cheeks were pink, and the sheepish way he was shuffling his steel-toed boots was so endearing.

She fingered the petals of the multi-blossomed stems in various colours from pastels to bolds, and a few two-coloured ones tossed in for extra variety. The scent was heady, sweet, and so Nova Scotian. "Normally one gives something like roses or another flower to say that. I've never had an apology given to me over lupines before."

He grinned awkwardly. "Well, uh, I thought you'd like them over anything else."

She lifted the bouquet to her nose and smiled as she inhaled their familiar and welcoming scent. "I do. They're my favourite flower." How could she stay mad at a guy who paid attention to the little things like that? Giving her a bouquet of lupines was like giving another girl diamonds. Her anger evaporated.

"Alexis, I really am sorry for Saturday night. I shouldn't have pulled you into the pool. It was stupid and careless of me, and you could have gotten hurt. Can you ever forgive me?" There was a pleading tone in his soft words.

She nodded with a roll of her eyes. "I'll forgive you this time. However, the next time you do something idiotic like that, consider yourself a dead man. The glass of water was only the tip of the iceberg of my ways to get payback."

They grinned at each other, Alexis was relieved a truce had been called. Seth seemed to have had a weight lifted off his shoulders because he immediately straightened. *He is such a pussycat.* His ex-wife must have had the IQ of a rock not to see what a sweet guy she had.

Her smile faded into wide-eyed shock when Seth looped his arm around her waist and hugged her. The feel of his lean musculature made a shimmer of desire travel down her spine. It felt natural to lean into him and hug him back while he rested his cheek on her temple. He smelled of sawdust under-lined with a hint of male sweat like a man gets after they put in a full day of hard work. It wasn't unpleasant. It was stimu-lating.

She mentally kicked her libido as another image of their bodies entwined in passion rose to the front of her mind. She could almost see his eyes darkened in passion, smell his ex-citement and hear his groans as she caressed him. She wanted to feel the weight of his body as he spread her legs open, and his rigid cock entering her soaked slit—

We're friends, don't go there! She lifted her head to stare at him and almost gave in to the urge to kiss him when he nuz-zled his forehead against hers. His lips were a scant heartbeat away. She could feel his breath caress her mouth, and she could almost taste him. The instant his lower lip bumped hers, she grabbed her desire around the throat and choked it down.

She shifted an inch away from him. "I'd better put these in some water before they start wilting," she murmured, hoping he wouldn't be insulted she backed off so fast.

Seth pulled back with a nod. "I'll leave you to it. See you tomorrow."

Just as he was turning to walk down the hall, she called after him. "Seth?"

He stopped and grinned at her over his shoulder. "Yeah?"

She beamed at him. "Thanks."

He gave her a mock salute in reply. As Seth walked away, Alexis leaned against the doorjamb with a sigh of feminine appreciation for the male form. With a jolt, she remembered her vow to tell Seth the truth about her past. *Shit. Another opportunity gone. If I had only told him before, we could be in bed right now.*

She slapped herself, hard. "Don't go there, girl," she muttered as she went back into her apartment and tried not to slam the door.

Tuesday morning started off with Alexis humming under her breath, and a comfortable note in the air. Things were progressing seamlessly with the renovations. The men were closing in on finishing the construction phase of it, and they would start painting and installing the shelves the following week.

Alexis was happy that the sounds of saws and hammering nails and the dust would finally be gone, so they could finally have things back to somewhat normal again. It had been an annoyance to have everything compressed into a smaller area while the one wall was blocked off from customers. The last couple of weeks had been busy, even with the tourist season on its wind down, and Alexis had to circumvent more than one curious person from going into the expansion area without permission. Some people didn't care about their safety, even with signs telling them it was an employee and construction crew only area.

Friday saw the saws and heavier equipment being taken away in Blaine and Seth's trucks and the sawdust being cleaned out of the store's addition. That afternoon, Alexis poked her head behind the plastic curtain and grinned when she saw the new walls, the clean and stripped floor, and the various touches waiting to be put into place stacked around in their designated spots. Her gaze latched on to something new in the far corner, and without thinking, she walked over to inspect it. Her eyes widened as she beheld the new and unpainted shelving unit, which stood a foot taller than she did.

When her fingers caressed the silky wood of its middle shelf, she recognized Seth's design. Its outer edges were carved with the same ivy design of the archway and soon-to-be-painted sign. It was an intricate piece that appealed to her, and it fit in with the rest of the shop perfectly.

"Do you like it?" Seth's voice came from another corner of the room.

Alexis grinned at him over her shoulder. "I love it. It fits in perfectly with the new theme and Mirrie's personality. I didn't know she was getting this because she didn't tell me."

He walked over to stand by her and grinned at her. "She didn't know she was getting it either. Something was missing back here, and it hit me that she needed some shelves to continue the theme through the shop. So I made this one, and she loved it and asked me to make a few more."

Her mouth watered a little when she saw how his jeans moulded to his legs, and the t-shirt was stretched tight around his chest. Feeling suddenly uncomfortable, she turned her attention to the shelving unit. "So this won't be the only one?"

"I'm sanding down the second one now, and the third one will be started next week when I have a chance. It's going to be four in total, two for each section of the store." He shoved his hands into his jeans pockets and stared down at her.

"You've been working on them in your free time? Don't you ever sleep?" She smiled up at him.

"It's been too hot to sleep most nights," he said quietly.

She shrugged. "That sounds like a good reason to get an air conditioner installed. You've said that a lot this summer." She wondered why he didn't just go out and do it. There were days that he complained about the humidity and heat, even if it was a comfortable temperature outside. Either he was part Inuit or Scandinavian, meaning he was used to colder temperatures, or he was trying to hide a darker reason for his insomnia. *Meh, whatever it is, it's his business, not mine.*

"There's no point in getting one this late in the year. I'll get one next summer." He reached out to brush a few grains of dust off the top of the piece and followed the lines of the intricate carving down the side with his thumb. "I don't mind it as much, especially if I have something productive to do, and doing this for Mirrie makes up for it."

"Are you going to just stain it, or are you painting it?" *I hope he paints it. It would be absolutely gorgeous if it matched the rest of the store.*

Seth's grin was bright, and it sent a tingle of awareness up her spine. "I was hoping you'd help me paint it to match the sign and the archway."

She eyed it with excitement, and she could almost see the splashes of colours for the ivy combined with the different coloured tulips. "I wonder if I can con Mirrie into watching the counter for me."

His rich laugh penetrated her senses, and her stomach flipped when he elbowed her arm. "Remind me to hire you the next time we do something like this. We need someone on the team who likes painting this kind of thing as much as I do. The guys aren't great at it, and they always bitch about having to do such *silly* painting jobs."

"Their problem, not yours. When do we start?" She dove for a stack of paint cans to the right.

"Down, girl," Seth said with a laugh. "We'll do the sign and archway first, and then we'll attack the shelves."

"Aw nuts," she muttered as her sneakers squeaked to a stop on the uncovered cement floor. She pouted for a second, and then she stuck her tongue out at him. "You're not my boss. I can start painting now."

"Mirrie is going to die for setting you loose on me." His body shook with restrained laughter.

If there was one thing Alexis loved more than drawing, it was painting. She loved the challenge of taking colours from a palette and combining them. "Aw, come on, Seth, be a sport.

We can do it tonight, as a surprise for Mirrie."

He sounded annoyed, but she could see his eyes twinkling. "I suppose we can pick out a few of the colours you want for it."

Alexis beamed and skipped over to the paint cans.

"No painting, Alexis. There's also a condition to me letting you do this."

She gave him a wary look and held up a small can as if it was a baseball, ready to pitch. "Yeah? What's that?" *I'll kill him if he forces me to do something I hate.*

"After we're done, we're going to go home, get cleaned up, and we're going out for a while," he ordered.

Oh yeah? Says who, asshole? She tossed the can in the air a few centimetres and neatly caught it. "For what?"

"I think you owe me the chance to regain my title as the best pool player in the group, and the sooner, the better." His eyes narrowed into a mock glare. He was shaking, which was an indication he was trying to hold back a laugh.

Beating him at billiards was not only fun, but it also knocked his ego for a loop. In Alexis's opinion, Seth was over-confident in his skills as both a pool player and a male, and it was a pleasure to kick him down a few notches. She hid an evil grin as she lowered her hand slightly and shrugged. "Fine with me, but don't whine when you get your ass kicked again. Hearing you cry like a little girl doesn't suit you."

He raised an eyebrow at her.

Alexis batted her lashes in return.

"Fuck." He let out a long, irritated sigh. "You'd better get the covers open if you want to get a jump on things. You have fifty-four minutes left."

CHAPTER FIVE

Monday Morning
Mirabelle's Shop

Seth arrived at the store early. Alexis was already there, with open cans of coloured paint, several brushes and different charts for each unit, the archway and the sign laid out on a work table. She frowned at a paper in her hand as she tapped the handle of a small brush against her lips and shook her head after a moment. The movement made the chandelier earrings tinkle softly and her bangs swish gently. *She's so damn cute, and any heterosexual man would fantasize about her.*

A second later, he mentally kicked himself and shut down that train of thought. *As much as I would love to have some raunchy sex with Alexis, I can't. Janie took too much out of me when she left. I don't want to do that again if things go south. I don't think my sanity would survive if we started dating and broke up. Alexis is too important to me as a friend. Losing that would kill a part of me.* He deliberately made a little noise as he entered the main part of the expansion, so she'd know she was no longer alone.

She turned her head and grinned at him, which made his stomach clench and his heart race. A shiver of something travelled the length of his body to lodge in his groin, and a fine coat of sweat appeared on his upper lip. His eyes slammed shut, and his hands started to shake. He had seen a similar grin from the girl in the dream near the end of it.

A whiff of flowers and soft fingers brushing his arm made the odd feelings evaporate. He still felt a little sweaty, but it was minimal. "Seth, are you sick again?"

He took a deep breath and shook his head. "I'm fine. Why?"

"You had that odd look on your face again," she said and reached upwards to touch his forehead.

He shook it off with a frown. "I'm okay."

She raised an eyebrow at him as she studied him. Finally, she shrugged and turned back to the worktable. "Sorry about the mess, but I got here early and couldn't resist getting a jump on things."

Relieved she believed him, he nodded. "I was counting on it, that's why I'm here a little early, too."

"I even brought a smock so I wouldn't get covered in paint," she said as she picked up a huge white shirt splattered with various streaks and spots of different colours.

He nodded and pointed to the paper on the table. "Put it on after we map where which colour goes, and we'll get to work."

Just after opening that morning, Mirabelle peered at the colour layouts for everything with a nod of approval. "It looks great, and it'll make the expansion even prettier."

"Thank Alexis for that. Her eye is better than mine is," Seth said with a grin, pleased that Mirabelle liked the colour scheme.

Alexis gave him a light push. "It's not all me, you goof. You picked out most of the colours. I decided where they would look best."

Seth egged her on by gently tugging on her braid, where it rested against her nape. "Yeah, and thanks to your creative genius, the flowers and vines are going to look fantastic."

Alexis giggled and swiped at his hand. "That tickles, you dork."

He did it again and backed up a step when she tried to kick

him in the shin. Laughter made her eyes sparkle, and she looked so damn appealing with her cheeks flushed to a soft pink. *Damn, those lips are made for a man to kiss.*

He focused on his best friend's wife to keep his mind and libido in check.

Mirabelle grinned at him and nodded. "It's going to look great when it's finished."

"I hope so," Alexis said. "I'm going to stay late in the evenings to paint. I'd like to have this done soon."

"Yeah, I'll stay with her, just to make sure she doesn't go crazy with putting too much colour in the wrong spot." Seth couldn't resist teasing her. She was so easy to joke around with.

Alexis pushed him in the side with a shoulder. "Asshole."

He stuck his tongue out at her jokingly. She mirrored it.

"Neither of you two have to stay late to get things done." Mirabelle glanced between them. "Alexis, you can work the store in the mornings and paint in the afternoons. I can deal with customers."

"What happens if you get busy, or a shipment comes in?" Alexis asked.

Mirabelle smiled. "I'll manage, and if I can't, I'll come get you. How does that sound?"

"Sure, that's fine," Alexis said.

Seth could see her twitching with barely concealed excitement. *She must really love to paint. I should hire her for jobs like this in the future. I wonder if Mirrie wouldn't mind loaning her out once in a while.* "Awesome, at this rate, those shelves should be done sometime next week, even with drying time and putting a top coat on them."

"Do the trim first. That way, it's up and ready before the shelves," Mirabelle said before she walked into her office.

Seth shook his head and glanced down at Alexis. "It's a damn good thing you brought your smock, huh?"

"Can't blame a girl for being prepared." She was almost

dancing in place.

"Speaking of being prepared, she's trying to weasel me into another blind date this weekend, and I had to lie to her."

Alexis frowned. "Oh? What is it this time, some cousin of a friend of a friend of a friend?"

"Something like that. I told her I had a date that night, but she doesn't believe me." He hated blind dates. The women Mirabelle had set him up with seemed nice and were smart, just as he liked, but for some reason, there was never that connection.

Then again, having what Janie did to him at the back of his mind didn't help him either. *Fucking bitch. Why can't I get over what she did to me?*

Alexis let out a long snort. "Who did you tell her you were taking out this time? She's not going to believe it until she sees you with another woman, you know."

Seth grinned evilly. "You."

"Me?" Alexis's eyes were huge behind her glasses.

Gotcha. Don't say I didn't warn you. "Don't you remember our deal?"

"I didn't think you were serious." She frowned, making her glasses slide down her nose a little.

"I am, and I thought you were." *Weren't you? Aw, shit, don't be mad for me being an ass and assuming.*

She let out a long breath and shot him a dirty look. "Fine. Let me know what's going on and when, so I'm ready on time."

Whew. That was a close one. I thought she was going to kick me in the balls for reminding her of our deal. "Friday night, at our usual bar. Seven o'clock. I owe you one."

"You can pay me back by doing the same when she gets up my ass," Alexis muttered. Her dark eyes shot fire.

He leaned forward to murmur in her ear, "With pleasure."

When he pulled back, their gazes locked. Alexis's breath hitched a little, and it sent a huge jolt of sexual awareness into his groin. The urge to crush her perfect soft pink lips under his walloped him between the eyes, making his vision blur. She was temptation personified, and Seth was losing his ability to resist her siren's call.

An image of his cold, manipulative ex-wife rose in his mind, which put out the flames of desire. *Argh. Why can't I let go of what Janie did to me?*

With a long sigh, he tweaked the tip of Alexis's nose in fun, gave her a wink, and turned to walk into the main part of the store.

Friday night, they were at their favourite hangout and playing pool again.

Halfway through a game, Alexis lined up the nine-ball and sank it in one swift move.

"Cheater," Blaine joked.

"Blame yourself, it was your shot that set me up perfectly," she shot back.

Alexis lined up to shoot at the number fourteen-ball. Seth came up behind her and said in her ear, "Watch out!" She jumped as the stick hit the cue ball, and it went off-kilter, rolling two inches.

She elbowed him in the gut and smiled when she heard him groan. "That's cheating, you jerk," she said over her shoulder. *Don't do that, please. I have enough problems concentrating without the smell of your aftershave around me or the feel of your body pushing against mine.*

"It's the only way we can win. Give us a break, Alexis," Blaine choked out around a snicker.

"Just for that, Alexis can take another shot," Mirabelle said with a dark look at her husband. Seth got a filthier look.

The men groaned.

Alexis shrugged. "Cheating is cheating. No mercy. Nine-ball in the center pocket," she stated with a smirk and lined up her shot. It went in with a loud clang and rolled into the ball holder deep inside of the table. *Take that, assholes.* The next three balls were gone in no time, and five seconds before it went home, Alexis called, "Eight-ball, corner pocket."

Seth's filthy look sent a jolt of satisfaction up Alexis's spine. "You asked for it," she told him and handed him her cue stick. "I'm thirsty, and I'm going to take a break. Hang that up for me, please."

He didn't reply, although his dark expression was so adorable in Alexis's eyes. *Typical man, he can't stand a woman showing him up. You'd think he would be used to it by now.*

She sat down beside Mirabelle at their usual table, not far from the billiards area.

Mirabelle leaned toward Alexis and asked, "Are you two a couple? Seth told me he already had a date, and I was not expecting to see you."

Alexis smiled. "No, we're just friends. He thought getting his ass kicked again was more fun than meeting some poor girl he'd never see again." *I completely get that. I'd rather hang out with Seth than some guy I would probably dislike on sight and hardly talk to.*

"You know he needs a woman in his life, and he can't meet anyone if he's always hanging out with you as friends." Mirabelle shook her head and sighed.

"Seth is a gentleman, and he thinks the poor girl you were setting him with was someone who wanted to be on a blind date as much as he did. He was trying to be nice and let you both off gently." Alexis smiled, hoping to reassure her boss that Seth wasn't ready to date anyone yet.

Mirabelle sighed and tapped a fingernail on the glass countertop. The blue polish looked almost purple in the low lighting. "Erin wasn't impressed that Angie wanted her to meet Seth in a double date setting either."

"So it's not only him. The women don't like it either," Alexis said pointedly.

Mirabelle nodded.

"If she wants to meet him, bring her to one of your barbecues, but no setting them up as a couple. Let them decide if they want to go on a date or not. If you try forcing a relationship, it may go boom in your face. Let them meet on their own terms," Alexis suggested gently.

"I was only thinking of Seth." Mirabelle frowned.

Alexis understood. Mirabelle adored Seth and had expressed that he deserved someone kind and loving after going through hell with Janie. Alexis covered Mirabelle's hand with her own. "He knows that, and he appreciates it, but you have to admit, he's not fully struck on the idea of meeting women he'd rather not date. He only does it to make you happy, even if it makes him miserable."

Mirabelle smiled sadly. "That's so typical of him. Always willing to suffer for my sake."

"Seth loves you like a sister, and he'd rather be tortured than disappoint or hurt you."

"He's like the brother I never had," Mirabelle said and sighed. "Fine. I'll let him go as long as he's open to dating again when he's ready."

"You'll be the first to know." Alexis smiled. She had a feeling Seth wouldn't say anything to Mirabelle when and if he was ever ready to start dating again. He was a man that preferred to do things his way, and Mirabelle's ideas for his perfect woman were way off the mark. Alexis had met Erin, the woman Mirabelle had in mind for that night once before. Erin was sweet but too docile in Alexis's opinion. *He needs someone bolder, who isn't afraid to put his male ego in its place when the testosterone is flying around.*

Mirabelle frowned again. "There is something odd with him."

"What is it?"

"How fast he warmed up to you, and I didn't set you two up at all." Mirabelle peered at her.

Alexis squirmed a little under the scrutiny. "That's probably why he doesn't mind me. I'm not some girl who is being
set up by a common friend or family member, and I'm not out
to get him into bed either."

"Well, he was always the one to take the safe route, except
for Janie."

"I'm as safe as they come, and he knows it. That's why he
asked me to tag along." Or was it? Seth had been acting a little
strange lately. The other day, she'd thought he was going to
kiss her, but he pulled back at the last second. *It's not like I
would have minded on one hand. On the other, I haven't told him
anything yet. I keep putting it off. I have to tell him, the sooner, the
better. If he wants to start something after that, I won't stop it.*

Mirabelle took a long gulp of her draft beer. "What if I said
I had a perfect guy in mind for you?"

Alexis smirked. "I'd tell you I had a date and bring Seth."

"You two worked on this together, you little shits." Mirabelle glared at her.

Alexis laughed. "It's better than being set up with someone
we'd probably never speak to again."

"What if I tried setting the pair of you up?" Mirabelle asked
with a sly smile.

"Me and Seth? Get real." *No, Mirrie. Don't you dare go there!
I don't want to be pushed on him, and I'd rather not have him
pushed on me, either. If something happens between us, it'll be because we wanted it to, not because you forced it.*

"You two are comfortable with each other, and you get
along great."

"We're friends." *And that's all it's staying unless we decide
otherwise.*

"Friends can turn into lovers," Mirabelle said with a wink.

"Or they can remain friends, which is what we'd prefer, so
no bright ideas." *Shut up, Mirrie!*

"Your choice."

"Exactly." *As much as I'd love to have a romp between the sheets with Seth, it won't happen. Not as long as he doesn't know how we really met five years ago.*

"Too bad, because it would have been perfect if you two were a couple. If you were, I wouldn't have to worry about putting up with another bitch like Janie." Mirabelle shrugged and sighed. "I can only hope he learned that lesson and sees the warning signs the next time."

"If he starts dating someone like her, I'll say something to him, I promise. I don't let a friend make the same stupid mistake twice," Alexis said with an evil grin.

"What were you two talking about?" Seth asked Alexis later that night after the pool cues were put away and the foursome had decided to stay to listen to the live music. They were on the dance floor during a slow song. Seth's hands were on her hips, and hers were on his shoulders as they moved to the music, with their fronts brushing from time to time.

It was perfection personified, but still bittersweet to Alexis. *I'm starting to want him more and more, yet I can't let him touch me – pure torture.* "Not much, other than I got you off the hook permanently," Alexis replied.

He shot her a confused glance.

Alexis leaned forward and said in his ear, "Mirrie promised not to set you up on another blind date unless you ask her." She pulled back and smirked at him.

"Really?" His teeth flashed in the dim light. "How did you get her to back off?"

"She thought we were a couple, and it was either have her up my ass about how we started dating without her realizing it, her trying to set us up, or come clean. I thought the truth was a lot less painful for all of us."

Seth cringed. "I'm so glad I didn't have to hear her grumble about me staying single."

"It wasn't that bad, especially when I reminded her that most of the time, you and the blind date never spoke again.

She really thought about it after I said the other woman probably liked being set up as much as you did."

"I owe you one. I've been trying to get away from Mirrie's schemes for a long time."

"I know, and you don't owe me a thing. We're friends, right?" *Keep it at that. Don't let my heart get involved, not now.*

He slid his arms around her waist and grinned down at her. "Right, and I couldn't ask for a better friend than you."

"Right back at you," she said with a wink.

Painting the trim for the archway was finished the following Tuesday. On Thursday, Seth started nailing it into place, starting with the part that went inside the expansion.

"That looks fantastic," Alexis exclaimed and caressed the north border of it with her fingers.

He grinned and stood back to admire it with her. "It does because I had a great helper." He nudged her arm with an elbow.

"Your design, not mine. I only chose the colours for it," she said as the chime above the door tinkled. "I'd better get that."

"You helped," he shot at her retreating back and bent over to pick up the connecting section. *She's a damn fine helper, too. The work went a lot faster with a pretty girl to talk to.*

He was fitting the connecting part into place when Alexis bellowed, "Get the hell out of here and never come back!"

Puzzled, Seth poked his head around the corner toward the front of the store. He blinked to alleviate some of the glare from the sunshine and used a hand to shield his eyes. Through the glare and the rainbows caused by sunlight going through various glass items, he could see Alexis. She stood between him and the windows, an arm raised to a right angle from her body and her finger stabbing the air toward the door.

"Aw, come on, baby," a male voice whined. "I said I was

sorry!"

"I don't care if you are or not. I said I don't want to speak to you again, and I thought a restraining order would make that very clear. Leave, or I call the cops," she snarled.

Seth's internal warning system went on yellow alert. Alexis never yelled at anyone, not even a wasp, so hearing her hollering at someone meant trouble. Restraining orders were only given out if there was a threat to someone, or if there was proof of physical assault or abuse.

The unknown male moved closer to Alexis, out of the glare, to reveal a thin face with sunken eyes and cheeks. He was reed-thin, and his hands shook as he gestured rapidly.

Seth's entire being stiffened, ready to pounce if needed. Anyone who was that jumpy was more than likely on something illegal. He slowly stood up and quietly moved toward Alexis and the intruder, using the shelves and clutter as a shield.

The other man grabbed her arm, which made the edges of Seth's vision turn a hazy red.

Alexis leaped backwards, her braid slapping against her back as she put distance between herself and the intruder. "I don't care if the restraining order ran out a month ago or not. I don't want to have a damn thing to do with you, Brett!"

Brett's eyes narrowed. He moved forward one step, his face darkening.

Seth's teeth ground together. *Shit, he looks pissed, and being on something could only add to it. This may escalate fast if something isn't done. Now.* He had to finish it before someone got hurt. *Not Alexis. I'd kill someone if this asshole laid a finger on her.*

Soft footsteps came from behind Seth. Without moving his gaze from Alexis and Brett, he hissed, "Call the cops. Now."

"Gotcha," Mirabelle whispered, and soft footsteps quickly zipped away.

Seth focused on the situation at hand. *I'm going to shoot this guy unless he leaves within the next five seconds!*

Brett whined, "I thought you'd be happy to see me, Al." He pouted.

"Not after what you did to me, you lousy jerk! I told you it was over, get it through your thick skull!" Alexis took another step backwards and stopped. She couldn't move any further because her back was against the counter.

Seth's stomach clenched painfully. *Fuck. Come this way, sweetheart. He won't touch you if I have anything to do with it.*

"I still love you, and I said I'm sorry." Brett's puppy dog look didn't arouse Seth's sympathy.

Yeah, I bet he still loves her, in the way he loves everyone — when they can do things for him — fucking asshole. Seth kept his gaze on them and slinked forward a few steps. He stopped just out of sight of the combatants, behind a shelf, where he could see everything happening via the openings between items. Alexis glared at Brett, but her hand shook when she shoved her glasses up higher on her nose. She seemed scared of him. What had he done to her?

"You never loved me. You told the cops I was selling the drugs, not you, and then you tried to beat the shit out of me when I wouldn't sing the same song!" Alexis snapped.

Hate for Brett—who Seth suspected was Alexis's ex-boy-friend—rose in his gut. His jaw tightened, his hands fisted, and veins popped out on his arms as he tried to control his temper. Men who hit women were vile creatures in Seth's opinion. Only pedophiles were lower on the list of scum. *He touches her again, and he's a dead man walking.*

"I was going to jail if they caught me. I had to keep you in line somehow. Else you would have done it again. If you did what you were supposed to do instead of defying me, I wouldn't have had to hurt you, Al!" Brett shouted. His hands flailed wildly, almost hitting a glass shelf filled with crystal ornaments to his right.

"Sure, blame someone else for your stupidity and nasty side, just like you always do. You haven't changed one bit, and you never will!" Alexis looked ready to fight, although Seth could see she was cowering despite her bravado. Her body was visibly shaking, and he could see her lower lip tremble as she barked at her ex-boyfriend. Hell, he could hear the fear in her voice.

Damn that mother-fucking pussy. Too bad it was illegal to beat up people like him because Seth would gladly show that loser the time of day.

"I have changed," Brett grumbled. "I wanted to tell you I stopped delivering stuff. That's why you left me, right? I didn't want you to leave me. I still love you."

"I left you because you're an asshole, and you beat me senseless when the urge hit you," Alexis fired back. There was a soft tremor in her voice.

Seth closed his eyes in sympathy for a second. *Stand tall, sweetheart. Don't let him know you're shaking in your shoes.* He focused his gaze on her and prayed Brett would leave.

Alexis's anger must have started coming to the surface because she suddenly straightened and spat, "If you really cared about me, you would leave me alone and let me move on, Brett. How long did you stalk me before you decided to come in here? A month? Two months?"

"This town always made you crazy, Al. I think it's time you came home and let me show you how much I still love you." Brett reached a hand toward her. It was grubbier than his filthy hoodie.

Brett's slimy voice made Seth's stomach revolt. He recognized the same tone Janie used to use on him to manipulate him into doing something she wanted. If he didn't follow her orders, there would be hell to pay. He had to repair a lot of damage to his house after Janie left. Holes in the walls, smashed windows, and furniture torn to shreds or smashed, the list was endless. *I should have sued her ass off when she left — the destruction of property. But by then, I was done with her and wanted it over with.*

Brett moved another inch or so closer to Alexis.

Seth almost growled — his loathing for the miserable creature was going beyond his control. He'd land in jail for murder before Brett hurt Alexis again. Where were the police?

Alexis's eyes narrowed behind her lenses, and she straightened to her full height, a bare inch below Brett's. "This town suits me perfectly fine, thank you," she replied primly.

Brett leaned forward and shook his head. "The cops here brainwashed you, else you'd see the truth. Come home with me, and you'll be fine."

Yeah, so you can beat her and brainwash her into thinking you're perfect? Not on my watch, asswipe. Seth's jaw clicked as he fought to keep silent. *A few more seconds, and I'll show my cards. Let Brett the lowlife dig himself a bit deeper.*

Alexis folded her arms across her chest.

Seth wanted to cheer when he saw the defiance in her stance. "I am perfectly fine, and they didn't brainwash me. You did. They let me go because they saw I wasn't the real troublemaker," Alexis shot back.

"Shut up!" Brett bellowed, and his hands fisted as he took another step toward Alexis.

That son of a bitch! He's going to meet his match. With a glare at Brett, Seth eased out from behind the shelves and casually hooked his thumbs in the front pockets of his jeans. "Hey, Alexis, do you need some help taking out the trash?"

When she saw Brett, Alexis had been terrified for her safety and Mirabelle's. *Until Seth arrived.* Somehow, she knew Seth would tear her ex-boyfriend apart if he dared to touch her. *Hopefully, he didn't hear all of it, because he won't talk to me once he remembers.* The thought of losing Seth's friendship sent a stab of agony into her heart. Alexis kept her glare on her ex-boyfriend and shook her head, although she was visibly shaking and ready to faint from anxiety and fear. "I'm fine, thanks,

Seth. Brett was just leaving."

Brett glanced at Seth and sneered, "Yeah, right."

Seth mocked, "Yeah, right." He was just inside of her line of vision, and he sounded pissed.

Brett spit on the floor close to Seth's steel-toed boots. "Keep out of this, asshole. It's none of your business."

Brett, that was dumb. Stop being a shit disturber and get lost before Seth lets you have it. Alexis had no doubt that Seth would tear Brett apart if provoked. Seth was protective of those he cared about, and she was one of his friends. It would be a bloodbath if Seth lost his temper.

Seth snorted sarcastically. "I'll go if Alexis wants me to leave."

"It's a public place. You don't have to leave at all if you don't want to." *Please don't go. He'll cause a lot of trouble if you leave.*

"Sorry, pal. It seems you're out of luck." Two footsteps later, Seth stood beside her. He was so close that his arm brushed hers, and she could smell the turpentine he'd used to wash his hands a while ago. His presence made her feel safe. Alexis wanted to hug him but stood her ground. Brett used other people's weaknesses to get his own way.

"Fuck off, asswipe." Brett gave Seth the finger.

Seth clicked his tongue. "That's not the kind of language you use around a lady. Apologize to her."

"What lady? All I see is a stupid, useless bitch. I ain't apologizing for something she deserves." Brett hawked loudly and spit on the floor by Alexis's sneakers.

Seth nonchalantly straightened his shoulders and smirked. "Looked in the mirror, did you?"

Brett's face turned red, and he snarled.

Seth smirked.

Brett's hand fisted, and a heartbeat later, he took a swing at Seth.

Seth caught Brett's hand and held it firmly. His fingers

started to close together. Brett grimaced in pain. "So, you think using your fists is the way to get people to listen to you, huh?" Seth hissed.

Now you've done it, Brett. Throwing a punch at Seth was really stupid. If he breaks your fingers, I'll testify it was in self-defence. Alexis remembered the security cameras. *I'll just back them up. Mirrie could be watching this from the office, and I hope she called the police. Brett won't bugger off until he knows they are on the way.*

Brett whimpered in pain, his face contorted, and his knees started to buckle.

The veins in Seth's forearm started to bulge as he applied more force.

Brett's knees hit the floor, and he gasped in pain.

Seth leaned forward and muttered, "You have three choices, Brett. You can go now, before the cops come, and never come back. Secondly, you can face the music and let the cops charge you with attempted assault. You're on camera, so it'll be hard for your sleazy lawyer to get you off this time."

"And my last choice?" Brett demanded in a groan.

Seth grinned evilly. "I'll show you what a wimp like you deserves for laying a finger on a woman."

"What if I don't choose?" Brett's words were strained.

Dumb move, Brett. Shut up and go before Seth tears a strip off your smelly hide.

"I'll pick number three because I want to give a little shit like you the time of day."

"Women deserve to be put in their place, especially a whore like her," Brett said with a smug smile.

Alexis's eyes widened — what a stupid comeback. Fighting Seth would land Brett in the hospital, and Seth in deep trouble with the law.

The first sounds of a siren entered the store. *Thank fuck. I hope they catch Brett this time. I'm so fucking tired of running from him.*

Seth's fingers tightened slightly. Brett yelped as his knuckles started to crack. "I'll leave her alone! Please let go of me!"

Seth tightened his fingers again. "Do you give me your word you'll leave this town and stay away from Alexis from now on?"

"Yes, yes, I give you my word!" Brett whimpered.

Seth dropped him.

Brett had only enough time to let out a gasp before he was dragged to his feet. Seth held Brett by the front of his hoodie, the men were eye to eye, and Seth glared into the pale greenish face with red-rimmed eyes.

"If I ever see you within ten miles of Alexis again, you'll have more than a sore hand," Seth hissed, and his voice was full of malice. His eyes were almost black with hate, and his entire face looked carved from granite.

It was a terrifying sight for Alexis, although deep down, she knew Seth wouldn't hurt her. Her instincts said he would never hurt a woman intentionally, but people like Brett were fair game.

Brett's face took on a deeper greenish hue. "Yes, sir!" he snivelled with wide eyes.

Seth let go of Brett, who slowly backed up a few steps without removing his terrified stare from Seth's. He jumped when his back touched the front window, and with a loud sob, he bolted through the door.

As Brett disappeared from sight, Alexis closed her eyes, let out the breath she had been holding, and started shivering despite the summer sunshine and warmth. *That was so fucking close! How did he find me? I didn't think he'd look for me here. Why does he keep following me? I told him we were done five years ago.* She bit her lip and tried to hold back a sob.

"Alexis, did he hurt you?"

She opened her eyes. Seth was staring down at her with concern. His jaw was in its normal position, his eyes were back to their beautiful navy, and his frown was gone.

She trembled as she shook her head. "He didn't hurt me."

Seth touched her cheek. His fingers were warm and strong and felt so good on her skin. "He's gone, and if he's smart, he'll stay away from now on." His voice felt like silk to her ears.

She closed her eyes and took a few shaky breaths. *I hope you're right, Seth.* Brett had found her before, which had made her run on several occasions. Now that he knew where she worked and who she hung out with, he'd wait until she was alone and strike. He kept showing up, no matter where she had lived in the last five years since she'd had enough of him and his terrible behaviour.

Her lips trembled with unshed tears as she whispered, "He's not done yet, Seth. He's going to come back when he thinks I'm alone here or at home."

His reply was cut off by a town policeman walking into the store.

"What's the problem?" the officer asked.

Alexis opened her eyes, and her stomach sank when she recognized Sargent Boutillier, one of the two officers she'd dealt with after her arrest five years ago. *Great, my day got even better!*

Chapter Six

Mirabelle gave her statement at the store, and the officers took the surveillance videos as evidence. Alexis opted to give hers at the station, away from Seth. She wanted to tell him the truth in private, and after she was calmer.

She tensed up when she realized Constable Manning was taking her statement. The same officer who interrogated her after her one and only arrest, five years ago, and in this same room. *Does she recognize me?*

The female officer flipped open a file and smiled at her reassuringly. In return, Alexis's smile was nauseated. She felt dizzy, queasy, and ready to cry. Why did Brett keep causing trouble for her wherever she went? She was sick of being stalked, having him show up every few months, and most of all, sick of moving. *I want a normal life, and Brett won't let me do it. That bastard causes trouble wherever I land.*

Constable Manning scanned a paper in the file. "Miss Graves, your ex-boyfriend isn't a stranger to us. According to our records, Mr. Galloway was arrested in Bridgewater about five years ago, on suspicion of drug trafficking." Her voice was level, calm, and reassuring.

Alexis's stomach started sinking. "Yes, he was." She started playing with her rings like she always did when she was anxious.

"You were with him when we took him into custody." There was sympathy in Manning's blue eyes.

Alexis nodded and remembered she had to respond verbally. "Yes." Her stomach felt wobbly, despite the officer's obvious attempts to keep her calm.

"I interrogated you, and if memory serves, he was interviewed by my partner. You were later released because you were clean and had no prior record." Manning tapped her pen against the pad of paper.

"That's right." Alexis didn't budge her gaze. *Short, sweet and to the point when it comes to me. Details galore when it comes to Brett.*

"It's required that I ask, and I'm sorry about this. Are you still seeing him?" There was a layer of sympathy in the officer's soft voice.

"Absolutely not. I broke up with him not long after his Bridgewater arrest." Alexis had enough of Brett's antics when he tried hitting her the next night. She'd grabbed what few things she owned, including her clothing, and left him two days later.

Constable Manning nodded with a smile and made a note on a legal pad. "I didn't think you were, going by your actions today. Did you have any contact with him after your breakup?"

"Yes, but not as his girlfriend. I've moved around a lot, and he still manages to find me." Her fingernails painfully dug into her palms with frustration. She went on to explain why she'd broken up with Brett and how he kept finding her, no matter where she was living.

"So, even though you had a restraining order in place for two years, he was still bothering you? Why didn't you contact the Mounties or the local police?" Constable Manning asked. She seemed puzzled but still sympathetic.

"I did, several times, but by the time they got there, he was gone. He'd show up again, and that would be it for me. I would move to another place after that. He would hide for a while, start looking for me again and eventually catch up to me. Hell, he found me even when I was living in New Brunswick two years ago."

Manning looked at the file in front of her again and sighed. "According to our records, he's been linked to several gangs across eastern Canada, and they share information from time to time. For a price, of course." She shook her head and frowned at the file. "It looks like they will search for someone who went underground, too, and it looks like that's how he's been finding you. I'm sorry, Alexis." The officer let out a long breath.

Shock rippled through Alexis, and she stared at the cop in disbelief. The edges of her vision started turning yellow, and the grey, sterile room started turning hazy. *No. He didn't. He wasn't using his gangster friends to stalk me.*

Was he? She thought about the times she'd thought he wouldn't find her because she was in such a small town, or in a large city far away from Stellarton, Nova Scotia, their home town. He still showed up, almost like clockwork, about three to four months after she arrived in each town.

It was almost exactly three months since she'd moved into her tiny apartment in Bridgewater. Her shock turned to rage on a dime. *Son of a bitch! That rat bastard! So that's how he's doing it. I knew I shouldn't have stayed with him the first time I caught him swallowing balloons of heroin. He was a mule for years, and I didn't want to see it. He had me believing he was the best lover and sweetest guy in the world. That's what I get for being stupid. I am getting a taser. Today. I want one that delivers the biggest zap possible. Brett deserves to have his balls burned off!* "That son of a—" Alexis cleared her throat and tried to swallow her fury.

The constable shoved a box of tissues across the table, compassion shining through her gestures. "I want to hear your side of today's incident. Take your time. We want this done right, so we can prevent him from stalking you again."

Alexis's hands shook as she took a tissue and gave her statement, only stopping to answer any direct questions from

Constable Manning.

After half an hour, Alexis was finished telling Manning everything she remembered.

"Would you like to press charges? Even though the restraining order has run out, you can still hit him with harassment." Manning smiled at her reassuringly.

Alexis tore a corner off her already shredded tissue and sighed. "Can I let it go until he bothers me again?" *I'd rather not deal with this. Not now. I just want to go home and get into bed. I want to forget this day ever happened!*

"It's not recommended, but if that's what you'd prefer —"

Alexis sighed. "Yes, it is. He'll bother me just for this, somehow, somewhere. I think the more you guys know about him before I hit him with anything, the better."

Constable Manning nodded and wrote something down. "I'll make a note of it, and we'll keep an eye out for him."

"Thank you."

The blue-eyed officer gently peered at her. "The next time you see him, even if it's in passing, call the Mounties or us. Since he's still bothering you five years after your breakup, that means he's a threat, and today's incident will look insignificant compared to anything he may do in the future." She leaned forward and patted Alexis's hand.

Grateful for the officer's kind words and offer of assistance, Alexis nodded with a small smile. "I will, thank you."

As Alexis stood, she remembered her vow to get personal protection. She turned and asked Constable Manning, "Before I go, do you know where I can get a legal taser or something like pepper spray?"

Alexis entered the lobby of the station, looking for Seth. The room was deserted. Not even the dispatcher was in her spot at the desk. Somehow, despite the sunshine streaming through the tinted windows, it made the place look more foreboding, more sterile.

Fear rose in her gut, her hands shook, and tears burned her eyes as everything started colliding in her mind. In the one town she'd hoped Brett would be smart enough to avoid, he had found her. *I was so stupid to believe him when he told me that we were only coming down here to visit a friend. Friend, my ass!*

She closed her eyes, and the events of that long-ago day played out on the canvas of her eyelids. One flash saw them in one of the unlit portions of a wooded park in town, and Brett was talking to a man she had never seen before. The second flash was of Brett handing the other man a parcel, and in return, the man handed him a wad of cash.

The air turned to concrete, and her body felt leaden as an image of gunmetal flashed in the light from Brett's lighter whipped through her mind. She could almost feel the iciness of the gun's barrel against her cheek and the memory of Brett's harsh threats, backed by his harsh, moonshine scented breath in her ear.

Don't move, bitch. Stay put, or you're swallowing a bullet.

He had been aroused, too. He always was when he was threatening her somehow, and he always had to get off after the deeds were done. Her mouth, her ass, or her cunt were plummeted repeatedly with his lust, depending on his mood.

She tried to hold back the terror, but the sight of the stark grey walls and remembering Brett's actions in the store were too much. She crumpled to the floor with a low moan, covered her head with her arms and curled up.

Hiding.

Seth's interrogation took a little longer than Alexis's, despite her history with the suspect. He went over every detail more than once, to show Sargent Boutillier he was telling the truth, from how he had waited until Brett tried manhandling Alexis, to who threw the first punch and why.

He kept his anger buried. The last thing he needed was to

be known as a hothead to the police. They needed to focus on catching Brett — or as Seth called him, *pussyface* — not be on the watch for Seth to lose his cool.

Finally, Sargent Boutillier looked at Seth with a reassuring smile, the first Seth had seen from the tall, silver-haired officer. "You're free to go, Mr. Mitchell. You were protecting Miss Graves, and any actions against Brett Halloway were self-defence on your part. It was all caught on the security cameras in the store, and it exonerates you."

Seth stood and shook hands with the almost military-like Sargent. Although they had met a few times before, it was the first in a formal setting. Seth was glad he wasn't a criminal, Boutillier could get a nun to confess to murder if he wanted to.

It's a damn good thing the cops around here know I'm not a shit disturber. He glanced at his watch when his stomach growled and was surprised to see it was mid-afternoon. *No wonder why I'm hungry. Hopefully, Alexis is up to getting a steak and playing some pool. She needs to relax after this morning.*

Seth exited the questioning area. According to Constable Manning, Alexis was finished with her statement and in the lobby. A weird sense of Deja-vu came over him as he exited the back part of the police station. He glanced around, saw the stark gray cement walls, the hum of the lights overhead, and sunlight streaming through the tinted windows. Although his throat closed, sweat formed along his upper lip and under his arms, and his legs shook, he took a step toward the main door.

A sob to his right made his insides freeze.

Seth knew what he'd see if he turned his head.

He took a deep breath and moved his gaze. His symptoms of Deja-vu evaporated when he saw a flowery blue blouse and faded blue jeans instead of the blackness that blended into the shadows of the room. The only resemblance she had to the other girl was the way she was sitting, with her feet pulled against her bottom, her face pressed against her knees, and her forearms and hands wrapped around her head.

Oh shit. No, don't cry, baby. He's gone. He's not going to hurt you again, not if I have anything to do about it. Seth took five steps across the lobby and crouched in front of her. "Alexis," he whispered and touched her sneakered foot.

Her head shot up. Their gazes met. A stronger sense of foreboding hit Seth in the gut, and he could taste bile on his tongue. Alexis's expression was identical to the one he had seen only in his dreams. She was wide-eyed, her face was wet and shiny from tears, her lower lip trembled, and her eyes held fear and resignation. She wiped a tear away with her sleeve, which made her more vulnerable. Seth wanted to hold her tight and protect her from the evils of this world. *Don't cry, sweetheart. I'm not going to let that asshole hurt you ever again.*

When she blinked and bit her lip, his world turned over, the air turned to titanium, and his throat felt like it was full of stinging wasps. *No. This isn't happening. Alexis can't be the girl from my dreams. Alexis is real. The girl is not.*

Sourness rose in his throat, and the sounds of the police station faded.

"You seem like a smart girl, don't waste your life on someone that won't do anything other than cause trouble for you and others." His voice echoed in his ears. He closed his eyes and saw everything clearly, from the way the girl was sitting in his dream, to the sound of her sobs, and even the greying laces in her white sneakers.

Like the core of a dying star, every piece fused into one.

Holy shit. It's not a dream. It's a memory.

Something touched his arm, and the sounds and sights of the room came back to him.

"Seth, you're not overheated again, are you?" Apparently, she thought he was experiencing heatstroke like he had led her to believe each time portions of the dream came to him when she did something that reminded him of the girl's.

White-hot rage filled his chest. *It's been more than six weeks since I met her. It was five years ago. Problems with the law be damned, and who gives a flying fuck her ex-boyfriend was a piece of shit.* Lying about their first meeting was unforgivable in Seth's eyes. It was akin to murder to him after what that cunning and cold bitch Janie did to him for their entire marriage.

He kept his gaze on hers as he reached up to cover Alexis's hand on his arm with his own. He would wait to yell at her about it when they were not in a public area. A line of rage-filled words was firmly swallowed, and he replied in his calmest and quietest voice, "I'd better get you home." He stood and held out a hand.

Alexis gave him a funny look, and tentatively, she allowed him to help her to her feet. She kept a foot of space between them as he gestured toward the exit.

He didn't want her to run away on him, so he took her elbow. Her arm felt tense, and she tried pulling away from him. He gently and firmly held on to her, through the door and on to the sidewalk facing Dufferin Street. Seth felt his jaw tightening each time he heard her breathing. He was pissed enough to chew plutonium. *How dare she? Mirrie told me that Alexis knows what Janie was like. Why didn't she say something instead of waiting until now?* He guided her toward his truck, trying not to stomp his feet as they turned the corner on to Exhibition Drive, toward the parking lot behind the Bridgewater town police station.

Alexis was dragging her feet. He could feel the resistance as she slowed her pace. Seth forced himself not to pick her up and throw her over his shoulder. "What's going on?" she asked, her voice small and wary.

"I'm driving you home." He pulled the keys out of his pocket and hit the unlock button on the keyring. The clicks sounded loud over the traffic on Dufferin Street.

She stopped and pulled her elbow out of his hand. "You can drop me off at the store. I'll get my car."

Annoyance shot through his gut. *Yeah, she knows something is up. Too fucking bad. She fucked me over. No way am I letting her get away without letting her have it.* "I said I'd drive you home, Alexis." He kept his voice cool.

She squirmed back an inch. She sounded terrified when she replied, "I know, but you don't have to. My car is at the store, and —"

Annoyance fed his fury, and it was all he could do to contain it. His reply was short, snappy, and filled with quiet rage. "You and I need to talk, and not in a public place." He could feel the cords in his neck start to bulge. If he didn't get her in a private place soon, the cops and anyone within earshot were going to get one hell of a show.

Alexis's eyes widened behind her glasses, and she took a step backwards, hands in the air. "We can still do that. I'll follow you home in my car."

"Be quiet and stop arguing with me, Alexis!" he growled as he let a tiny part of his anger loose.

She cringed away from him and held her hands over her head defensively. It was something he had seen other beaten women do in the past, and guilt washed away part of the anger. *Wait a second, is she doing that for sympathy? If so, that's another mark against her.* He took a deep breath to keep his temper in check. *I can't believe I was starting to think about asking her out, or that she was cute. Women. They're all alike. You can't trust them at all, only Mirrie and Mallory. The rest are conniving twats, including Alexis.* He opened the passenger door of his truck and gestured for Alexis to get in.

She cringed away from him.

Seth let out a long, annoyed sigh. "Get in, Alexis. Now." When she hesitated again, he added, "Don't worry, I'm not a useless dirt-bag like your ex. I don't hurt women, even lying ones like you."

She blinked several times, probably to hold back the crocodile tears, before she crawled into the cab.

Seth climbed into the driver's seat and started the engine. He glanced over at Alexis.

She sat with slumped shoulders and her head on her chest. Her body visibly trembled, and her voice shook. "Seth, please tell me what's going on."

As he donned his seat belt, he turned to face her and hissed, "Oh, I will, *after* you tell me why you didn't tell me about your previous arrest in Bridgewater, and why you lied to me about how we *really* met five years ago."

Her head shot up, and as her wide-eyed gaze met his, she burst into tears.

Tension crackled out of Seth as he drove toward her apartment building. His fingers dug grooves into the steering wheel, and he had to monitor a heavy foot on the gas pedal. His teeth ground together, and veins in his arms were popping out as he tried to control his fury.

He deliberately took his time maneuvering his truck along the streets, to allow the consequences of her actions to sink into Alexis's brain.

He could see her huddled against the passenger side door, as far as she could get away from him while wearing a seat belt, and she trembled as she tried not to cry openly. She seemed terrified of him and his anger, and he wondered if it was because she was truly sorry for lying to him, or was sorry she'd been caught. She had been a good friend, someone he liked a lot, and he enjoyed being around her. All of it had been shattered when her treachery had been exposed. It hurt him a lot, and for that, Seth didn't think he could ever forgive her or forget it.

On impulse, he drove past the turnoff for her apartment building and directed his truck toward his house, a one and a half story residence in Wileville. Normally, he was proud of his home. It was his first major project, built on the edge of his parents' farm, and it was his oasis.

Why are you taking Alexis there? If you're going to scream at her, do it at the store or her place. Don't fuck up your private space. He ignored the voice and determinedly made a beeline for his house. *Better to yell at her where no one can hear us.* His house was more than a kilometre off the road and surrounded by trees in its own little haven, across the old fields from his parents' home that was still standing one hundred years after it was built.

Seth spared a glance to his right. Alexis's eyes were closed, and her sniffles echoed in the cab as the pickup covered the miles between the police station and his home. She didn't lift her head until he turned off the pavement into his driveway. Her expression didn't change. Tears were still leaking out of her eyes, and she looked like her world had ended. A shot of sympathy rose in his gut, and it was tamped down immediately. *She's a liar. Don't let her manipulate you.*

Seth navigated the gravel drive toward his house. It was a bitch to clear in the wintertime, but the privacy and quiet of the woods balanced it out. They made the last turn, and pride rose in his chest. Made of weathered grey wood with a grey metal roof and a single attached garage, it blended in with the quiet of the forest surrounding it. Even the row of solar panels on the front part of the roof seemed like they were a part of the natural surroundings.

He parked the truck in front of the porch and put it in park. After flipping off the key and extracting it, he reached across Alexis to open her door.

She sniffled loudly and wiped her nose on her sleeve.

Seth didn't feel like offering her a tissue or anything else. He was still boiling with rage. It calmed a little when Alexis unfastened her belt and slid out of the truck. The door shut quietly behind her.

Although somewhat calmer, Seth glared at her and gestured for her to follow him before he stomped up the three steps onto the porch. Softer, quieter treads behind him told him Alexis was complying with his silent orders. He unlocked the house, and without looking over his shoulder, entered. The dark brown of his living room welcomed him, and so did the faint scent of lemon cleaner, an indication his mother had been there, cleaning for him again.

He turned left, past the stairs, and into the kitchen. Sure enough, there was a note on the counter, propped up against the toaster oven.

S – Your dad wanted lasagna for supper last night, and I made too much again. There's some in the fridge. Reheat at 350 for about 20 minutes, and don't burn it! Love, Mom.

Seth grinned at his mother's handwriting. It seemed she was always making too much food, and she wound up bringing a lot of the leftovers to his house, or his brother's place in Newcombville. Karen Mitchell loved her children and tended to fuss over her youngest, Seth, because he wasn't married like his brother, David.

She always leaves too much for one meal. Seth sighed. If only Alexis hadn't been such a liar, he'd ask her to stay for supper and help him clean up the usual big pan of pasta his mother left for him. With a shake of his head, Seth balled up the note and tossed it into the paper recycling bin by the edge of the countertop, in the dining area.

He turned and faced Alexis. She was still quiet and had followed him silently into the house. He could see her looking back and forth from time to time as if she was trying to see everything without being obvious about it.

Seth narrowed his eyes at her and cleared his throat. She jumped a clear foot off the floor and took a large, shaking breath. He went into the dining area, grabbed a chair, and placed it between the sink on one side of the narrow kitchen and the stove on the other side. "Sit," he said in a calm, cold tone. The placement was deliberate. It was easiest to intimidate her into confessing her lies. Part of Seth wanted to put the fear of God into her. He hated liars, especially women who lied. *Damn.* Janie had fucked him royally.

Alexis eyed him warily and hung back. She seemed to shrink in upon herself. She quickly shook her head.

He leaned forward and hissed, "Sit, or I'll tell Mirrie you are open to blind dates."

Alexis swallowed hard with wide eyes, and her butt was in the chair in less than three seconds. She didn't look at him and hung her head as her shoulders drooped.

"Start talking," he ordered in a snarl and leaned back against the counter with a glare and his arms folded across his chest.

Alexis took a deep breath. "Seth, I know you don't believe me, but I am really sorry—"

"You're right. I don't give a shit how sorry you are. You lied to me, and that's a big deal-breaker in my book." His entire body shook with rage. He could feel the cords in his arms stretching his skin as he tried to keep his irritability in control.

Sobs shook her body. "I didn't lie to you."

"Yes, you did. Instead of saying how we *really* met five years ago, you let me believe it was the first time we met when Mirrie introduced us a few weeks ago," he hissed between clenched teeth. Her words ignited his anger. "Fuck," he growled, and his clenched hand connected hard with the lower cupboards behind him.

Alexis jumped and whimpered, "You didn't seem to remember me at the time. I was going to tell you when the time was right, but things kept messing it up."

"Well, it backfired on you, and what a fucking mess you're in now. Don't like it much when you're caught, do ya?" He couldn't help it. Every single bit of rage, disappointment, and pain she had caused him came out in his words. He wanted to slam his fists against the fireplace until they were smashed and bloody, then curl up into a ball and let the agony flow out of him like arterial blood, crimson against the hardwood floor.

Her sobs echoed in the kitchen and into his heart. "I'm sorry because I hurt you, Seth."

"Bullshit," he snapped, his fingers dug into the varnished wooden cupboard behind him.

She lifted her head and met his gaze. Spiky eyelashes were visible behind the lenses of her glasses, which were wet with tears. "Obviously, you're not in the mood to believe me," she choked out and started to get up. "Take me home, please."

"You're staying put until I get a few more answers. Sit down. Now." The command was clear despite the agony behind the words.

She stared at him with wide eyes and a trembling lower lip as her butt connected with the chair again.

"Spill it," he bellowed when she didn't start talking.

"We did meet five years ago, and yes, it was at the police station," she whispered, so softly that Seth could barely hear her. "Brett had been arrested for trafficking that night, and since I was with him, I was brought in, too. He had gotten a call from someone down here. We met his contact in the park. I can't remember which one."

She glanced up at Seth and continued, "Uh, it turned out the contact was really an undercover cop. I guess they knew there was a line down this way, and somehow managed to find it, and Brett." She played with the now soggy sleeve of her blouse and didn't look at him.

Seth's rage eased a notch downwards. The police officer had said the same thing during his own questioning.

Alexis took a deep breath. "They let me go once they realized I was clueless about what was going on, and I didn't have anything to do with it. I didn't run because I was surprised and was scared out of my mind when I realized we were in deep shit. I was only there because Brett demanded it, so he could turn the blame on me if he was busted. I found that out while I was being questioned, and I was so upset that he'd do something like that, I started crying, right in front of the officers."

That much had been said in her and pussyface's argument that morning. Seth's anger started to dissolve a little more, although his trust in her was still shattered. "Do you have a record?" he asked.

She shook her head. "The police in various towns know I was one of his associates, that's it."

Seth nodded. That had also been mentioned in his talk with Constable Manning's partner, Sargent Boutillier. His anger cooled by a few more points.

Alexis pushed her spectacles higher on her nose and whispered, "I think you were on your way out, and you saw me in the corner. I had been there all night, and wasn't sure what time it was, only that it was sunny that day."

"It was in the morning," he said quietly as the memories from that day became clearer. "I had stopped in to see a friend of mine who was an officer, to let him know his cabinet was ready and he could pick it up anytime. He wasn't there, so I left a note telling him to call me on my cell."

She gave him a small, sad smile. It was enough to melt the remaining rage in Seth's chest. "The reasons why you were there don't matter as much as how nice you were to me that day. Those few minutes changed my life forever." She held his gaze and whispered, "If you hadn't talked to me that morning, I don't think I could have left him."

He stared at her, surprised. "You're kidding."

She glanced away and back at him. "I hadn't had a guy talk to me like that in years before that day. I was used to being talked down to by Brett and his friends. You treating me like an equal made me see that not all guys are useless jerks like he is. You were a gentleman and let me cry on your shoulder, even though you didn't know shit about me or my life."

How she'd looked that day was forever engraved in Seth's mind. "I remember your hair was black, and it sort of blended in with your sweater at the time," he said with a wry grin, despite still being a deeply hurt at her dishonesty.

"I am sorry about not saying anything. When I moved here, I didn't think Brett would follow me. He knows the police in this town will watch him if they know he's here. He got off on a loophole, thanks to that sleazy lawyer his boss hired for him.

"I was wrong for keeping my mouth shut. I should have said something to you right away, like thank you for being there for me. I hoped you wouldn't remember me at all, so I could pretend I wasn't arrested here. You're one of my best friends, and I really didn't want to hurt you like this. You're a sweet guy, and I trust you a lot." She sighed and sniffled loudly. "It won't happen again. No more hiding for me." She glanced up at him. The tears in her eyes looked genuine. "If you'd rather not talk to me again after today, I get it."

Seth's anger was replaced by sorrow for harming her in return. The remaining tension left his body, and although still hurting, he understood Alexis's motives for not being truthful from the start. He pushed himself away from the counter and motioned to her. "Come here."

She stared at him warily as she rose from her chair, still crying a little.

He lifted her chin with a hand and stared down at her.

Their gazes locked for eternity.

He brushed a stray tear off her cheek with his free hand. "I forgive you," he said quietly.

Alexis beamed at him through her tears, and she threw her arms around his neck.

Seth's forgiveness released the tension around Alexis's heart. She had been terrified of losing his friendship, so much that she had been willing to eat white-hot coals to prove that she hadn't meant to deceive him or omit how they had truly met years ago.

He froze with his arms hanging at his sides when she hugged him. *Oh shit, too much too soon after the argument?*

A second later, his arms were around her, hugging her so hard that her feet left the floor. She savoured the feel of his muscles pressing against her breasts and stomach, along with the delicious feel of his arms tight around her waist. *Whew. He's not mad. I probably surprised him.*

He set her down. She dropped her arms and smiled at him.

His lopsided grin made her insides quiver with longing and her knees go weak. On impulse, she stood up on tiptoes and softly kissed his cheek. He smelled so good, like sawdust, paint, and that amazing spicy aftershave she remembered from the exhibition. His cheek was a little rough against her lips. *Either he gets a five o'clock shadow, or he didn't shave this morning.* The intimacy of feeling his whiskers against her lips made her toes curl in her shoes.

He stared down at her and blinked as she backed up a step. "I hadn't properly thanked you for helping me that day," she whispered and gave him a shy smile.

His grin reappeared. "You're welcome."

His gaze seemed to linger on hers, and it sent a weird current down her body, one she recognized with a splash of reluctance.

I want to fuck him. It had been ages since she'd felt it for anyone, and the knowledge made her freeze in place with a dry mouth, trembling hands and nausea bubbling in her gut as they stared at each other for an eternity. *Why now, and why Seth?*

"Maybe I should take you back to the store."

His husky, gentle words broke her musings.

"We've had a long day, and you look like you're about to drop where you stand."

There was a lot of concern in his voice, and it sent a shiver of warmth into her chest.

As he navigated his truck toward the store and her car, her mind churned. She wanted to dig out her heart with a white-hot poker. *Why did you have to choose Seth? He is giving you the impression he wants to be friends, and nothing more.* She glanced over at him with a mournful and heavy feeling in her chest. *I'll never be his. God, I am such a fucking idiot for falling for him.*

CHAPTER SEVEN

Thursday, Mirabelle's Store

Seth was getting annoyed. Alexis had been avoiding him for the last week. She was listening to music again, like she had been every day since Friday. Seeing the earbuds plugged into her ears and the cord tangling in her earrings drove a shot of irritation through his gut. He hated having to tap her on the shoulder to get her attention, little as she paid him, instead of an instant response when he called her name.

Her back was to him. She was humming and moving her hips to a rhythm he didn't understand or hear. The sight of her delectable derriere in her tight, faded skinny jeans made a shot of longing stab his heart. *What the fuck is her problem lately? I'm lucky if I get a one-word response if I ask a question.* He thought they had gotten a lot closer after Brett showed up and their fight in the aftermath. He sighed when she untangled the earbuds cord from her hair. *She's acting like I'm not here.*

With a shrug, Seth turned back to his task and tried focusing on carving another part of the trim for the second shelving unit. He fit the chisel between the two pencil lines and gently started pushing it forward.

Alexis walked between him and the windows. The sunlight streaming in shone through her blouse, showing him the perfect outline of her breasts.

The wood suddenly turned to nothing. He glanced down at his hands and, with a sigh, realized he had cut a line three times deeper than needed. "Fuck me. At least it wasn't like I messed up the last bit of trim on that piece," he grumbled. It was the start of one for the second shelving unit, so it wasn't like he had wrecked an entire piece. It could be adapted for something else. Waste not, want not.

He glanced at Alexis. If she'd heard him swearing, she'd ignored it. She was humming along to her music, still putting details on a tulip. *She's been working on that same spot for half an hour. Shouldn't she be done by now?* The bitter taste of irritation landed on his tongue. He heaved the ruined piece of trim into the scrap pile. The urge to yank the mini speakers out of her ears and force her to talk to him was getting stronger with each passing second. *She'll punch me if I try that. I'll be no better than Brett if I touch her in any way other than to make love to her.*

A hot jolt of sexual awareness for her zapped through his body, settling into his groin. His cock, encased in his usual tight jeans, came to life as an image of her lying in his bed, naked, with her hair spread around her, her lips swollen from his kisses, eyes half-closed and almost black with desire while she fingered her soaking wet pussy splayed across his vision.

He blinked, and the image disappeared, although his cock was still ready for her. *Where did that come from? She's a friend, right up there with Blaine and Mirrie. Why am I suddenly daydreaming about fucking her?* He let out a long sigh, grateful for the carpentry apron hiding his erection. He took a few deep breaths and focused on the scents of paint and wood, two of his favourite things in the world. After a moment, his body calmed down, and he chose another piece out of the pile that was cut for the shelves.

Alexis bent over to put her paintbrush into some turpentine. His gaze moved to her backside, and he felt a grin of masculine admiration spreading across his face. *She's even cuter when she's ignoring me.* With a mental slap, he grabbed another piece of wood and started tracing his trim design on it. *Don't go there. She's still recovering from a shitty relationship. Brett did a lot of damage, and it's going to take her a while to get over that. Be there as a friend, don't try to hump her leg.*

The chime above the door rang, and Alexis disappeared into the main part of the store. Her soft perfume lingered around Seth for a moment. He savoured it, although it stabbed him in the heart. He could hear her soft voice through the wall, but he couldn't make out her words.

Having her ignore him hurt more than Janie's accusations of cheating. It was worse than watching Janie smash treasured family keepsakes. Alexis's indifference was the worst pain he'd ever felt, even more than losing his beloved grandfather.

His hands fisted and connected softly with the board in front of him as his eyes closed, and a tremor travelled from his head to his feet. He felt like he was standing on the edge of a cliff, on the verge of stepping off. He could almost feel the air rushing around his face and ears and taste the bitterness of it on his tongue. Somehow, dropping into the unknown felt safer than staying on the precipice. But, what was over the edge? It was shrouded in haze. He rubbed the back of his hand on the bottom of his chin and let out a soft grunt. The odd feeling went away. *Jesus, what the hell was that?*

He glanced at the wood in front of him and rolled his eyes. He couldn't concentrate, not with Alexis pretending he wasn't there. He wanted to see her, so he weaved his way through the shelving units in the store, glass in the middle, wood around the perimeter, and stopped in view of the counter.

A lady with short brown hair and wearing a blue and green hound's-tooth print dress had her back to him, and she was shaking her head. "I don't understand," she said.

Seth couldn't see what the woman was referring to, but Alexis was visible.

She smiled at the customer and flipped her braid over her shoulder. "I'll show you again. You press this button and flip this open at the same time." A click echoed in the room. "Now twist the button to the left, and it should open."

Alexis lifted the item in question. It was an oval ceramic jewelry box, dark blue, hand-painted and had a white button at the top, and the entire box was eight inches across. There was a hidden compartment in the cover, and it was tricky to open. Seth remembered Alexis practicing with a smaller version of it between customers not long after she started working at the store. She'd had it figured out in less than five minutes without instructions.

The customer sighed. "Please show me again."

Although Alexis kept a smile plastered on her face, Seth could see the lines of stress forming around her mouth. She repeated her actions, slower this time. "You try it." She pushed the box closer to the other woman.

Seth couldn't see what was happening, but going by the frustrated noise that the woman let out and her head shaking, he guessed she didn't get it the first time. He moved a little closer to the counter, pretending to study the trim around the archway so he could get a better look.

Alexis stared at him blankly for a moment before she smiled at the customer again. "I'll talk you through it. Press the white tile on the underside of the cover. No, not that one. Yes, that one." She pointed to something inside of the cover. "Hold it down while you flip this tile up. No, you don't press on it. Lift it with your fingernail, like this. See what I mean?"

"No, I don't," the woman said irritably. "Do it again."

Alexis blinked at the woman and shrugged. She lifted the cover and repeated her actions for a third time, really slowly. "See how it locks open when you do it?" Her smile seemed fake, almost doll-like.

Not good. She looks like she's about to eat the customer alive. Seth held back a snicker.

The customer shook her head. She drummed her fingers on the counter a few times. "I still don't get it. Why did they make it so damn hard to open?"

"It's supposed to be for hiding things like jewelry, watches, and money."

Seth could almost hear Alexis wanting to add *Yeah, that's what a secret compartment is for, stupid. Alexis has the patience of a saint. If I were dealing with an idiotic bitty like that, I'd tell her off in no time.* A growing admiration for Mirabelle's only employee rose in his chest. He could see why Mirabelle had hired her.

The customer clicked her tongue a few times and sniffed. "I was hoping you'd have something similar, but not so hard to open."

"That's the least complicated hidden compartment box we have. Would you like to see some without the extras? We have some silver filigree ones that arrived yesterday, and they are beautiful." Alexis smiled and gestured to the woman to follow her.

The customer held up a hand and shook her head. "I don't think so. My niece was hoping for something she could hide a few treasures in, not something obvious that people would want to snoop into."

Alexis nodded. "If you want to leave your name and number, I can call you when we get something a little more suitable for her." She pulled out the scribbler containing their customers' contact details from underneath the register.

The woman snorted. "I'd rather not. This store isn't as good as it was supposed to be. I won't be back." She sniffed loudly, raised her nose in the air a few notches, and primly turned on her heel.

In Seth's opinion, her face was as ugly as her personality. It looked like she had a permanent frown on her face, and her eyes squinted behind thick glasses. Her short brown hair looked permed, and the wrinkles on her face made her seem ancient, but not wise. *What a fucking douche. She won't be back because she was too fucking dumb to get a simple mechanism?* Seth hated people like that.

The woman departed, the happy tinkling of the chimes

above the door sounding odd in the air.

Alexis stood beside the counter, frowning at the door after failing to make the sale. Her eyes narrowed behind her glasses, and she growled softly. She tapped a sneakered foot a few times, and her jaw clicked twice.

"Jesus, what a fucking old bitty," Seth said with a chuckle. "She couldn't find her way out of a bunch of wet toilet paper with directions."

"Yeah, she's pretty stupid." Alexis drummed her fingers on the glass countertop and let out a long, annoyed sigh. She sounded distant again like her thoughts were elsewhere.

Four words, that's a record for this week. Keep her talking. "How many times did you show her how to open it? Three? Four?"

"Five."

Her aloof monotone was like fingernails going down a chalkboard, and the tone made him cringe. *Ouch.* "Jesus, I swear some people can't see what's right in front of their face."

Alexis turned her frown on him. "Yeah, obviously," she said, the words laden with sarcasm. She snapped her headphones on, and with a glare at him, she stuck her nose in the air, turned and stomped back to the employee's area of the store.

Seth's ears burned, and confusion rippled through his body. Did she just tell him he was missing something that was right in his face?

He closed his eyes as the pain in her words and how much he missed her chatter hit him. The cliff appeared in his mind's eye again, and this time the wind in his face and hair echoed with the cries of sorrow and loneliness. The haze in the chasm was lighter now, no longer black, but a dark blue. Through it, he could see sunshine, a glimpse of joy.

He opened his eyes, and a purpose rose in him. His lips flattened, his shoulders straightened, and Seth let out a long, calming breath. With a nod to boost his courage, he whipped around and firmly strode to the employee's area at the back of the store.

Alexis dived into the storage room and slipped out of her headphones. She covered her face with her hands and tried not to cry. When she looked at the clock, there were two more hours until she could leave and head to the employment office to print off copies of her resume. After that, a hot bubble bath, a glass of non-alcoholic wine, and a good cry were in order. Being around Seth and not being his girlfriend was taking a lot out of her. It had been so hard not to joke around with him after that last customer left. It would have been fodder for a lot of gags and laughs for a week in the days before Brett resurfaced. *That's what happens when you fall for your best friend and he doesn't return the feelings.* She wiped a stray tear off her cheek and let out a shaky sigh.

The door behind her opened. "Alexis, what's wrong?" Seth asked from behind her. He sounded concerned.

"Nothing. I'm tired," she replied over her shoulder.

"Nothing, my ass. You pretty much bit my head off a minute ago."

"Go back to work. I'm fine. Thanks for checking." She fingered the bracelet on her right wrist and wished he would disappear so she could regain her balance in private.

"Not until you tell me what I did to upset you."

"You did nothing. That last customer was a doozy, and I'm sorry if you think I took it out on you." It was true. That woman was a moron in Alexis's opinion.

"She was, but that's not what got you going. It's me, isn't it?" He sounded desolate.

Fuck a duck! She shook her head and played with her headphones.

"Bullshit. One minute we're best pals, and the next, you're acting like I have the plague. What's wrong?" he demanded, pain layering his words.

"Nothing. Go back to work. I'll be along in a few minutes. I need to catch my breath."

"No," he replied firmly.

Alexis couldn't keep all of the agony out of her voice. "Please go back to work. I haven't been sleeping well the last while. I'd rather not take it out on you." Not a lie—her decision to avoid him had given her horrible insomnia, and she always wound up crying herself to sleep in the wee hours of the morning. She sniffled loudly and bit her lip.

"That's not it. I did something to upset you, and I'd like to know what it is."

"Leave me alone," she snapped over her shoulder.

"I'm not letting you hide again. You're too damn important to me," he responded.

She turned around and glared up at him. The tears in her eyes made him blurry, the blue of his jeans mixed with his black t-shirt. "I'm not hiding!" she whimpered in denial.

"Dammit, yes, you are. Stop it and start talking to me. Please."

Was he really that upset that she had pulled back from him? *Please leave me alone. I can't take much more of this.* "Seth—"

His fingers brushed a tendril of hair off her cheek, his calloused thumb wiping away a rogue tear. His skin felt amazing against hers, and although her lungs burned with the agony of unshed tears, she wished he would never stop touching her.

"Whatever I did, I hope you can forgive me, sweetheart. I never want to hurt you," he whispered.

Alexis was sure her agony was echoed in his words, and she laid her palm over his hand and leaned into the tender caress. His gaze latched on to hers and held it. Through her tears, she saw he was almost crying, too.

"Alexis, I—oh, to hell with it," Seth murmured. Without removing his gaze from hers, he reached back with his free hand and shut the door behind him. He took a step toward her, so close that their bodies brushed. He cupped her face in both hands and pressed his forehead to hers. His breath was warm, soft and smelled like coffee.

She closed her eyes. The sight of the pain on his face was too much for her.

A heartbeat later, he groaned, and his lips touched hers.

Shocked that he was kissing her, in the back of Mirabelle's store of all places, it took a moment for Alexis to respond. His mouth was hot, firm, and felt heavenly. Alexis's toes curled in her sneakers, and she moaned softly, shivering in delight. One of her hands slid up to his neck, to delve in the soft thick hair at his nape. His long deep groan of pleasure sent a spark of triumph through her body.

It was better than all of her fantasies wrapped into a single heartbeat.

He slid his tongue between her lips. Something nudged her stomach, above her pelvic bone. The distant realization he was aroused made her knees go weak, and a gleeful shock of desire lodged deep in her pussy. She wanted this man more than she wanted anything in her life.

Too soon, Seth eased his mouth from hers. His breathing was ragged, and his hands trembled against her cheeks. There was a new spark in his dark eyes, and his gaze was tender. She reached up to touch his face with her fingers, still unable to comprehend what had just transpired.

He kissed her forehead, slid his arms around her, and sighed quietly.

Alexis snuggled against him and suddenly trembled as something hit her.

She wanted Seth all right, but not as a bed partner.
She wanted him for life.

Kissing Alexis seemed to be the only way to get her attention, but the instant he felt her soft, full lips under his, Seth knew there had been an ulterior motive.

He had wanted to kiss her, and it had seemed to be the right time to do it. He hadn't counted on the feelings she provoked in him, even before it happened. Not that he regretted it. It had been building up for a while, and it was past time for it to happen.

It was something to talk about another time, in another place, not right after their first kiss. The first of many, many more, Seth hoped. "Am I forgiven?" he asked softly.

She stared up at him, her soft pink and swollen lips parted, with a dazed and happy look in her eyes, half-hidden behind her spectacles. "Uh-huh," she replied, almost distractedly.

He nuzzled his mouth against hers again. Her perfume swirled around his head, hypnotizing him. It was heaven. "That's not an answer," he whispered against her lips.

"Huh?" she mumbled.

Seth nuzzled his lips along her cheek to rest against her ear. "Say I'm forgiven for whatever I did, sweetheart."

"We were fighting?" Her voice had a dreamy, distant quality that made him chuckle.

He pulled back enough to stare into her eyes. Damn, she was beautiful, staring up at him with those dark eyes filled with trust. "You were pissed at me."

"I was?"

"Yeah, you were."

"I'm not now," she whispered. Her fingers touched his lips. "Why was I pissed at you?"

"I don't know. You wouldn't tell me." He brushed a tendril

of hair from her cheek, which felt like bronze velveteen. *She's so soft, loving, and so pretty. How can anyone hurt her?*

He sought her mouth with his, and joy surged through his veins when he found his target. When she responded, his knees started getting a little rubbery, so he leaned back against the closed door and pulled her with him. Her body fit against his perfectly.

His cock twitched painfully. Seth hoped his leather carpentry belt was enough to mask his eagerness for her. Alexis didn't need to see how strongly he desired her, not yet. There was lots of time to show her how much he wanted her in his bed. His reassurance that he wanted her in his life was enough for now but as more than a friend.

She snuggled deeper into his embrace and tangled her fingers in his hair. Seth tightened his arm around her waist and delved his tongue into the sweetness between her lips. She mewed softly and opened her mouth wide, giving him full access.

A hard, heavy note of desire twanged all of his nerve endings. *Not now. Wait until she adjusts to having you as her lover. That pussyface did a lot to her, and she needs time to think about things before you shove your cock in her face.* He forced his body under control and let his feelings for her surface. He liked Alexis, so much that one day of her silence felt like a decade. The last week had eroded at his patience, his heart, and his soul. Alexis was like a balm to his nerves, soothing and healing him. *I need her. She makes me want to be a better man. I'm me with her.* Her mouth moved under his. *She needs me to be the best I can be, too.*

His phone rang with his favourite country song, startling him. "Fuck," he muttered against Alexis's lips. With a long sigh, Seth reached into his pocket, located the power key and hit it once to cancel the call. He hoped whoever it was would bugger off. He was enjoying the tender moments with Alexis too much to have the world invade their bubble. *Leave a message, dammit.* He focused on her mouth, so pretty and inviting. "Kiss me, sweetheart," he said in a soft command.

His phone blared music a second time. Seth's teeth ground together. "Jesus fucking Christ," he muttered. *Who the fuck is bothering me? Can't they wait a few more minutes?* He finally had Alexis speaking to him again, and they had just had their first kiss. *Screw other people.* Alexis was his priority, no one else. He pulled the phone out of his pocket, saw Blaine's number, and hit ignore. "He can fucking wait a few more minutes." The phone was shoved back into his pocket.

Alexis slid her arms around his waist and stared up at him. There was a new shine in her eyes, one that had been missing all week. She looked so happy, like she had been given the world

Seth kissed her nose, and joy surged in his chest. His entire body felt lighter with the air cleared and a new path in front of him. *Fuck me. I hit the jackpot with Alexis. She's funny, sweet, loving, and kind. She's everything I want in a woman.* His mouth found hers again.

His phone twanged with country lyrics for the third time. "I'm going to fucking kill him," he snarled.

"Who?"

"Blaine." He sighed.

Another shot of music reverberated in the air. "Maybe you'd better get it."

Deflated, he rested his forehead against hers. "I'll make it quick, I promise."

She smiled and nodded. He couldn't resist caressing her mouth with his one more time. With a low growl, Seth yanked the phone out of his pocket.

Alexis started to pull backwards. Seth tightened his arm around her waist. "Stay put. This won't take long. I'm not

done with you yet," he murmured, adding a layer of huskiness to his voice.

She relaxed and rested her head on his shoulder.

He hit answer. "What the fuck do you want, Blaine?" he
snapped into the phone.

"Aren't you supposed to be carving the trim for the shelving unit?" his partner asked. Blaine sounded a bit pissed.

"Yeah, so?" Seth couldn't help barking into the phone.

"So where the hell are you? Have you seen Alexis? Mirrie
is freaking out, thinking she quit."

Alexis lifted her head and stared up at him with wide eyes,
the quiet in the back room allowed her to hear both sides of
the conversation.

"Sorry," he mouthed to her.

"It's okay," she whispered back and kissed the underside
of his chin.

He pressed his cheek against the top of her head in reply.

"I'm in the back room. Alexis had a problem with a customer and needed to take a few minutes. I'm talking her
down."

"Tell her Mirrie's looking for her, they need to get things
cleaned up and shut down for the night."

"Got it." He hit disconnect before his partner could reply.

Alexis was staring up at him, her dark eyes almost glowing
behind the lenses of her glasses. "Back to the real world,
huh?"

Seth nodded reluctantly. "Are you free tomorrow night?"

"That depends on who's asking."

"Do you want to go dancing or something?"

"With you?" She smiled a little.

"I'm not that bad of a dancer." He couldn't resist grinning
at her.

"I remember. Hmm, okay."

Joy flooded his body, making his chest puff out a bit. Those two words made him feel like he had conquered the world. "Seven o'clock okay with you?"

She fingered the collar of his t-shirt. "It's perfect."

"So are you," he said and gave her a long, slow kiss that had them both trembling and breathless. "Back to reality," he reluctantly muttered as he pulled back.

Alexis nodded and caressed his cheek before sliding out of his arms and opening the door.

Anticipation for their first date had Alexis's heart racing each time she caught a glimpse of Seth the next day.

He looked extra sexy in tight worn jeans and a pale grey t-shirt that seemed to mould to his muscular arms and chest. Each time their gazes met, he marginally winked at her, which made her knees weak and a thrill quiver in her pussy. Those stolen moments kissing the day before had shown her a side to Seth that she never expected.

Yes, he was a gentleman to the core, but she'd never realized how tender and thoughtful he could be as not just a friend, but as a potential lover. She had imagined he would be a little more forceful in showing her his desire, not taking his time and kissing her so gently that her entire body tingled in pleasure each time she thought of him.

Unconsciously, she pressed her lips together as she watched him help Blaine level a shelf beside the archway. Her gaze wandered downwards to Seth's backside, covered in taut denim. *Mirrie's right. He does have a nice ass.* She jumped a clear foot off of the floor when someone dropped something onto the counter in front of her.

"Alexis, are you okay? You seem distracted today," Mirabelle asked and opened the till. She was adding more change, as Alexis had requested ten minutes earlier.

Alexis took a deep breath and let it out slowly. "I'm fine,

thanks, Mirrie. I didn't sleep much last night." It was true. How could she sleep when her body and mind ached for a man who seemed to understand her and treated her like she was the only person in his world? If Mirabelle knew the real reason why Alexis was distracted, it would feel like the Spanish Inquisition. Nope. That was not happening yet. She wanted to keep her new relationship with Seth to herself. Telling Mirabelle would be like asking the guys at CKBW, one of the local radio stations, to announce it six times a day.

"Get a cup of coffee. That should help." Mirabelle closed the till with a firm click and picked up a stack of papers. Alexis recognized order forms for office supplies. Mirabelle must be making an office store run on Monday.

Alexis took the cue and almost ran to the back room. It was the perfect excuse to disappear for a few minutes, catch her breath, and bring herself back to reality instead of drooling over Seth. She shut the door behind her and exhaled loudly. "Christ, girl, get a grip on yourself," she muttered and glanced at the coffee maker. The carafe was empty, and whoever had drained the last few drops of brew hadn't bothered to set another pot going.

"I will shoot whoever did that," she grumbled as she grabbed the carafe and started filling it with water. She loaded the tank at the back of the maker, pulled out the basket, and dumped the used filter and grounds into the compost bucket, to be disposed of later.

She inserted a new filter and opened the can of fresh coffee, ground by Mirabelle that morning. Alexis took a long sniff and sighed happily. Chocolate mint, one of her favourites. Mirabelle had been sneaking in treats like this for the past week, ever since Brett showed up at the store.

A scoop landed in the filter, then Alexis's gaze was drawn to the photo of Blaine and Seth on the wall above the table. It was a commemorative of ten years in business together. Her gaze lingered on it, and she scooped out a few more spoons of coffee from the can.

Footsteps approached from behind her. "Hey, sweetheart. Mirrie wants a cup, too." A thrill travelled up her spine when she recognized Seth's voice. His fingers brushed her bare forearm, bringing a round of goosebumps and a warmth that spread into her chest.

Alexis glanced over her shoulder, saw his handsome face, and hoped her grin wasn't too goofy. "Sure. I have to make a new pot. Someone drained the last one." She took another scoop while staring at him.

Seth's brow furrowed. "Aren't you supposed to put the coffee into the basket?"

She blinked at him. "What?"

"You're making a mess."

"Huh?"

He pointed to the counter in front of her, and she turned her head and cringed. Coffee grounds were piled on the counter around the coffee maker. "Aw, fuck!" she muttered. She looked into the basket. Only one small scoop of coffee grounds had landed into the filter. "Double fuck!"

"Here." Seth was holding a dustpan out to her.

Did she hear a chuckle in his voice? If so, he was a dead man. With a long sigh, Alexis took it and started swiping the grounds into it with a hand.

Seth's body pressed against her back, his heat a comforting distraction from her task. Her hands stilled, and she stared at him over her shoulder. It was so tough not to lean into him, but if she did, the coffee wouldn't be made, and Mirabelle would guess something was up. That was the last thing they needed.

Seth locked his arm around her waist from behind and lightly kissed her temple. "Be glad it's coffee grounds, and not something dangerous. I almost cut off my finger while sawing a piece of wood for the shelf," he snickered in her ear.

Hell with it. She needed to get closer to him. Let Mirabelle think whatever she wanted. Alexis wanted five minutes alone with Seth. "You, too, huh?"

"Yeah." His fingers caressed her stomach, which made a shiver go up her spine. "I've got it bad for you, sweetheart. Tonight can't come soon enough."

"Should I pack an overnight bag?"

"I don't sleep with a woman on the first date, especially one I like as much as you, even though the thought of you in my bed is enough to make me almost come right now."

She shivered at the heavy lust in his voice, and her slit became soaked as an image of him on top of her and groaning in pleasure popped into her mind. "Hearing you talk like that almost made me finish," she whispered.

Seth's mouth claimed hers, hard, and she moaned in delight as his tongue thrust between her lips. He wasn't wearing his carpentry belt, so she could feel his erection pressing against her bottom. Her knees nearly buckled from the weight of her own readiness threatening to overtake her.

Abruptly, he pulled back and let go of her. He was breathing heavily, there was a thin layer of sweat on his upper lip, and his eyes were almost black. He inhaled sharply through his nose, and his nostrils flared for a moment as they stared at each other. "I'd better go before I wind up fucking you here," he panted.

Good idea. I'm about ready to jump your sexy bones, Seth Mitchell. Alexis nodded. "I can manage this on my own, thanks."

He gave her one last soft, lingering kiss before he left, the spicy and ultra-male scent of his aftershave and sawdust lingering in her nose.

Alexis sighed dreamily and managed to make the coffee without any more mishaps.

CHAPTER EIGHT

Alexis's Apartment Building
Friday Evening

Five minutes to seven. Seth couldn't hold back the grin as he turned into Alexis's apartment complex's parking lot.

She was already outside, standing by the security door. He climbed out of the vehicle and sauntered toward Alexis. She looked amazing in her pale pink blouse, white skirt, and white sandals, with bare legs. Her dark hair was down, and curling around her shoulders, but pulled back with a jewelled comb on the right. A pair of long silver earrings peeked out from behind her hair, and a white lace choker circled her throat.

Seth's mouth watered as he approached her. She looked like a pink and white cupcake, ready for him to savour. Or was that devour? He stopped in front of her. Alexis smiled, almost shyly. It sent a protective quiver up his spine, one he hadn't felt in a long time. Years. "Ready?" he asked and held out a hand.

Alexis placed her hand in his, which sent another loving zing through his body. She was wearing a couple of rings with pink stones, ones he had never seen before. "More than you realize," she whispered.

Their fingers entwined, and he started guiding her toward the parking lot. Alexis looked around with a puzzled frown between her eyebrows. "Where's your truck?"

Seth grinned and hoped she would love the surprise. "I

didn't want to drive it tonight. It's filthy, and for work." He stopped walking and hit the unlock switch on his keychain. The forest green year-old muscle car beside them beeped its horn and flashed its lights.

Alexis's eyes widened. "Yours, or did you borrow this from a friend?"

"It's mine. I wanted something nice for special times."

"I love it. It's a gorgeous car." She ran a hand reverently along the lines of the hood. "I'm happy you think tonight is special enough for it. I would have been happy with your truck."

A twang of envy zoomed through him. He wished she was caressing him instead of the car. "You deserve to be driven around in something nice, not that junk pile I normally drive." He touched her cheek and turned her face toward his. Their gazes locked.

"I'm not special." Her smile had faded, and her eyes were downcast.

He stroked her cheek lovingly. "To me, you are."

"Seth—"

His thumb tapped her lips. "I mean what I say, and I think you're amazing."

She smiled briefly and touched his wrist. "You're important to me, too."

The look in her eyes made his heart quicken. Unconsciously, he reached up with his free hand and caressed her temple with his thumb.

She leaned forward expectantly, and Seth almost gave in to the urge to kiss her. Not in public, not yet. It was too new to share with everyone. "Later," he promised as he pulled back to open the door for her.

She nodded and took the cue to climb into the low slung car.

The instant his door shut behind him, he reached over and

pulled her as close to him as they could get across the middle console.

Alexis sighed when he crushed her mouth under his.

The soft sound made desire burn through his veins, along with something else, something he couldn't identify. A thrust of his tongue between her lips, and mint ran across his taste buds. Her flowery scent swirled around him, a siren's call, one that he was losing the will to resist. He pulled back, gasping for air. He had to get some semblance of control. Alexis deserved to know what dating him was going to be like. He wasn't using her for sex, and tonight was supposed to be proof of it.

His control almost snapped at the dazed look in her eyes, her swollen lips, and the soft sigh that hit his eardrums. Her small breasts rose and fell quickly with shaking breaths.

Her nipples poking through the soft material of her blouse were designed to make a man weep with pleasure. *Damn.* She was almost too much woman for him to handle.

"I was going to ask you if something was wrong," she whispered after a minute.

"Why?" He couldn't resist touching her face again.

She rubbed her cheek against his fingers. "You didn't kiss me right away."

He flipped on the engine and smiled as it caught with a loud purr. "I don't like kissing a girl in public. Who you're seeing is no one's business but yours, and I didn't want to embarrass you in front of the entire neighbourhood."

Her hand touched his arm. "Thank you."

"For what?" He covered her fingers with his free hand.

"You're a gentleman."

A smug sense of satisfaction rolled up his spine. "If you think I'm one now, wait until I get you into bed."

"How so?"

He leaned over and murmured in her ear, "I plan on making you come so many times that you're not going to remember anything other than how to scream my name." He nipped at her ear to emphasize his point.

Her sharp inhale and the throbbing vein in her neck sent shockwaves of lust through him, making his cock react with a painful hard-on.

Her gaze lowered. He shifted slightly to let her see his reaction to her. When she raised her gaze to his again, he almost lost it as he saw his desire reflected in hers.

"Not tonight. Let's wait a few days," he replied to her silent question.

"Then let's get out of here before I drag you up to my apartment."

He grinned at her, put his feet on the clutch and brake, and shifted the car into first.

When Seth told her she was special, Alexis believed him. It wasn't how he didn't kiss her in public that made her feel like that, or the way he touched her cheek in the parking lot, it was the honesty and gentleness in his gaze that reflected the truth in his words.

He looked so sexy that night, in a button-down shirt, dark blue pants, and shoes, a nice change from his usual attire of faded and worn jeans, a t-shirt, boots, and his carpentry belt. The navy shirt highlighted his eyes, and the pants emphasized his muscular thighs and tight butt.

Her mouth wouldn't stop watering as she watched him foot the brake and clutch, then shift the car into the higher gears. Watching a man drive a vehicle with an automatic transmission wasn't as interesting as a standard. She licked her lips as she watched the muscles play in his legs as he maneuvered the car toward the highway.

"Where are we going?" she asked.

"Mahone Bay, there's a little restaurant there I thought you'd like." He glanced at her with a smile and shifted the car into fourth gear.

"And afterwards?"

"Nowhere in Bridgewater. I'd rather not have Mirrie or Blaine getting wind of this yet." He glanced at her. "Do you have to work in the morning?"

She shook her head. "Mirrie gave me the weekend off."

"I took it off, too. Halifax, it is then."

"Sounds great to me."

The café was at the head of the bay, with a breathtaking view of Mahone Bay's picturesque and brightly coloured buildings from across the water. The yellow building housed an intimate setting with soft classical music in the background and the smells of delectable entrees wafting through the dining area. Soothing tones of beige and tan dominated the room, highlighted with mahogany wood accents and burgundy chair cushions. It was the perfect backdrop for the view.

Alexis tried not to gape as the hostess sat them at a table by the windows and below the skylights. The sun was on its decent, but one of the most photographed scenes in Nova Scotia blossomed before her in all its splendour. The dramatic spectacle of the three churches dominating the skyline along Edgewater Street had her mesmerized. The spires of the Anglican and Lutheran churches reached skyward, while the castle-like bell tower of the United Church stood regal beside its taller counterparts. The golden yellow and reddish-brown exterior of the Anglican church to the left set off the black and white of the Lutheran in the middle and the pure white of the United Church on the right. The green leaves of the trees were the perfect backdrop for the beautiful houses of worship, and their reflections in the mostly calm waters of the bay heightened the grandeur of their magnificence.

Alexis sighed happily and grinned. It was a sight she had only seen in photographs or video until that night.

Seth's chuckle made her blush. "It's something else, isn't it? I never get tired of that view."

Alexis set her purse on the chair beside her and smiled. "It's gorgeous. I can see why so many people take pictures of it. It's even better in person."

Seth opened his menu and winked at her. "Something told me you'd appreciate it."

She rested an elbow on the table, leaned her chin into her hand and batted her lashes at him. "How so?"

Seth blinked at her slowly and smiled. "You're a woman who appreciates the little things in life. A lot of women wouldn't take an apology over anything less than a dozen of the most expensive roses, but you were ecstatic to get lupines I picked up off the side of the highway. You were happy at the exhibition. Other women would have taken that as an insult to their intelligence and maybe even demanded something more upscale." His smile faded.

When Alexis saw the storm reflected in his eyes, she lowered her gaze to the open menu in front of her, bit her lip, and fiddled with her condensation-covered water glass. "You mean your ex-wife."

A strong hand covered in callouses caressed her fingers, and a strong zap travelled from her arm into her heart. Every single nerve ending tingled happily, especially in her pussy. Her pink lace panties were not going to survive too many of Seth's gentle touches. She was soaked now, and they had only shared one long but steamy kiss so far that night.

He sighed. "I was hoping we wouldn't talk about her."

Alexis raised her gaze to his. His eyes were dark, a frown marred his mouth, and stress lines framed his lips. She hated seeing him like that. "Then we won't talk about your ex. Let's focus on other parts of our lives." She turned her hand and linked her fingers with his.

The darkness faded from his face, followed by a slow, easy smile. "Tell me about yourself."

Alexis blushed and bit her lip again. "I told you I'm not interesting."

"You don't have any brothers or sisters? Are your parents still alive?" Seth's smile was open, relaxed, and felt non-judgemental.

Alexis gratefully smiled up at the waitress who arrived with a complimentary bread basket and what looked like real butter on the side. The contents looked fresh and smelled amazing. The fiftyish waitress, whose name tag read Camille, smiled. "That batch came out of the oven about half an hour ago. It may be hot in places, so be careful. The butter comes from a dairy in Lunenburg. It is amazing."

Alexis mumbled her thanks and turned her gaze to the menu. The café's main items were from the sea, mostly shell-fish, which was no surprise, since fishing was one of Nova Scotia's top industries. There were a few safe items, like steak and duck and finned fish. She adored lobster and clams, but unfortunately, an allergy to bivalves like scallops as well as crustaceans like crab kept her from enjoying such delicacies.

"What are your specials?" Seth asked.

Camille's voice was perky. "We have lemon roasted salmon with a side of Mediterranean salad, roasted duck with herbed potatoes and vegetables, T-bone steak with your choice of potatoes and vegetables or salad, pan-fried halibut with mixed greens, and beer steamed lobster tails with garlic bread."

Alexis sighed. All of it sounded heavenly.

"The T-bone steak sounds amazing. I'll have that with a baked potato, garden salad, and a dealcoholized beer. Alexis, order whatever you want."

There were no prices listed on the menu. None of the food

listed looked cheap.

"Don't worry about prices. I've got it covered," Seth said and took her hand.

She looked up and smiled at him. "I'll have the halibut, please." It wasn't the most expensive thing on the menu. The costliest item was probably the king crab with lemon butter.

Camille jotted down their choices on a pad and scooped up the menus. "It'll be along in a jiffy." She disappeared.

Seth's navy eyes bored deep into Alexis's. "You never answered my questions."

She took a long gulp of water. "What questions?" Her childhood had been rough. That was why it had been so easy to pack up and leave Stellarton behind without looking back.

"Do you have any siblings?"

Alexis shook her head. "No." She didn't, not any that she could remember.

Seth nodded. "What about your parents?"

She fisted her hand around her cream-coloured napkin. "Gone. They passed away when I was two." The agony of never knowing her mother or father still radiated through her soul. She didn't remember them, only knew their faces from photographs and their voices from videos taken before their passing.

His full lips turned downwards, and a hand covered hers. "Geez, I'm sorry, sweetheart."

She turned her gaze toward the churches, standing so regally across the bay. "They had taken my older sister to a play. She was six. I was sick that night, so I was with my grandparents. Nana said it was from the blizzard. They went off the road on the way home, about two miles from Nana and Grampa's house, over an embankment. They rolled several times before hitting a tree. Uh, Nana said they died instantly, but Grampa said my sister was still alive when the police found them. She died from hypothermia at the hospital." She kept her voice level. Although she didn't remember any of them, the crushing pain in her chest was a reminder she was an orphan and never had the big sister she had wished for as a child.

"Jesus," Seth whispered, and his fingers tightened around her hand. "Did you stay with your grandparents after that?"

Alexis nodded. "Grampa died when I was ten, and Nana passed away not long after I met Brett."

Seth's eyes darkened slightly. "Did she meet him?"

"Yup." Mirth rose in her chest when a picture of her maternal grandmother's face popped into her mind. Cassie Gordon was courteous that day — she was a true lady and was brought up to be polite even to those she hated — but her normally smiling face was pinched, and her lips puckered like she had taken a shot of the nastiest cold syrup in Canada. Her blue eyes had taken a stormy hue and were narrowed behind her glasses.

Alexis raised her glass to her lips and took three huge gulps of water so she wouldn't laugh too loudly in the quiet restaurant.

Seth's eyes twinkled, and he smirked. "What's so funny?"

Alexis sniffed. "Nana didn't like Brett, as you probably guessed."

"Yeah, I got that impression by the look on your face." There was a snicker behind his words.

She leaned forward and murmured, "Nana said he walked like he had a load of shit in his pants, and he wouldn't know a good woman if she kicked him in the nuts, slapped him with a piece of moose meat, and shot him point-blank with a thirty-thirty rifle." Alexis remembered the can of spray from Constable Manning, neatly tucked into her purse. She may be out on a date, but she wasn't taking any chances with the pussy-face, as Seth had labelled Brett. Better safe than sorry.

Seth's upper body shook in mirth. "I think I would have

loved your Nana."

Alexis smiled wistfully and sighed. Nana had been gone over ten years, but the hole in Alexis's life was still a gaping wound. Nana had been her entire world, the only mother Alexis remembered. She missed their talks, and how Nana always seemed to inject humour in the worst situations. *If she hadn't died, I might not have stayed with Brett. I would have gone to university or community college and done something better with my life.* Unfortunately, ovarian cancer was a sneaky disease in older women. Cassie's had spread to her liver, lungs, and brain before it was caught. She died less than two months after her diagnosis, leaving her devastated only grandchild behind.

There's still time to go back to school. Alexis stroked his fingers. "Nana would have adored you. She would have told me to scoop you up and never let go of you."

Strong fingers tightened around hers again. "I'm glad you scooped me up. You're a good person, and I love spending time with you."

Alexis felt her cheeks warming, and her heart skipped a few beats. A melting feeling spread through her stomach and into her heart. "You're a sweet guy." It was all she could say with vocal cords that felt like they were drowning in syrup. It was a damn good thing she was sitting down, because his bright smile always made her knees weak and made her crotch yearn for his touch, his mouth, and his cock. She wanted to have his firm lips against every single centimetre of her skin.

Camille returned with their drinks.

Alexis's ardour cooled enough for her to remember they were in public and it wasn't a good idea to jump Seth in the middle of the café. She flipped her bangs out of her eyes and cocked her head to the side. "I saw the note from your mom last week before you bawled me out."

Seth rolled his eyes skyward. "The one with the line about

the leftover lasagna?" He made a quoting sign with his left hand.

Alexis giggled. "That one."

"I'm really close to my parents. They're amazing people. So are my brother, David, and his wife, Vanessa. I'm an uncle three times over—Dakota is fourteen, Ava is twelve, and Mikaela is eight." There was a heavy dose of pride in his voice.

The sour taste of envy burned Alexis's tongue. Unlike her, Seth had memories of his parents and brother. He had two nieces and a nephew that he loved dearly. She sighed quietly, letting the jealousy leave her system. There was no point in it. Their lives might have been different, but it didn't affect her feelings for this amazing man sitting across the table from her. "You'll have to show me pictures of them sometime."

"Later. I'd rather focus on us, not my family. I love them dearly, but tonight is about you." There was a deep streak of affection in his words, which sent another shot of longing through Alexis.

Their food arrived, and Alexis's tummy rumbled. Halibut was a delicacy her grandparents had splurged on numerous times during her childhood, and it always brought back memories of love, laughter, and contentment. It was the perfect thing to eat on her first date with Seth because of the warmth it inspired. One large fillet was served with mixed greens tossed in a lemon-oil dressing. It was perfect.

Camille smiled as she set a plate in front of Seth. She glanced at Alexis. "Your halibut was brought in fresh overnight. Most of the food here is locally sourced."

A strong warmth invaded Alexis's chest. Her grandfather had worked as a fisherman in his younger days, so anyone supporting local tradesmen like him was extra special in her book.

"Thank you," Seth said before Camille disappeared. He grinned at Alexis and picked up his fork.

The halibut tasted heavenly and sweet and brought forth warm memories of her grandmother cooking it, perfecting it. No one had been able to mimic Nana's way with the fish, until now. She had a knack for getting it perfect every time, no matter how she prepared it. Only the café's chef had come close to Nana's level of perfection. Ten stars. *I'll give the café a rave review on their website later tonight.*

They ate in silence, communicating with smiles and winks from Seth. Each time their gazes met, her heart twitched happily, and a warm tingle zinged through her nerve endings. She stretched her leg out under the table, found his with her foot, and rubbed her heel along his shin.

His gaze latched on to hers, and there was an underlying hint of desire burning in his deep blue irises. Alexis's pussy twitched with the knowledge that she was affecting him.

"Keep that up, and we won't get to Halifax." His voice was low, husky and vibrated with secrets only lovers shared. Secrets they were yet to discover.

Alexis batted her eyelashes.

"Dammit, woman, don't start." Seth pointed his fork at her with a smoky look in his eyes, and one of his grins that made her nipples tighten and her slit scream in need. "You may wind up getting kissed until you can't breathe, for starters."

Her pussy felt like it was pouring rivers of nectar. If they kept this up, she would soak the chair beneath her. She blew him a kiss and turned her attention back to the window and the amazing view of the churches. The sun had sunk lower in the sky, making them glow. It was so comforting to look out across the water and behold the little town. Alexis felt right at home, even though it was the first time she had been in the café. She grinned at him. "Thank you for bringing me here. I love it."

"We'll come back again sometime soon," Seth said. He smiled at her and wiped his mouth with his napkin.

Damn, he is sexy even when he's doing something mundane. Her chest felt like hummingbirds were bouncing around her ribs. *I don't know if I am in love with him, but holy shit, I'm close.* Alexis smiled back, a bit bashfully. *If the rest of this evening is as wonderful as dinner was, it will be the best night of my life.*

Two hours later, Seth parked the car behind a brick building not far from the Halifax Waterfront. At the front of the building, the large sign spouting *The Haven* was lit in a blue and green scrolling font. They entered through the main door, where a heavily muscled man sat behind a desk, watching various monitors. His jeans and shirt looked casual, but the gold name tag reading *Jonas Porter, Security* in black lettering showed he was all business.

"Evening, Jonas," Seth said to the man.

"It's good to see you, Seth." Jonas looked about thirtyish, with short, tightly curled black hair, deep brown eyes behind frameless glasses, and his chin sported a goatee. "Who is this lovely lady?" He stood up and held out a hand to her. Alexis guessed he was easily six-foot-six, if not taller. He towered over her, but she didn't feel intimidated. He was gorgeous, he had high cheekbones and straight white teeth, but he wasn't as handsome as Seth. His bright smile was open and relaxed. She took his hand and smiled back. He lifted her hand to his lips and kissed it, which made her blush. The chivalrous gesture was really sweet, and not many men had kissed her hand.

She grinned shyly. "Hi," she whispered.

"This is Alexis." Seth slid an arm around her waist and winked at Jonas.

Jonas nodded with a smile that looked conspiratorial to her. "Understood. Your private area is ready, and Sally is on standby with your drinks."

Seth grinned and shook Jonas' hand. "Thanks. Has it been a quiet night?"

Jonas sat down in the comfortable looking leather swivel chair behind the desk and waved toward a wooden, highly varnished door behind him. "Nothing more than usual."

Seth nodded. "Thanks. We'll see you later, maybe during your break."

Jonas smiled. "Sure thing, Boss."

Boss? What is that about? Did Seth work there? If so, it was news to her. Working in a bar was strong, honest work. She had no problem with it. What did he do? Was he a bartender? A waiter? *No, Jonas said boss.* He must be a supervisor of some kind. She shrugged it off and decided her questions could wait until another time. The night was about spending time with the amazing man beside her and showing him how much he meant to her.

Seth guided her around the desk and to the door. Alexis could hear the twang of a country song, and she cringed. *Yuck.* Modern country music made her twitch, and she wanted to roll her eyes each time a country song came on the radio at the store. Thankfully, the older of Bridgewater's radio stations, CKBW, played a mixture of genres, so she had a variety to listen to. She hoped the DJ played different genres or else she might rip her hair out.

They walked into a large and comfortable looking room. The bar was long and narrow, occupying the left wall. It was hard to see what colour it was in the low light, but several fluorescent lights above the bartenders allowed them to see what they were doing. One was a dark-haired woman in her 20s, with a low cut blouse and a big smile. Another was a tall and thin blond man, who added a bit of showmanship to creating his orders. He flipped the drink mixer around, catching it and twirling around to the delight of the few patrons at the bar. The man looked like he'd been doing it for years and was an expert at it.

"That's Daisy and Reggie, both have worked here for a long time," Seth explained as he waved to them.

To the far right, a DJ booth holding a blonde woman wearing headphones and glow-in-the-dark lipstick graced the edge of a dance floor, which was filled with several dancers. The music changed from something country to light rock. *Thank god.*

Seth took her elbow with a grin and guided her around hardwood tables and chairs strategically placed around the large central room, toward the back of the open area. He smiled and nodded to several people, shaking hands with a couple of gentlemen on the way toward the back. Daisy smiled and waved from her spot behind the bar, while Reggie gave him a thumbs-up in between manoeuvres.

They stopped at a dark coloured curtain at the very back of the venue, in the left-hand corner beside the bar. A lit-up sign saying *Private: Only with Permission from Owner* graced the side by the counter. Seth pulled back the curtain with a grin. "How's this for now?"

It was a corner booth that housed a highly polished fake marble-topped table with a padded loop-around bench in a rich blue. Several throw pillows and a couple of velvety royal blue throws graced a shelf above the back part of the bench. It was luxurious, cozy, and deliciously private.

She sat down on the soft, comfortable bench and slid around the table until she was at the back, facing the curtain. Seth dropped the curtain and slid in beside her, his hip pressing into hers. With the curtain down and the low lighting in the booth, it felt like they were in their own world. *What a great idea for a first date.* "You come here often?" she asked.

Seth slid his arm around her shoulders with a grin. "Almost every weekend."

His spicy aftershave wafted around her, and the feel of his body against her side felt amazing, and it sent her desire for him up a few notches. His mouth was barely an inch from hers. It was so tempting to kiss him. "That much?" She nuzzled her bottom lip against his.

He inhaled sharply. "Mm, yeah. That much." His arm tightened around her.

"Seth?" A woman with straight blonde hair poked her head around the edge of the curtain. She looked around thirty, with perfectly applied makeup and big brown eyes.

A touch embarrassed that they were almost caught in the act, Alexis shifted uncomfortably.

"It's okay, she's safe," Seth whispered in Alexis's ear. He turned and grinned at the waitress. "Hey, Sally. This is Alexis."

Sally walked in, carrying a tray with a bottle of Seth's favourite dealcoholized beer and a can of Alexis's favourite diet cola with a glass. No ice. Sally grinned as she set the beer in front of Seth and the glass and can in front of Alexis. "Aunt Karen said you were finally seeing someone, and she can't wait to meet her. Looks like I get first crack at showing her what the family can do. Nice to meet you, Alexis. Enjoy your time at *The Haven*." Her smile was warm and felt a little familiar to Alexis.

Alexis returned the smile. "Thanks."

Sally turned to Seth. "Pierce is looking for you." Her lips went flat, and she shook her head.

Seth let out a long breath. "He knows I took the weekend off. He can fucking well wait until Monday." He sounded a touch annoyed.

Jonas called Seth boss, and now another worker is looking for him. That means Seth must be a manager or assistant manager. Alexis's appreciation and respect for Seth grew. He was working two jobs—as a carpenter during the week while moonlighting working at a bar on the weekends. She cracked open the can of cola and started slowly pouring it into her glass.

Sally shrugged, and her eyes rolled skyward. "I know, but tell him that. You work more than he does, and that's saying something. You deserve to take a weekend off once in a while. Hell, you deserve every weekend off, in my opinion."

Seth stared at the waitress. "If I did that, you'd hate it."

Sally stuck her tongue out at him. "Yeah, I would, but only because you're my cousin."

Seth flipped her the finger. She mirrored it.

Alexis snickered and relaxed more. She'd already met a member of Seth's family, and Sally seemed to like her a lot. She loved Sally so far. She was warm, silly, and really funny.

"Anyway," Sally muttered, "I'll tell him to fuck off and leave you alone."

Seth twisted the cap off the bottle of near beer. "I'll give him five minutes. After that, he's on his own until Monday." Seth took a sip from his bottle and sighed.

"If I had it my way, he'd bugger off and not bother you at all. You finally have a date, and he can't let you enjoy your-selves. Screw him." Sally folded her arms across her chest and glared at the table.

"I am his supervisor, and if something went wrong, I would like to know about it." Seth drummed his fingers on the table.

Alexis glanced at Sally. Her lip was curled into a grimace, and her brown eyes blinked a few times. "All right. I'll time him. If he isn't done in five minutes, I'll drag him out of here and lock him in the office."

"Be gentle. The place can't run without him, as you know." Seth pointed his finger at Sally.

Sally let out a long, annoyed-sounding breath. "Yeah, yeah, yeah." She picked up her tray and smiled. "You enjoy your-self, Alexis, and don't let that old bear Pierce bother Seth too much." She winked, flipped her hair over her shoulder and disappeared behind the curtain.

Seth rubbed his free hand down his face. "Do not be sur-prised if I have to bail Sally out of jail if Pierce comes in here more than once. We grew up together, and she's more of a sister than a cousin to me."

Alexis grinned. "She looks a lot like you, but more girly and with blonde hair." Sally was gorgeous, and she seemed to have a tough but kind personality.

"Her family lived on the same farm, and their house was within view of ours. We were always at each other's houses for meals or playing when we were kids."

A small stab of jealousy over Seth's large family hit her chest. "It must have been great growing up with family so close."

Seth grinned. "It was. Mom used to joke she had three boys and a girl instead of two boys. Sally is the only girl between the two families — Mom and her sister, my aunt, Pam — so it was interesting and fun to have her around. Sally can hold her own. She's the toughest of the four of us."

"Am I going to meet the rest of your family sometime?" Alexis fiddled with her empty pop can, suddenly apprehensive and unsure of her place in Seth's life. Were they going to be fuck buddies, or was this a serious thing for him, too? She was already half in love with him. It wouldn't take much more to fall over the edge.

"Mom and Dad are in Scotland for their fortieth wedding anniversary right now, but I can arrange for you to meet them when they get home. Are you sure you want to meet them?" Seth gently grasped her chin and forced her to turn her head to look at him.

Relief spread through her when their gazes met, and she felt his arm tighten around her waist. She nodded.

He grinned. "Good, because my mother can't wait to meet you."

Her stomach churned nervously. *Seth's mom wants to meet me. Me. His new girlfriend. Oh fuck.* The delicious dinner they'd had in Mahone Bay suddenly felt heavier than a black hole in her stomach, and her fingers began to shake. A shot of cold went from the top of her head to the soles of her feet. *Fuck. I'm not the girl next door. I have a lot of problems and an ex-boyfriend who can't get the message to fuck off and leave me alone.* A frosty drop of sweat ran down her back and she shivered. *She's going to hate my guts.* Was Seth the kind of guy who had to have his parents' approval when it came to women, especially after the snafu with his ex-wife? No way would he see her if his parents hated her. Her muscles stiffened, her heart began racing, and her breathing quickened as her flight instinct started to kick in, and she began to prepare herself for their eventual breakup.

Seth brushed a tendril of hair off her face. Alexis closed her eyes and savoured the tenderness of the gesture. He was always so kind to her, even when they were arguing.

"Hey, whatever you're thinking, don't go there. Mom and Dad already know you are a lot different than Janie and were ready to meet you long before we got together. Mirrie told them about you, and they were going to ask you over for a family barbecue, as a friend. We happened to get together before it happened. You don't have to worry. Mirrie has them loving you already." His voice was low, soothing, and felt amazing to her ears.

The glacial feeling oozed out of her body, and her skin started to warm up. Her stomach felt normal again, and her suddenly tight muscles relaxed. It took an extra moment for her heart to slow down. She blinked at Seth. His gaze locked on to her mouth. She moistened her lips with the tip of her tongue and felt desire crackling in the air between them.

When his mouth claimed hers, Alexis started to tremble. She felt like she was standing on the edge of a chasm, about to fall over into the abyss. The feeling grew stronger when his tongue slid between her lips. She wasn't sure how much time passed. It could have been a minute or sixty. The only thing she was conscious of was Seth, feelings of safety, warmth, and joy coursing through her with each touch, every kiss, and the way his arms tightened around her from time to time.

It wasn't until after they came up for air that she realized lust hadn't invaded her mind once during the time they were kissing. She had been happy just to be with Seth, whether they were talking or not. As she stared into his eyes, the cliff disappeared beneath her feet, and she fell into the chasm. It was more intimate than sexual attraction and acting upon it.

Holy shit, I'm in love with him.

The soft scent of Alexis's perfume wafted around Seth as they pulled back a little, making him dizzy. *I can't get enough of her.* He softly groaned as he slid a hand to the nape of her neck and tugged her closer. Her mouth opened beneath his. She trembled against him when he eased his tongue between her lips. *She smells and tastes so damn good.* At that moment, all he wanted to do was make her feel like the only woman in the world.

A reverberation bounced through the side wall and into the seat. *Who the fuck is bothering us?* Seth kept his arm tight around Alexis as he lifted his head and barked, "This better be important!"

Pierce poked his head between the curtains and glanced between Seth and Alexis. His face turned red. "Oops, sorry, Boss!"

Fuck. There goes my quiet time with Alexis. Five minutes, that's all he's getting. Sally can handle anything else if Pierce gets too jumpy. Seth sighed and glared at the bar's night manager. "What's up, Pierce?"

Pierce pushed his way into the booth, the curtain swinging shut behind him. "I thought you'd want to hear about last night's sales."

Seth resisted the urge to snap at Pierce. The first Friday night he took off in months, and he couldn't get away from sales figures or the rising cost of booze. Figured. "I'm not working tonight, Pierce. I'm busy," he said firmly.

"I see that." Pierce smiled at Alexis.

"Alexis, this is Pierce, the annoying shit that runs the place. Pierce, this is my date, Alexis."

"Hi," Alexis said. She returned the smile and pulled away from Seth's side an inch.

He tightened his arm, squeezing her hip against his again. She relaxed and fiddled with the empty soda can on the table.

Pierce smiled. "Ma'am, sorry for the interruption." He turned to Seth and said, "It's nice to see you finally come with a lady, if you don't mind me saying so, Boss."

"I do mind it. It's none of your fucking business," Seth muttered with narrowed eyes.

Pierce snickered. "I'll make sure only Sally comes by, or I'll look after you myself."

I'll let him live, this time. Pierce was the soul of discretion, just like Seth's cousin. "Thank you."

"Anything to help you with a special lady. You two enjoy yourselves, you hear?" Pierce glanced at Alexis with a nod.

"We will." Seth glanced at the curtains and back to Pierce, a hint for Pierce to move his ass out of the room.

"Ma'am." Pierce nodded at Alexis and flipped open the curtain. Seconds later, it swished shut behind him, leaving Seth and Alexis alone in their private bubble.

She turned her head to stare up at him, her dark eyes narrowed and her lips pursed. A trickle of uneasiness crawled up his spine when she leaned forward and tapped him on the nose.

"What?" he asked, half terrified of her reaction to his position at *The Haven*.

"Why didn't you tell me you owned the bar?"

She doesn't sound pissed. She sounds curious. Thank fuck. "I didn't think it was necessary."

"Why not?" Her eyes narrowed to thin slits.

"I wanted a spot where we would have privacy, but at the

same time, be able to dance and have fun around others. I didn't think you'd like it if I told you I owned the place." *Shit, she looks like she's planning some sort of retaliation for that. I'd better watch my back.*

She glanced around the booth with a smile. "I love it. Is this your private area?"

"Yeah. People are only allowed in here with my say-so." He gave her a sheepish grin.

"You didn't answer my question about why you didn't tell me right away." Her temple brushed his chin, and the scent of wildflowers rose into his nostrils.

Be honest. She hates liars as much as you do. "I thought it would make you nervous. Are you okay?" he asked as he nuzzled his mouth against her ear.

"I'm fine. I was confused for a while, but I like knowing you own it." She burrowed deeper into his arms and sighed. "How long have you owned this place?"

He nipped at her earlobe. "Since about a year after my ex-wife left."

"Oh. I didn't think she was on the conversation log tonight." Alexis immediately straightened and tapped a fingernail against her glass.

Fuck. Me and my big mouth. Slightly pissed at himself for breaking the mood, he let out a long breath and closed his eyes. They might as well clear up a few things about that fucking ice-cold bitch. "How much do you know about Janie?"

Alexis fiddled with her glass. "Mirrie told me a few things."

Fuck. Leave it to Mirabelle and her big yap. Annoyed, he muttered, "Like what?"

Alexis didn't look at him as she mumbled, "Like she only married you because she thought you were rich, and how she acted like a spoiled brat when she found out you weren't."

Seth's jaw clenched, and his free hand fisted. *I'm going to fucking kill Mirrie once I get my hands on her. She had no right to say shit to Alexis. It's my place to tell people about that cold fish Janie, not hers.*

Alexis's knee tapped his. "Don't be mad at her, Seth. She considers you family and thought I should know so I'd understand you better."

He opened his eyes and stared down at Alexis with a blink. "Mirrie thought you didn't get me?"

"She was trying to set us up at the time," Alexis said with a sheepish grin.

I'm still going to kill Mirrie, for trying to set me up behind my back, again. Jesus. "That would do it. Mirrie always likes to run her yap when she's setting me up on a blind date."

Alexis turned her head and kissed his jaw. "If you're worried that it made me feel sorry for you, it didn't."

Her mouth on his skin felt so good. *Keep it up, love. Maybe I won't strangle my best friend's wife and go to jail.* "That's good."

Another kiss on his jaw, this one was close to his ear. He could feel her soft breath on his skin, and the warmth of her mouth made his dick tingle with anticipation. "I want to yank Janie's eyes out with a white-hot poker." There was a touch of evil in her quiet words.

Seth choked on a laugh. "I'm not surprised you would like to do that."

"She's not a real woman." Her tongue flicked against his earlobe.

His cock twitched, and a shudder of lust tickled his heart. "How do you know that?"

"Any woman that can't stand a man like you touching them is out of their fucking minds." Her voice was low, husky, and filled with assurance. She snuggled closer to his side and looped an arm around his waist.

The loving actions made a shiver of smugness zoom up Seth's neck. "You think so?"

She leaned back to stare up at him. "I do. I don't want you to stop touching me as long as we're seeing each other."

The physical side of a relationship was important to him, too, even if it was just a kiss or holding hands. Sex with his ex-wife had been an ordeal, Janie always acted like he was raping her, even if she had initiated it. He turned to masturbation more and more in the years after their wedding. Janie had acted as if he was cheating even if he spoke to another woman. Having her permission to have sex with someone else while they were still married would have been out of the question. She didn't want him but didn't want anyone else to have him, either.

"If you ask me, Janie is a frigid twat." There was a hint of malice behind her words.

Seth laughed as a picture of his ex-wife staring down her nose at him rose in his mind. "That's a great description of her."

"I'm not frigid." Alexis's eyes were as smoky as her low voice.

His dick started to harden. "Going by the way you were kissing me earlier, I'd say not."

She fingered his shirt collar. "I happen to love sex when it's done right."

Thank fuck. I won't feel like I'm violating her. I hoped she'd love sex, and I got my wish. "Pussyface wasn't your first?"

Alexis's eyes rolled skyward. "No, thank heavens. I was sixteen, and my first was a really sweet guy, Duncan." She sighed wistfully and shifted a bit in her seat. Her legs squeezed together, and she moaned a little.

"Did he make you come?" Seth asked, intrigued by her actions. She looked like she was trying to have an orgasm. *Not without my fingers, tongue or cock down there, sweetheart.*

"Yes," she breathed, her voice barely audible.

His cock went from half-mast to a painful, demanding hard-on. "I'm going to make you come, too, so much you'll think I was your first," he groaned as he trailed a finger between her small and perfect breasts. Her skin felt so silky against his.

Her breath caught, and a pulse began fluttering at her throat. "Just like I plan on making you see stars each time you orgasm."

His nostrils flared slightly as the primitive instinct to mate rose in his gut. They were in a private area, with orders not to be disturbed unless he texted Sally. They could have a quick fuck if they wanted to. *Shit. I don't have any condoms.* No way was he making love to her without some sort of contraception. He wasn't ready to have kids. Hell, he didn't know if Alexis even liked kids. It was their first date. They had plenty of time to figure out their future, however long it lasted.

"How many girls have you brought here?"

Her quiet inquiry knocked his arousal back a few notches. He stared at his empty bottle of near beer and mumbled, "You're the first." He never had any urge to bring a woman into his private realm. Alexis was different. She was special to him.

"Really?" she asked with a note of disbelief.

He sighed and sheepishly smiled at her. "They were casual. I didn't see the point in having the staff ask questions about one girl only to see me with another one a few nights later."

"Uh-huh. And how many were there between that frigid twat and me?"

Seth winced at the jealousy in her voice. "Only a few, but I still don't think it's anyone's business who I'm fucking."

"You brought me here." Alexis's eyebrow went up a notch.

"You're different." He reached out and touched a tendril of her silky hair. *I can't wait to run my fingers through that when I'm fucking you, sweetheart.*

"Yeah, you're not fucking me yet." She sighed and pouted.

"It's not that, sweet girl." He trailed his thumb along her jaw.

"Then what is it?"

God, she looks so delectable with her lower lip thrust forward. It made him want to rub the head of his cock around her mouth. He shifted uncomfortably, from the rush of blood to his balls and dick and admitting how he felt about her. "They were not my girlfriends. You are."

A light appeared in her eyes, and she smiled. "You want us to be exclusive."

He nodded and grinned. "I do. I care too much about you to see anyone else."

She touched his cheek. "Likewise," she whispered.

He cupped her face in one hand, his fingers against her jaw, lowered his head and gave her a long, slow kiss. She tasted of cola and the promise of tomorrow. *Damn, she's perfect.* His heart drummed hard against his chest, matching the beat his fingers felt in her neck. Slowly, he moved his hand downward and deliberately brushed his fingers along the outer side of her breast as he stroked her upper arm. She shivered, and her breath started coming faster. Goosebumps tickled his finger-tips as he lightly stroked her arm again.

She pulled back and pressed her forehead against his. "Mm, we'd better stop for now," she murmured.

"Why?" he asked as he tightened an arm around her waist.

She rolled her eyes. "You promised me we'd dance tonight, and so far, all we've done is kissed and talked."

"I thought you were enjoying it."

"I am, but I also want to show off my new man."

Damn, she's so cute when she wrinkles her nose. "I said—"

"I know, it's no one's business but ours, but I still want to dance with you tonight." She stared up at him with her beautiful dark eyes twinkling.

Seth jokingly groaned. He couldn't resist that look, and he suspected Alexis knew it. "Let the disc jockey know what you want to hear, and I'll make sure she plays it."

She grinned and clapped her hands happily. "When do you want to dance?"

"Anytime you're ready, love." He kissed the top of her head and sighed.

CHAPTER NINE

Seth cringed at the loud, screaming guitars and heavy bass blaring out of the speakers. "Heavy metal? You want to dance to this?" he asked with a grimace.

Alexis narrowed her eyes at him. "What's wrong with it?"

"You don't look like a metalhead." He pointed to her with a confused grin.

Her brow creased, and she tapped her foot. "What is a metalhead supposed to look like?"

He gestured to her blouse and skirt. "Metalheads wear leather, chains, and spikes. They look tough. They ain't soft and pretty like you are."

Amusement bubbled in her throat. It was hard to hold back a snicker at the obvious confusion on his face. She put a hand on her hip and leaned forward. "You think I'm soft?"

He rolled his eyes. "I mean, you wear a lot of lace and look girly. I don't remember seeing you wear leather," he mumbled.

She shot him an evil, knowing grin. "I don't wear it very often, only on special occasions."

"Like when?" His eyebrows went upwards, and there was a half-nauseated look on his face.

She smiled slyly and snickered. "That's for me to know and you to find out." She added a slow wink and wagged her eyebrows to get her meaning across.

He stared at her, puzzled for a long moment before his eyes widened and a grin appeared on his face. "I'd love to see that."

She tugged on his hand. "Another night, I promise. Come on, the song's half over. You did promise me we'd dance to a song of my choice."

Seth grumbled something she didn't quite catch but followed her onto an empty corner of the dance floor. He wasn't great at keeping the rhythm to a heavy metal song, but she gave him points for trying. She closed her eyes, sighed, and let the music flood her senses. The heavy beat, the screaming guitars, and the singer's hoarse lyrics reverberated across her nerve endings, which sent zings of pleasure along every cell of her body. Unconsciously, she began to gyrate her hips to the beat and swing her upper body in time with it.

Her eyes opened after a moment to lock with Seth's, and a shot of smugness zipped into her core and upwards into her heart. The raw hunger in his eyes almost drove her over the edge. Slowly she started dancing toward him, mouthing the lyrics, her gaze never wavering from his. She stopped a hair's-breadth away from him and kept dancing. The front of her body brushed against his as the music soared.

Tingles of sexual desire made her shiver when her engorged nipples brushed his chest, just below his pectoral muscles. Seth's nostrils flared, and his eyes were almost black in the dim light. She could feel his erection brush against her abdomen when she moved a little closer to him. His fingers brushed her hip, a cue to dance with him. She obliged by turning around and snuggling her back against his front.

A low groan vibrated in her ear when she nuzzled her backside against the hard ridge of his cock. A hand on her hip kept her in place when she tried moving away.

"Stay put, I don't want the entire place to see me with a hard-on," he murmured in her ear, barely audible over the roar of the music.

She nodded without missing a beat and ground her ass harder into his groin. His low grunt of pleasure made a smile flicker across her face.

"Don't do that too much. I'll blow up." His low, husky tone reverberated in her ear, into her soul.

Reluctantly, she stopped her motions and stared up at him over her shoulder. "Better?"

"Yeah." His arms slid around her waist. "Maybe we should slow it down a bit."

"Us? Isn't that a little presumptuous, considering how we were almost fucking in the booth?" Thank god the song was so loud no one could hear her yelling in his ear.

"Not us, the music. You're dangerous when you're wrapped up in a song," he retaliated. He kissed her temple and signalled the DJ, Jennifer. She grinned knowingly and nodded at them.

Alexis could feel Seth subtly taking control as the louder thrashing song ended, and a softer, slower country song started weaving its way out of the speakers.

"Perfect," he groaned against her ear and gently eased her around to face him.

Automatically, her arms went around his neck as his fastened around her waist. She unconsciously rubbed her forehead against his jawline and inhaled deeply. A pleasantly spicy and purely male tang sent a shiver of pleasure through her senses. His cheek pressed against her temple, and one of his hands gently grasped the back of her neck.

Desire's hurricane evaporated into a warm, gentle mist, engulfing her deepest emotions and pulling her deeper into its hold. Somehow, her tough, prickly exterior turned into a soft, loving girl whenever Seth touched her.

He made her feel perfect.

With a contented sigh, she snuggled closer to him and let the music take control again.

Alexis's Apartment Complex

Four hours later

"Mm."

Seth reached over and took her hand. "Are you tired?"

Her grin flashed in the dim light emanating from the dashboard of his car. "No, I'm just thinking it was a great night."

Good. "I'm glad you had fun."

She sighed happily and lifted his hand to her face. "We have to do it again sometime."

"We will, probably next weekend, if I can talk your boss into giving a weekend day off." He winked.

Alexis giggled. "Mirrie will allow it if it's you asking."

Smugness crawled up his spine. "Mirrie can't resist it when I use my puppy dog look on her."

"What woman can resist it?" There was a teasing note in her voice.

A picture of his ex-wife popped into his mind, and he growled a little. *Fuck. Why can't I get away from that bitch and what she did to me?*

"Shit, I forgot about her." Alexis's soft cheek rubbed against the back of his knuckles, and a soothing calm penetrated his being.

"Eh, fuck her," he muttered dismissively. His ex-wife wasn't worth his time or energy. She'd left him after treating him horribly. She no longer deserved the time of day.

"Not literally, I hope," Alexis said.

"I wouldn't wish that on my worst enemy," Seth replied, his voice full of his disgust for the woman he once believed he loved.

"Dead fish," Alexis stated.

Dammit, I love it when Alexis reads my mind. She's right. Janie is a dead fish in a lot of ways. She felt like one, too, cold and dry. Yuck.

"Are you ever going to tell me more about her?"

Seth let out a long sigh—a touch annoyed that Alexis

wanted to know more about the abuse he undertook while still with his first wife. "I don't know. Maybe sometime. I try not to think of her much nowadays."

"Because she hurt you." There was a lilt of understanding in Alexis's words.

Like pussyface hurt you. "Maybe, but she also tried scamming Blaine and Mirrie out of a lot of money."

"She was a real piece of work, wasn't she?" Alexis's brows furrowed together.

"One of the ugliest people I've ever met." He resisted the urge to tweak the end of Alexis's nose.

"She won't cause trouble if she thinks you're seeing someone, will she?" Alexis asked warily.

"Janie won't if she's smart. Mirrie has a baseball bat with Janie's name on it, and I think Blaine has a few things he'd like to say to her, too." His best friends were pissed at Janie for what she'd done to him, even more so for trying to blackmail them by threatening to call Child Protection Services to file a false child abuse report if Blaine and Mirabelle didn't dole out several thousand dollars and let her blackmail them for life. They had called her bluff, and the call wasn't made. They knew Janie had to give her name and sign the report. CPS would eventually discover it was done out of spite, and Janie knew she would have been in trouble for filing a false report. Seth had been glad his friends outsmarted his narcissistic wife. Janie didn't deserve more than to be tossed into a rubber room and the key tossed away.

"I hope they do get a chance to wallop her. I'd love to get my hands on her, too," Alexis muttered, her hands fisting.

Seth had to laugh at the image of tiny Alexis ripping into his tall former spouse. "If Janie does start something with us, I'll make sure you're at the start of the line. Mirrie and Blaine can wait."

She leaned over the console and kissed him. "Thank you."

Fuck, she tastes like sunshine, something I've been craving my entire life. "There's a condition to it."

"I see." Her voice carried a wary, almost feral note.

"You let me have first crack at pussyface, if he shows up again."

She snickered. "Deal, as long as you hide the body."

"Who says there's going to be anything left when I'm finished with the douche?" Seth retorted evilly.

Alexis's laugh tinkled in the cab, making Seth's heart ache at the possibility of having a real relationship with a real woman. "It looks like I'm going to have to get some heavy-duty grease cleaner, just in case."

"Don't forget the full-body protection suits." He squeezed her fingers.

"The ones with their own supply of oxygen?"

"Exactly."

"Why?" She sounded confused.

A shot of arrogance shot through his chest. "No one hurts my woman and lives to tell the tale."

Her teeth flashed greenish-white in the lights from his dashboard. "Just like no one touches my man and lives."

He snickered. Alexis was turning out to be an even more loyal girlfriend. He loved it, and he loved the way she growled when she said he was hers. He also loved the way she had snuggled against him while they danced. Her willowy body fit perfectly against his, and the top of her head brushed against his cheek as they swayed together. Janie had been almost eye to eye with him. He hated it. He preferred to be taller than any of his dates.

Alexis's scent wafted into his nostrils again, and his cock immediately reacted when she started caressing his leg through his pants and kissing his jawline. He turned his head a little, and their lips met in a searing kiss that made his insides shiver in delight. Her tongue thrust upwards between his teeth, and her taste and the scent of her perfume were making his dick feel like it was going to explode.

He pulled back abruptly, and their harsh breathing echoed in the cab. "Baby, go inside," he panted.

"Only if you come with me." Desire made her voice low and husky like they were already fucking.

His cock twitched at her overt innuendo, and he almost gave in to her silent demand to ride her senseless. "Alexis, go. Now."

"Seth—"

"I'm so fucking turned on, I'll probably wind up jizzing in my pants before I can pull it out."

She kissed his neck. "Do you want a blow job?" Her fingers trailed down his chest and stopped at his belt. "It wouldn't take much to give you one."

Her soft words made him cling to the edge of his sanity, and his cock felt like it was going to burst through the fly of his pants. "I would love to come in your mouth, just not tonight."

"Are you sure?" Her fingers caressed his thigh, almost touching his member.

Oh god, if she touches me, I'll fucking blow my load. "No, but we agreed not to fuck or do anything like that on the first date."

"That's your rule, not mine." She pouted.

"Rules are rules," he reminded her.

"And sometimes they're meant to be broken."

With a sigh of resignation, he murmured, "I'll make it up to you later."

"Promise?" There was a sly sparkle in her dark eyes.

"Yes."

"How?"

Seth grinned. "I'll think of something." He reached over and deliberately grazed the outside of her left breast with his right knuckles.

Alexis's sharp intake of breath made his balls clench painfully, and he could feel a little pre-cum soaking his shorts, hot and wet. *Damn. At this rate, I'll be masturbating three times a day until I fuck her senseless, and even then I'll still need to do it. She's perfect.*

A hard kiss against his mouth, then a loud click, and warmer air filled the cab. "Damn it, I'd better go before you explode," Alexis muttered. "See you later!"

The door slammed shut, and she was gone.

Seth watched her go, his cock still hard and waiting, and his libido was screaming for release in the flowery scented air she left behind.

His dick was going to get a few poundings that night. One wasn't going to be enough.

CHAPTER TEN

Seth's house
One week later

"Fuck me!" Seth bellowed as he hurled the phone across the room. *Great, the only night Alexis and I have left this weekend, and Mirrie fucks it up. She knows Alexis hates parties. I wish she'd take her craziness and drive it so far up her ass it hangs out her nose.* They were supposed to be watching movies there, and he was hoping to start the sexual side of their relationship. Seth didn't think his hand or his dick could handle any more masturbating. He wouldn't be surprised if he was getting carpal tunnel syndrome from whacking off so much. A smoky glance from Alexis was enough to send him into such a tizzy that he'd come after three strokes.

His room was prepped for her to spend the night. There were brand new freshly washed sheets on his bed, lots of battery operated candles to create ambiance, and lots of pink cloth flowers—mostly lupines—in vases around the room. Seth hoped Alexis would love it. He had never been so anxious to have everything perfected for a woman he was dating. Alexis deserved the best after what she went through with pussyface.

He rubbed a hand along the back of his neck. "Christ." A picture of Alexis naked formed in his mind, and his cock reacted painfully. Damn, he needed to get laid. Now.

Unfortunately, the universe never gives me a break. Jesus.

A trill from behind the couch had him scrambling. Locating the phone on the fifth ring, he scooped it up, hit the talk button and barked, "What the fuck do you want?"

"Your cock in my mouth, for starters. What's up with the screaming?"

"Huh? Wait a sec, who—shit. Sorry, Alexis. I thought it was someone else." Relieved it was his girlfriend, he rubbed a hand over his face and sighed.

"Let me guess. Mirrie, right?" Snark flew across the airwaves.

"Yeah, how'd you know?"

"She texted me a few minutes ago."

Aw fuck. Don't tell me Mirrie bugged Alexis about it, too. "She wants you to talk me into going to her party tonight."

"Yeah." Alexis sighed loudly.

"Do you want to kill her, or do you want me to do it?"

"I want it. I'm so fucking pissed at her. I could shove her into a volcano!"

"Let me know if you need help." Yeah, Alexis was angry, all right. Hell, he was so pissed, he could have chewed uranium and loved it.

"You can have what's left. Are you going to that fucking shindig of hers?"

"Unfortunately, yes. She wouldn't take no for an answer."

"Jesus. Hang on." She was quiet for a second. "Oh my god. She just texted me again. Either I show up, or she'll come drag me out by my hair. That's it. She's a dead woman," Alexis growled.

"Fuck. Someone must have cancelled, or else she wouldn't be so forceful," Seth murmured. "Get ready. I'll pick you up on my way. Mirrie can't ruin our entire evening."

Alexis sighed. "Good, I get a few minutes alone with you before the insanity," she said softly. "I really missed you in the chaos this last week with Mirrie needing help setting up for the grand opening."

He snickered. "I have to get some time with you, or else I'll wind up killing Mirrie myself."

"So, I distract you?" There was a huskiness in her tone. It sent his libido soaring.

His cock went to half-mast. *Slow down. I'm not beating off now. I want to save it for Alexis. She needs me full on and ready for her.* "You always distract me, but in the best way possible. How's about I pick you up at six-thirty?"

"That sounds like a plan. Maybe if we're lucky, Mirrie won't notice if we sneak off a little early. I don't want to be too tired when we hit your place later on."

He could almost see her winking to emphasize her point. His dick turned to concrete. *Shit, I'm a walking hard-on, thanks, Alexis.* He couldn't get her to his house and in his bed and fuck her fast enough. "Keep your fingers crossed."

Mirabelle's backyard
After sundown

Alexis's fingers were linked through Seth's as they slowly backed into a shadowed area near the pool after sunset.

"An hour left, at most," he replied to her questioning look and snorted as she turned a glare in Mirabelle's direction. "Then we'll head back to my house and watch a movie." *And hopefully, I can fuck you until we can't breathe or remember our own names.*

She grinned. "Which one? I don't want any of the cowboy movies you like."

"We could watch an action flick." He didn't mind them, as long as they had a great story.

She inhaled slowly and reached up to trail a finger down his front. "Or something else. You have pay per view as well as the monthly thing, don't you?"

Sparks tingled his skin through the material of his shirt.

Alexis's touch always made him feel amazing. "Yeah. Do you want to see what's on that, too?"

"We may as well. I'll pay for it."

Seth narrowed his eyes. "If it's at my place, I'm covering it."

He could barely see her face in the shadows, but her eyes twinkled softly in the dim light. "You're rescuing me from Mirrie. You've already done enough tonight."

"You can pay when we do it at your place sometime." He kissed her and ran a hand down her bare arm. Her silky skin became puckered with goosebumps. Smugness crawled up his spine, and he wondered if her nipples were sticking out, ready for his tongue.

"Seth," she rasped softly.

He tugged her a little deeper into the shadows, intent on having a moment with her away from prying eyes. "Seth, what?"

She took an extra three steps and tugged on his hand. "I don't have pay per view."

He grinned and pulled her behind a tall bush. "You can do it another way then."

"How so?" She kissed him.

Tingles of pleasure shot through his lips, down his chest, and settled in his gut. She tasted like coffee and lemon water, an enticing sample. "We'll figure something out."

Her gaze locked with his in the low light, and hands brushed his belt. "I think I know how."

Curiosity rose in his gut. *What's she planning now?* He wasn't sure if he liked that weird twinkle in her eyes. "What do you mean?"

She grinned and dropped to her knees. One of her hands slid around to his backside.

His cock started to harden. "Alexis, what are you doing?"

He gasped as she nuzzled her face against his fly. He went

from somewhat flaccid to full-blown aroused in two seconds. Fast even for him.

Automatically, his hands cradled her head, and he felt the softness of her hair against his skin as he involuntarily thrust his groin closer to her face. His hard-on became painful when she started to kiss him slowly through the taunt denim. He could almost feel her warm breath on his flesh.

"I'm paying up." Her free hand undid the buckle on his belt.

Oh god, if she touches me, I'm going to blow my wad all over her face. "We're going to have sex now? I don't have any condoms," he panted.

She flipped open the button at his waist. "We don't need one, not for this round," she replied and placed a kiss on the head of his cock through the denim.

The pressure of her lips made all rational thought leave his mind. His entire universe shrunk to nothing but Alexis and how she was on her knees before him. He panted harshly as her fingers slowly pulled down his zipper and tugged his jeans off of his hips. His engorged flesh flopped outwards, uncovered by underwear, and he groaned as cooler air hit him in a combination of pleasure and shock.

Her soft gasp of delight was almost his undoing. He felt a drop of pre-cum forming at the head, and without thinking, he started stroking his cock and showing her how much she was driving him crazy. She licked her lips a moment before her warm fingers slid beneath his length and caressed his balls.

Seth's eyes slammed shut, and he let out a harsh, low groan as her tongue licked the head. Her fingers tightened a little around his sack, sending a shot of pleasure through him. "Stop teasing me, baby," he gulped and thrust his swollen member toward her luscious, full lips. He needed to come between them. He wouldn't be satisfied until he felt his orgasm slide into her beautiful mouth.

Alexis shoved her glasses on top of her head and ran her tongue along the underside of his hot, swollen and highly sensitive cock.

Seth groaned in torment.

She blew a little cold air onto him.

He shivered violently and whimpered, "Baby, please!" Her teasing was too much. His lust had overtaken his entire being. *Two strokes, and I'll be done. Let me come somehow, sweetheart. I can't take much more of this before I lose it completely.*

Wet heat replaced the cold air, with a light sucking pressure. Seth saw stars and growled low in his throat as he drove his full length between her lips and fisted his hands in her hair. Alexis started bobbing her head up and down as she swirled her tongue around the sides of the head of his cock and sucked on and off.

Seth felt his orgasm building fast. He held her head steady as he pumped his hips, increasing in speed as he got closer to exploding. It felt amazing. *Damn, she knows how to give head.* "Gotta come," he groaned when he felt the warning tingle. Her fingers sank into his ass, holding him still. The tip of his cock hit the top of her mouth as she sucked, hard. His cock felt like it was three times its normal girth—he was so ready to blow. With a long groan, Seth's hips convulsed and his knees shook vigorously as his cock shuddered with relieved lust.

Seth's house
One hour later

"Where did you learn how to give a guy a blow job?" Seth asked. They were cuddled close on his sofa, his arm around her, and her legs were draped across his lap.

Alexis shrugged. She didn't really want Seth to know about her past. He knew about Brett, wasn't that enough? "Does it matter?"

"I just want to know if anyone else has experienced it. That was heaven," he said. He sounded happy and relaxed.

Well, maybe it's okay for him to know a few things. I have to learn to trust him. Seth knows I love sex, even though Brett treated me like shit and used me as a way to relieve his lust. "It wasn't Brett, if you're asking."

"You didn't—" Seth's fingers touched her face.

Her gaze met his and held it. "No, he didn't get that kind of a blow job. I held still while he fucked me in the mouth. Even if I had known the right way to do it back then, he wouldn't have gotten it. He didn't deserve it, and he's lucky I didn't bite his dick."

Seth cringed, and his left eyebrow twitched. Alexis couldn't hold back a snicker.

His gaze met hers again. "How did you learn to do it like that?"

Alexis smiled at the picture of a lover from Moncton rose in her mind. Gavin was a sweet guy, so gentle and understanding. "I learned from another man I dated for a while after I dumped Brett's lazy ass. He taught me what he liked and what areas most men like having licked, and so on."

Seth nodded and smiled. "How did he know?"

"He was bisexual and loved giving blow jobs as well as getting them. He wasn't shy about showing me how to do it properly either."

"You watched him with another man?" Seth asked incredulously.

She blushed, a little embarrassed. "Not just watched."

"You participated in it?" he asked with raised eyebrows and his jaw hanging low.

"I rode him while he blew off the other guy," Alexis admitted and sighed happily. It had been her first ménage, and it had been so erotic for her. She had relived it in fantasies for years afterwards. Thank heavens for vibrators.

Seth grinned. "You liked it."

She shifted in her seat. Her pussy was starting to tingle, and she could feel the wetness in her lace panties from her arousal. "I loved it. I've never experienced anything so erotic. Well, not until I was the one getting tag-teamed by both of them several times over the course of a month. That was the most amazing thing I had done up to that point." *That's it. I'm so fucking horny, I could scream. If we don't get to the fucking part of the evening soon, I'm going to lose it and masturbate. I can't handle this much longer.*

Seth coughed in shock. "I would have never thought it."

She trailed a finger down his chest toward his belt. "Were you ever in a ménage?"

He blushed. "I have a few times in college. It was me and two girls, roommates, who didn't mind sharing." He grinned smugly. "That was an amazing semester."

Being with that dead fish ex of his must have been a shock after his school days. "Do you want to have another ménage, but with me as one of the partners?"

Seth leaned back into the cushions of the couch and stared at her blankly. "You'd bring in another girl?"

Huh, that sounds interesting. I've never been inclined to mess around with another girl, but who says it wouldn't be fun? "I'd bring in another girl, but on the condition you bring in another guy. Balance." She added a wink and rubbed her palm on his stomach.

"I'm not sure if I could handle watching another person touch you, sweetheart. I'd kill them." He groaned, and his blue eyes blazed into hers.

"That's good, because I want only you, no one else," she whispered and caressed his jaw with her hand.

Calloused fingers stroked her cheek. "Sweet girl, you have no clue how happy that made me."

His hand felt so good on her skin. She wished he would touch her elsewhere. Alexis was already half out of her mind from the blow job, since she didn't get any relief herself, and talking about her ménage experience had her slit fully soaked and ready for him to do what he chose to her. She was ready to become fully his.

She moved to her knees and leaned in to kiss him. "Why don't you show me?" she whispered and boldly started unfastening his pants. She was delighted that he was already hard and ready for her. She caressed his length with her fingers and pulled him free of the denim. *Jesus Almighty, he has the most gorgeous cock I've ever seen.* It was standing straight up, ready for her, with a drop of pre-cum forming on the head. His pubic hair was almost black, much darker than and not as thick as the hair on his head. A dusting of hair ran upwards, under the cotton of his black t-shirt. She had to explore where it went and how much he had.

Seth leaned forward, whipped the shirt over his head and tossed it on the floor. Alexis grinned and licked her lips as she marvelled at the sight of his bare chest, covered in a dusting of dark hair that was thicker around his pectoral muscles and tapered toward his stomach. A soft sheen of sweat was starting to form along the bare patches of skin. His obvious excitement was a siren call to her.

She had to taste him again. His salty-sweet nectar felt and tasted marvellous, and the scent of his aroused body was intoxicating. She licked her lips again and leaned forward, so she was on all fours. Her lips found the head of his dick, and she slurped at it greedily.

"Fuck!" Seth yelped.

Alexis lifted her head and stared at him. His eyes were so dark, and his breathing was hitching every few seconds. Seeing him like this sent a surge of smugness up her spine. She was driving him insane. Another tap or two in the right direction and he would be out of his mind. "I thought you loved getting sucked off," she murmured.

He panted, "I do, but it's not fair for me to have two in one night, and you not have anything."

She smiled slyly. "I told you I love the taste of a man."

"You want me to fuck you, don't you?" His hips thrust upward.

"Later." She licked him from hilt to tip. *Shit, he tastes and smells even better the second time around.*

Seth's hips lifted off the couch. "No, now. I need to know what you feel like when you're coming," he panted and started pulling upwards on her blouse.

She sat up, allowed him to tug it over her head. She moved to a vertical position and unfastened her jeans. His hands impatiently shoved them and her lacy panties down as she undid the fastener of her bra.

"Let me look at you," he ordered.

Alexis slowly stood up and put her hands on her hips as she let Seth see her naked for the first time. She could feel the arousal in his gaze as he took in the view. She was slim and worked hard to keep herself that way. Those long walks around the Duck Pond behind the Desbrisay Museum had paid off.

His gaze moved upwards, back to her bare mound, lingering before it moved up to meet hers. The raw hunger she saw made her knees go weak and her pussy throb uncontrollably.

"Holy shit," he whispered after a moment.

Her cunt felt like it was on fire — she was so ready for him. She took a step toward him but stopped when he waved her back.

"Stand there for a minute. I want to really look at you."

His husky tones felt silky to her ears, putting all of her nerve endings on alert, ready for his fingers, his tongue, and his cock. Alexis smiled and did as he ordered, her knees starting to shake as she watched him staring at her.

Without moving his gaze from hers, he shoved his pants down to his ankles and fisted himself. Mesmerized, she watched as he started masturbating while his gaze roamed her body. He licked his lips as he picked up the pace, and she almost climaxed on the spot.

The two-men-at-once was trumped by the sight of Seth pleasuring himself as he watched her. *I need him inside of me. Now.* "Seth?"

He nodded with a loud pant. "There's a rubber in the drawer, just a second."

"I'll get it." She pulled open the drawer and secured the foil packet in seconds.

"Not yet." He set it on the couch beside him.

"Why not?"

He stood up, kicked off his socks and jeans, and lay down on the carpet. His cock stood straight up, the sac underneath it swollen and beckoning to her.

Puzzled, Alexis stared down at him and put her hands on her hips. "What are you doing?"

"Sweet girl, I need to taste you. I want you on my face. Now."

Her knees finally gave way, and she had to crawl to him to position herself properly.

"Fuck, you smell so fucking good," he groaned and nuzzled his face into her pussy when she was in the proper position.

Alexis moaned softly and instinctively pushed her groin closer to him.

"I love it when a woman shaves for me, much easier for me to fuck her with my tongue." He gave her full slit a long lick. "Mm, you taste amazing."

Pleasure shot through her body, eliciting a louder moan from her throat.

"Yeah, that's what I want to hear," he growled against her pussy and nudged her slit open with his tongue.

A jolt of pleasure zapped deep in her cunt. "More," she

cried out. Seth wiggled his tongue against her opening. "You're making me crazy." Her fingers dug into her legs for balance and to keep from mashing her cunt into his face. She didn't want to smother him.

"I haven't even started yet, you just wait." He shifted his head a little, dug his fingers into her ass, and burrowed his face deeper into her soaking wet cleft.

Her pussy felt like it was pouring out rivers of her lady juices. A muffled scream tore from her throat as he ran his tongue around her clit. Round and round, until Alexis felt like her head was going to blow apart.

He pulled back, blew cold air on her wet heat.

"Don't stop, Seth," she whimpered as she pressed her mound against his face.

"Let me hear you come, baby," Seth ground out and put more pressure next to her nub.

He shifted again. Alexis felt suction on her clitoris. Painful delight shot through her pussy, into her breast, and back to her soaked cleft. She couldn't hold back her peak, and she let out a long, high pitched scream of pleasure. She tensed up as the orgasm ripped through her. He increased the pressure, shoved a finger up her cunt, which sent her into a continuous strong orgasm that made her entire body stiffen and air freeze in her lungs.

He suddenly stopped, and she fell forward to rest her hands on the floor with her ass in the air. Her forehead hit the carpet, her eyes closed, and she panted as she tried to regain her senses. Seth's masterful tongue had driven her insane. *Fuck me. He knows what he's doing. At this rate, I'll want to ride his face all of the time.* She gasped for air and gripped the carpet with her fingers, her last shred of sanity evaporating fast.

A rustling behind her was followed by Seth's hands on her hips and a nudge against her still soaked slit. Her pussy started to tighten and demand to be filled as she leaned back into his groin.

"Fuck me, Seth," she groaned between pants.

His fingers tightened around her hips, and he thrust his engorged cock deep inside of her. His balls slapped against the front of her slit. She moaned in joy as she felt his cock scrape her g-spot. She needed more now. "Faster!" she demanded.

Seth let go of her hips and leaned across her back, his hands on the floor beside hers as he started plummeting her pussy relentlessly, their lust too far gone to take it slowly. After a moment, his thrusts started to become more powerful and more controlled, an indication he was getting closer to his peak.

Alexis squeezed her internal muscles tight around him, and her moans became louder as she felt his dick slide in and out of her. It seemed he knew exactly where to hit her inside to turn her into a delightful mess of pussy juices and lust. She could feel her clitoris tingling painfully, and her inner spots were screaming for release. "Seth, please," she whimpered and thrust her pussy harder against him.

"Dammit, your pussy is so fucking tight, I'm gonna come soon," he groaned in her ear and bit her shoulder as he drove into her and held still for a few heartbeats.

Alexis screamed. Her peak hit her so hard that she drove her ass deeper into his groin, and it made her elbows buckle.

Seth thrust again and again, each one giving her another peak, her pussy getting tighter each time he made her come. She could feel his cock getting larger and larger with each thrust, bringing him closer to his orgasm. "Hurry, Seth. I want to feel you come," she moaned and ground her hips into his.

He bit her ear, and one powerful and hard push had him tensing over her. Seth let out a strangled shout against her shoulder. Alexis could feel every one of his spams against the walls of her sheath as it emptied his seed into the safety of the condom. His damp chest pressed against her back, his hot breath brushed against her ear, and the last soft groans from his climax timed perfectly with the spasms of his cock and the ripples of her pussy.

He started to pull out of her, and she stopped him. "Stay with me, just for a minute."

Seth nodded and wrapped an arm around her waist as he kissed her neck. It felt good, comforting. Loving. They were sweating profusely, but she didn't care. Seth was the perfect lover for her. He seemed to know what drove her wild and how much she loved to feel a man's cock buried inside of her.

"What the hell just happened?" he panted.

"The best sex I've ever had," she replied. It was true. Seth was generous, loving, and happy to please her.

He moved a hand to her breast. "Mm." He kissed her shoulder and ran his hand from her breast to her pussy. A tingle of happiness zapped deep in her sheath, and she realized that despite all of the orgasms she just had, she would need at least one or two more rounds before she went home.

"What's that supposed to mean?" She craned her neck so she could look at him over her shoulder.

"It means it was the best I've had, too, and give me a minute to recover." He eased his now soft member out of her and started pulling back.

Alexis lay on the carpet and watched him. Seth was gorgeous when clothed, but when naked, he looked like a Greek god to her. Not a spare inch of fat was on his frame, and his lean muscles rippled a little under his skin as he lay down beside her and pulled off the used contraceptive.

After disposing of the condom in a nearby wastebasket, he cuddled her to his side and brushed her bangs out of her eyes. "I got a little rough. I didn't hurt you, did I?"

It was perfect. She smiled. "I like it rough."

"I do, too, but I also like it slow, gentle, and sweet." He stood up and held out a hand for her.

She let him help her stand and stood on tiptoe to kiss him.

Surprise ripped through her when he scooped her up and carried her to his bedroom.

"You're tired?" she asked as he set her down on the floor by the bed.

"Not yet. That floor is too hard for us to lie on, I thought you'd be more comfortable here. I wasn't planning to fuck you for the first time on the floor. I was going to do it in here."

Alexis glanced around, and her heart skipped a few beats. The room looked so pretty. Battery operated tea lights highlighted fake lupines, and the bed covers were turned back to reveal pale blue sheets, sprinkled with pink cloth petals. She sniffled happily. Seth's attempt to be romantic made her feelings for him strengthen and deepen. He was the perfect man in her eyes. "It was still hot doing it that way, but yeah, a bed would be nice once in a while. Keep this up, and a girl may fall in love." Not a joke. She was already there. *Who can resist him?*

He stroked her cheek with calloused fingers. "You keep smiling at me like that, and a guy may fall in love, too."

Without removing her gaze from his, she lay down on the bed and spread her legs wide. She fingered her pussy, her silky skin getting slippery again as she stuck a finger inside herself and wriggled it around. It felt good, but Seth's tongue and cock felt so much better.

He groaned, and his breath caught as he watched her.

Power surged in her veins when she saw his cock sticking straight out, and his balls tightening in preparation for another round. "Lick me all over, Seth. I need to feel your hands and tongue on me. Now."

With a low groan, he fell to his knees and buried his face in her pussy.

Alexis's victorious sigh was lost in a moan as Seth's tongue found her opening.

Worship me, my handsome carpenter.

CHAPTER ELEVEN

Monday Morning
Mirabelle's Shop

"Everything okay, Seth?" Blaine's voice came out of nowhere.

Seth yelped in shock and jumped a foot clear off of the ground. His chisel landed on his boot and created a huge clatter. "I was until you scared the living shit out of me," he growled. He bent over, scooped up the tool, and flipped the finger at his best friend.

"That's what I smell." Blaine clicked his tongue once and stared knowingly at him.

Seth glared at him before turning his gaze back to the carving in front of him. "Shouldn't you be working?" he asked in a snarl.

"I was about to ask the same of you." Blaine stared at him and poked a finger at the almost blank board.

Seth drew a line on the wood, a little embarrassed his lack of effort had been noticed. "I am working."

Blaine snorted and scoffed. "You call staring at the clock or the door for the last two hours working?"

"I've been doing a lot of thinking and didn't want to cut my hands while I was doing it." Seth drew another line, then erased both irritably. Neither was right. He kept his gaze on the wood, cowardly focusing on that instead of looking his best friend in the eye. If Blaine only knew what was bothering Seth, he'd never hear the end of the ribbing from all of the guys, and Mirrie would be over the moon.

"Thinking, eh?" Blaine sounded like he didn't believe it.

"Yeah, thinking." Seth started tracing out the lines of a flower. It made him think about Alexis and wonder where she was. It was two hours past her start time. She had told him she'd see him before ten that morning, and it was almost noontime.

"Was it about Alexis?"

The pencil went wayward, creating a jagged, dark line across the oak grain. He erased it with a growl. *Shit.* Blaine must have seen him staring at her. Play it cool. Seth started tracing another leaf for the flower. "Why would I be thinking about her?" he asked, trying to keep his voice level.

"Don't try to feed me that line of bullshit, Mitchell. You two looked pretty fucking smug when you came out of the bushes the other night."

Oh shit. Seth squeezed the pencil so hard it snapped in two. "I don't know what you're talking about." *Liar, liar, pants on fire.*

Blaine punched his arm. "I can see why you're hot for her. She's pretty, smart, warm, and fun. Nothing like that dead fuck you married."

"Yeah, I guess she's pretty," Seth mumbled as he dropped the broken pencil on to the board and pulled a fresh one out of his carpentry apron. He still couldn't look Blaine in the eye. Not yet. Seth hoped to keep things quiet for now and enjoy being Alexis's boyfriend. Apparently, the universe had other plans. *Fuck me.*

"Come on. She's your type. Even I know that," Blaine muttered.

Embarrassed someone had seen them despite being so careful that night, Seth could only shrug and stare at the floor.

"Are you happy with her?"

Seth raised his gaze to his best friend's and grinned. "Yeah. She's amazing. We've been on the way to this for a while."

Blaine's shaggy beard couldn't hide his sly smile. "Be glad it was me who saw it and not Mirrie. You know what she's like."

Mirabelle didn't know yet. *Whew.* "You didn't tell her?"

Blaine shook his head. "It's not her business. I thought you two should be allowed to fuck your brains out a few times before she stuck her nose into it and started planning your wedding."

Seth laughed. "We're nowhere near there yet."

Blaine gave him a pointed look. "I know that, but you know Mirrie."

"Too well." Way too well.

"I overheard her on the phone with Alexis this morning, and she won't be in until later this afternoon. Something about a doctor's appointment."

Concern immediately zinged up Seth's neck, hot and un-comfortable. "Is she okay?"

His best friend smiled knowingly. "Yeah, you've got it bad. I think it's just a checkup, because I heard Mirrie ask her several times if she needed more than this morning off."

"I'll ask her myself, probably after closing."

"I knew you would. Just don't let you-know-who see you kissing Alexis until you're ready."

It was code for no making out in the store itself due to the security cameras, or in the back areas if Mirabelle was around. "Understood."

"I'm glad you're with her. You need someone warm and nice like her."

Seth gave his friend a half-grin. "Thanks."

Chimes rang above the door around one o'clock that after-noon, and a loud exclamation from Mirabelle had Seth poking his head out of the extension into the main area. Relief hit him like a truck when he saw Alexis being escorted through the store by her boss.

Their gazes met briefly. She smiled at him, and the remaining tension left his body. Her silent message conveyed she was fine.

He still wanted to talk to her later about why she was at the doctor's office. *I didn't hurt her, did I?* He still had rug burns on his knees and ass from taking her on the carpet of his living room, and his hips were a little sore from having sex more in thirty-six hours than he had in the previous six months.

Seeing her sent shockwaves of tenderness through him. He wanted to touch her, kiss her and hug her tightly, and protect her from the evils of this world. Her perfume wafted his way when she walked by him. His dick went from zero to hard and demanding in less than a second. *I fucked her six times over the weekend, twice last night, and I want to fuck her again. Jesus.* His overly high sex drive was great for when they were alone, but not at the store. He turned back to his tracing with a curse at himself. Focusing on his task was the perfect thing to relax his arousal. Until a familiar scent wafted into his nostrils, then his cock went to attention again. *Thank god for my carpentry apron, I'd embarrass myself if it weren't for that.*

"That looks great, Seth," Alexis marvelled and traced a line with her fingers. She was close to him, and her arm pressed into his.

He glanced down at her and resisted the urge to kiss her temple. Mirabelle was in the main part of the store, almost within eyeshot. "I have another one ready, if you want to start painting it today."

Her bright smile made his pulse quicken. She turned back to the wood in front of them, took a pencil from him, and started tracing another flower. "Blaine said you were worried about me, being at the doctor and all." Her whisper barely reached his ears above the sound of the radio playing in the corner.

"He did?" Blaine had a big mouth sometimes.

"He knows about us." She sighed, drew another line, and shook her head.

"I know." His gaze met hers, and he nodded.

"I'm fine, Seth. Don't worry." She leaned into his arm and smiled up at him.

You're my woman. Worrying about you is my job, sweetheart. "As long as we're together, I'll worry."

"It's your way." She nodded and snuggled closer to his arm.

"Exactly." Her full pink lips tantalized him. It had been only a few hours since he last kissed her, yet it felt like months. He quickly glanced over his shoulder, saw no one in sight, and placed a soft, quick kiss on her mouth.

Her smile widened. "You can stop worrying now. I just went in to get a few things checked out, and I'm fine."

Relief flooded through him. "Good."

She pulled up a stool and sat down. Alarm shot up his spine when she cringed.

The chisel fell to the floor with a clatter as he clasped her elbow. "What happened? Did you hurt yourself?"

"I'm okay. I didn't realize my butt would hurt after the needle." She cringed and rubbed the spot near the seat of her jeans.

At that point, Seth didn't care if someone saw them or not. He reached down and caressed the area gently. "That's a weird area for a shot."

"It wasn't an immunization." Her cheeks were a darker pink than normal.

Why was she blushing? "They don't take blood from your ass, either." He gave her one last caress and lifted his hand to brush her bangs out of her eyes.

"It wasn't blood work. It was the birth control shot," she mumbled, and her cheeks went crimson.

"We use contraception. Why do you need the shot?" There were a box and a half of rubbers in his bedroom. There was no need for her to get extra birth control.

"The condoms made my pussy feel like someone took sandpaper to it after the fifth time around." She cringed and rubbed her denim-clad knee with a hand.

He blinked down at her and touched her cheek lovingly. "Why didn't you say something? We could have done other stuff."

"I was enjoying it too much. Besides, once we started using the lube, it wasn't so bad."

"You don't want me to use condoms?"

"Not once the shot has kicked in," she replied with a grin.

"I've never gone bareback before." He went from flaccid to fully hard in seconds. *Damn.* The thought of coming in her without anything there was enticing. A vision of Alexis on her back with his seed showing at the opening of her pussy was enough to make his knees weak and blood to thunder through his body. His heart thumped wildly, and his breath quickened.

Alexis's gaze burned up into his. "Not even with your ex?"

Shit. That cold fish again. His cock went back to its unaroused state. "She thought sex was messy, and she didn't want to risk getting pregnant. I was lucky if she let me come near her even with a condom on more than once every six or so months, longer the last going off."

Alexis put a hand on his arm. "I haven't gone without one either, but I want to with you. It doesn't feel right using a condom, for some reason."

He grinned. *Damn, if she keeps this up, I'm a goner.*

"What?"

He placed a soft kiss on her nose. "You are turning into the perfect woman."

"How so?" She sounded innocent. His Alexis was so sweet and needed the reminder once in a while.

He leaned forward and whispered, "You are a hell of a pool

player, and you give as good as you get, you like the occasional beer, and you're gorgeous. You're a hell of a wild ride in bed, you love to give blow jobs, and now you want me to fuck you without a rubber."

She discreetly leaned into his side. "Maybe I want to know I'm the first woman who ever had your spunk in her."

His cock twitched, hard, as the image of her with his seed oozing out of her pussy flashed in his brain. "And I want to know I'm the first guy who ever came in you without one," he panted in her ear.

She gasped softly with wide eyes. "Maybe I'd better work over there."

"What's wrong with helping me?" Had she soaked her panties again? He glanced around, didn't see anyone, and flicked his tongue on her earlobe.

Alexis's voice was a little shaky when she replied. "After the way you were talking, it's going to be hard not to jump your bones right here."

Seth grinned evilly. Yup, she had soaked panties, and that meant she would be jumping him the instant they hit his place. "Good point. Just stay where I can see you."

"Likewise."

Thursday Night
Mirabelle's shop

Seth had stayed late that day. He was painting a mural of Alexis's design along the top of one wall that she helped with him between customers. It was Alexis's idea, one he'd jumped on. It was the perfect way for them to spend time together without having Mirabelle hovering.

"I hate Labour Day," Alexis whispered on their way out the door that evening.

He scooped up his toolbox and draped his carpentry belt over one shoulder. "Why?"

Alexis shoved her glasses up on her nose and sighed. "It means the cold weather is on the way."

"You don't like snow?" He loved it and loved ice skating.

"It's so depressing." She locked the door, pulled out her key, and tugged on the handle a few times. Seth took it as making sure things were secured.

He touched an earring to send it swinging, its soft chimes tinkling in the early evening air. "Knowing Mirrie, she'll make sure you don't have much time to think. The holidays are her busiest time." They left the store on King Street, looped up a side street behind the building, and climbed the slope to the parking lot attached to Pleasant Street, the next street up the hill on the west side of the LaHave River. His truck wasn't that far from them, three spaces away. Seth pulled his keyring out of his pocket and hit the unlock button twice as they approached the vehicle. The locks opened, and Seth opened his door and placed his toolbox on the floor of the back seat. He got in and fired up the engine.

Alexis looked downcast as she crawled into the cab, slammed the door and fastened her belt. "Yeah, but what about after that? She told me it's so quiet in the New Year that she closes the store on Mondays and Tuesdays due to a lack of customers. I won't be getting as many hours, even if I use them as my days off."

He sighed as he fastened his own seat belt. He backed the truck out of his space and replied, "You won't be bored. I'll make sure of it." They stopped to check the street, and pulling out, he made the turn toward her apartment complex, not far from the Desbrisay Museum on Jubilee Road.

Alexis snorted. "How so?"

"You won't be stuck in your apartment alone. You'll be staying with me part of the week, especially if there's a snowstorm." He smiled slyly. No way was she staying home alone if he wasn't working. It was his job to look out for her and make sure she was fine. He glanced at her, and the sight of her bright grin made his heart skip a beat. "You like that idea."

Her fingers brushed his knee. "You have no clue."

"I'd rather have Mirrie catching us in the act than go a day without seeing you." He nudged her knee with his.

A click preceded a warm body snuggling up to his side. Seth grinned when she moved to the middle seat and snapped the belt around her waist.

Seth draped his right arm around her shoulders as she leaned into him. Her hand rested on his knee, and her head brushed the side of his jaw occasionally. Janie never did that. It would have messed up her hair. Alexis kissed his neck softly, and a shudder went through his body. Janie wouldn't have done that either—her lipstick would have gotten smeared.

Just like Alexis's is now. Damn, she looks so good with that dreamy sparkle in her eyes and her cheeks warm with joy. She gave him another bright smile, and an unnamed emotion hit him between the eyes, hard. It made his vision blur, and dizziness threatened to overtake him.

"Seth?" Alexis's voice, a little distant, had a panicked note to it.

The vertigo evaporated, and his eyesight cleared. He gasped and blinked several times, dimly aware that they were at a stop sign, his foot hard on the brake, and his knuckles white on the steering wheel. He shook for a few seconds and took a deep breath to alleviate the weird feeling that hit him.

"Seth, are you okay?"

She's going to freak if you don't say something now. He let out a long breath and nodded. Nothing was broken, and he could see again. "Yeah, why?"

"You zoned out for a bit like you used to when you had heatstroke over the summer." Her cool fingers brushed his cheek and neck. The caress was so soothing and felt like heaven to him. He loved her touch, and it made him feel like he was the only man in her world.

He cringed. If she knew what had really caused those spells, she would think he was insane. "I did?"

She nodded. "Yes, and it's a damn good thing we were already stopped. It could have been bad otherwise. Do you want me to drive?"

He shook his head. They were close to her apartment building. "I'll be okay."

Worry creased her brow. "Are you sure?"

"Yeah." He smiled at her to reassure her.

"I want you to rest for a few minutes before we head back to your house." An eyebrow went upwards, and she stared up at him with determination on her face.

He stared down at her. *Shit. She isn't letting go of it.* "You're worried."

She gave him a blank look. "No duh."

"Only if you rest with me, sweet girl."

"It won't be resting if I do." She smiled slyly and winked at him.

Oddly, his cock didn't automatically twitch at the smoky promise in her voice. Was the initial blush of lust gone already? No, but something was muting it somewhat.

She twisted slightly toward him on the seat and looped her arm around his front. He tightened his arm around her shoulders and placed a long kiss on her temple. The soft scent of her hair and her contented sigh penetrated his senses—his soul. The dizziness started hitting him again, but he was able to shove it away before he drowned in it. *I'd rather drown in everything about my Alexis.*

"Seth?"

"Mm?"

"There's a car behind us."

"Shit, it figures. I was enjoying this," he muttered as a loud honk reverberated the air behind them.

She kissed his jaw. "We'll just have to wait until we hit my apartment."

Seth eased his foot off of the brake and pulled her head down to his shoulder. "No arguments from me."

"Hi, Allie, someone was here, asking about you."

Alexis glanced over at her building's superintendent, Beverly, as she entered the foyer. She hated her nickname, but since Beverly was really sweet and had helped her a lot over the four months she had lived there, she allowed it. In return, she also helped the superintendent with airing out recently vacated apartments and occasionally showing empty ones to potential renters. Suspicion tingled her spine. "Did you know them?"

"No," Beverly replied with a shrug. "He seemed really agitated, though."

"How so?" Seth asked, his voice wary.

Beverly tapped her finger on her cheek and thought for a moment. "Every time a bird chirped or if someone made any kind of noise, he'd jump. Come to think of it, he couldn't stop moving his hands and talked really fast. I had to listen to him for a few minutes to understand what he was saying."

"What did he look like?" Seth's voice took on a deeper, darker tone.

"Well, he was wearing a hood, so I couldn't see him too well. I could see some long blond hair sticking out of it though, long bangs. You know my eyesight isn't the best, Allie, and I forgot to put on my regular glasses. I say he was a bit shorter than Seth and wasn't as good looking."

Alexis stared at her landlady in disbelief, trying not to believe what she was hearing. "What do you mean?"

"This one wasn't as broad-shouldered, and he was really

thin."

Fear crawled up her spine. *No.* He hadn't found her apartment building, had he? Alexis started stiffening, despite Seth's arm around her waist.

"Anything else?" This time, there was a bit of hate included in Seth's voice, an indication he was thinking along the same lines.

"Yes, he smelled. Really bad."

"Like what?" Alexis couldn't keep the panic out of her voice.

"It was like rotten gym socks, sweat, and booze. He needs a bath, too. I don't think he's had one since his mama last gave him one. I could smell the body odour from three feet away. It was disgusting."

"Okay, thanks, Beverly," she heard Seth reply as Beverly disappeared outside.

Anger, frustration, hate, and disgust coursed through Alexis, and panic started rising. *Fuck, that little prick found out where I live! Why did I ever think I'd be able to stay in this town and start over? I got too comfortable after Seth threatened him and chased him away.* She started to tremble. Nausea bubbled in her throat. She gulped to alleviate it and closed her eyes. *I was stupid to think that I could have a normal life, and I was stupid to think I could have a life with Seth. I have to leave – now. I can't have him going after Seth or anyone else I care about. He'll do it to spite me for leaving him.*

She let out a small moan of fear and pain. Seth's arm moved from her waist to her shoulders, and he hugged her tight to his side. Instantly, her trembling stopped, and the nausea started abating. *Shit. I can't leave Seth. I love him too damn much. What the hell am I going to do? Brett will keep coming after me until I'm dead, or he is.*

Seth's low growl made her jump. "Pack as much stuff as you can in twenty minutes. You're not staying here until that loser is in jail."

She had to stand her ground this time. She was done running and done putting up with her ex-boyfriend finding her wherever she went. "I'll be okay."

"He can easily get through the security locks, Alexis. All he has to do is buzz someone and say he forgot his key. Instant access to your place," Seth murmured in her ear, and concern made his voice shaky.

"He may not know which one is mine," she mumbled lamely, even though she knew it wasn't true. Her name was next to the buzzer for 3G, in plain view of anyone in the lobby.

"You know that's bullshit. If he asked about you now, he's been scoping this place out for a while, and probably knows your routine from sunrise to sunset, and even how many times you go to the bathroom."

Fuck. Seth was right. If Brett had appeared to Beverly, it meant he had been lurking for a while. Deflated, she nodded. "How long do you think I'll be there? I don't want to impose." For once, she wished she had adopted a dog, a large one, but she'd never got around to it. She had been too busy with her new life, and lately, her relationship with Seth.

"As long as it takes," he replied.

"What if it's for the rest of my life?"

His calloused fingers caressed her cheek, and his forehead rested against hers for a long moment. "If that's what it takes to keep you safe, yes."

"Seth, I think I'm—"

The rest of her words were cut off as he kissed her tenderly. She responded, feeling safe and protected for the first time since her childhood. A realization that Seth wouldn't let Brett near her made her tremble. It became a full-body shudder when she realized he'd die to protect her.

Please, don't let it come to that.

A scream echoed around the apartment building complex.

"A-lex-us, where the fuck are you?"

Seth whipped his head around as he shoved a duffel bag of Alexis's treasured items into the camper style storage area on the back of his truck. Sure enough, the little shit disturber was there, his back to Seth as he stomped up the walkway, bellowing for Alexis to show her face.

"I know you're there! I saw you bring down a suitcase. Are you running away from me again? You know I don't like that," Brett bellowed in a sing-song voice.

"Hey, asshole, why don't you go bug someone else?" someone yelled from a second-story balcony.

Brett flipped them the finger and screamed, "Go fuck yourself, this ain't your business, fucknuts!" His movements were jerky, uncoordinated, and he weaved a lot. That and the odd slurring in his voice made Seth wonder what he was on. Brett started swinging a baseball bat as he approached the main entrance to Alexis's building.

This was escalating fast. If it wasn't stopped soon, things were going to get really nasty, and someone was going to get hurt. *It better not be my sweet Alexis. I'll fucking kill him with my bare hands if he touches a hair on her head.* Seth's hands fisted as he started moving stealthily toward the drunken man's back, carefully watching to make sure he wasn't seen. It was easy, considering Brett kept his focus on the door as he screamed obscenities and demanded to see Alexis.

Within fifteen feet of Brett, Seth had to swallow hard due to bile rising in his throat. *Beverly wasn't kidding. He smells worse than summertime compost! What was he doing, rolling around in dog shit for a week?*

"Allie, Allie, Allie, come out! I have a present for you!" Brett sang hoarsely and whipped the baseball bat around a few times.

Don't let her come out, don't let her come out. Seth grimaced when she appeared on her balcony, hands on her hips and a glare at Brett. *Aw, fuck!*

"Go away," she snapped.

"I can't! I love you, Allie! Forgive me!" Brett cried.

"No, you don't. You only wanted me to be your fall guy and give you my paycheck so that you could blow it on drugs." Seth could hear the disdain in her voice. It carried around the parking lot. With a sideways glance, he saw several people gathering outside and others standing on their balconies, watching the scene unfold. *Fuck.* The last thing they needed was an audience.

A heartbeat later, he saw a few had their smartphones out. *Witnesses. Good. Maybe this time, the police will put this mother-fucker away for life.*

Brett continued in his singing voice. "I'm clean now, don't you see? Allie."

Her sarcastic snort echoed around the parking area. "What is it this time? I'm thinking some whiskey, and what else? Meth? Or is it cocaine again?"

Brett weaved in place. "Only a little shot of scotch." He fell down and managed to get himself upright by using the bat like a cane.

"One little shot? Uh-huh. You're tripping over your own feet, Brett. Nice try," she said sarcastically.

Her gaze met Seth's, and she blinked once, twice, three times before she refocused on her ex-boyfriend. Brett moved three feet closer to the building and stopped.

"I haven't slept in days. I'm so sick about not being with you!" Brett slurred loudly.

Seth used the noise level to move closer, almost within reach of the drunk, presumably high, and increasingly agitated man yelling at Alexis.

Brett started swinging the baseball bat around again.

Seth sneaked another step closer and swore, inwardly, when the sole of his boot connected with a small twig, creating a sound louder than a thunderclap to his sensitive ears. Brett whipped around with a snarl. Seth choked hard when the bat connected with his stomach. *Damn, it hurts like hell.* He hoped he hadn't broken any ribs. Winded, he barely managed to stay on his feet. Brett swung again, and Seth managed to dodge a shot aimed at his head. He backed up a few steps, trying to buy himself some time to regroup.

"You!" Brett screamed and started toward him with the bat swinging back and forth. "She's been fucking you, hasn't she? I knew she was a whore!"

Only Seth's quick reflexes kept the wood from connecting with his body, even though he was being forced to walk backwards. He never broke eye contact with Brett, not even to check if he was backing into a pole or a car—he had to focus on avoiding getting hit again. *Gotta stop this before he hurts anyone else or gets his hands on Alexis!* He carefully watched Brett's movements, hoping to see a pattern. They were random, awkward, and erratic. Sometimes the swings were at Seth's waist level, his chest, or lower. Another step backwards and Seth cursed, inwardly, when he felt the solid wood of a power line pole against his back.

Brett's glazed eyes widened, and his smug smile showed rotting teeth.

Seth almost vomited on his boots—the stench of Brett's breath was so brutal. He waited quietly, hoping for an opening.

In the distance, a faint whine turned into a louder one. Sirens. Seth silently thanked whoever had called the cops. He had been too focused on protecting his girlfriend to remember to dial the emergency number.

"Brett, stop!" Alexis screamed.

Seth glanced to his left, saw Alexis standing on the concrete walkway in front of the security door, and turned his gaze back to Brett. *Damn it, why did she come down? She was safer in the building!*

"Stay out of this! I have a score to settle with this jerk. I'll give you your present when I'm done with him!" Brett took another swing, but it went low.

Seth jumped as it almost connected with his foot, then landed on the ground in a roll. His ankle connected with Brett's shin and Seth smirked. Brett screamed in pain as Seth's steel-toed boot connected with his knee.

With a growl, Brett swung the bat again. Seth automatically raised his arms in front of his face in defence. Something connected with his left arm with a loud *crack* and he tried not to yell as pain screamed through it.

"Brett, stop," Alexis pleaded, her voice much closer.

Shit, go back inside, Alexis! Don't look at her, keep your eye on the pussyface! Seth kept focused on the other man, even with the yellow mist of pain blurring his vision. He pulled back a leg to kick out if Brett came any closer.

"Fuck off, Al!" Brett yelled and threw out an arm.

Alexis screamed.

Seth heard a loud thud on the ground not far from him. Through the haze of agony from his arm, he could see her lying on the ground next to him, her face pale, eyes closed, and redness along her left cheek. Fury rose in Seth's gut. The little bastard had punched her. Hate choked him, making his vision turn red. Brett shouldn't have touched her.

Brett loomed over him and snarled in triumph. Hate fueled Seth's actions as he kicked his foot upwards. The heel of his steel-toed boot connected with Brett's groin. Brett growled, stumbled, and almost fell. Seth kicked out again, connecting in the same spot. Somehow Brett managed to stay upright.

The third hit was hard enough to send him stumbling backwards and falling to the ground, dropping the bat in the process. Brett whimpered and curled up into a fetal position, vomited a few times, and started to snivel.

The sirens became deafening. Help had arrived, almost too late. Seth stumbled to his feet and moved to kick away the bat, but someone clamped his shoulder. "We'll take it from here," a man said.

Where's Alexis? Seth turned and saw she was sitting on the ground, with Beverly holding her up. Fury shot up his spine when he saw the bruise forming on her cheek. He glared at Brett, who was now flanked by the first man and another large, heavily muscled man, and Seth barely resisted the urge to pummel Brett to a pulp with his bare hands. Men who hit women were only a notch above those who hurt children.

"Seth?" Alexis's voice penetrated the anger.

She needs you free, not locked up in a cell.

"Seth? Are you okay?" Her voice sounded panicky.

He turned and held out a hand to her. *Calm down, fuckhead. She needs you to be strong for her sake.* "I'm fine, sweet girl," he replied as she took it and pulled herself to her feet. Automatically, his arms slid around her, and he hugged her tightly. *Let the authorities take care of him. We finally have enough on him to put him away for a long time.*

An officer locked Brett in handcuffs and read him his rights as he was led away. *Hopefully, it's for good. That motherfucking prick has caused a lot of problems for a lot of people, especially my sweet girl.*

Alexis trembled against him and started to cry. He held her close, not wanting to let go. "Shh," he whispered.

"Sorry," she sobbed, "I thought he was going to kill you."

Her tears were soaking his shirt, but he didn't care. She was safe. "He didn't. I'm fine, Alexis."

"I can't stop crying. I was so scared for you." She sniffled and lifted her head.

Seth kissed her, hard, needing the contact and reminder that she was okay. As her lips softened under his, the unnamed emotion struck him in the gut, his groin—his heart.

"I love you, Alexis. More than life itself," he murmured against her mouth.

She stared up at him, eyes wide and mouth agape.

"Miss Graves, Mr. Mitchell, sorry to interrupt, but we're going to need you both to come to the station."

With a long sigh, annoyed the mood was shattered, Seth turned his head to nod at Constable Manning. "How'd I know you'd say that?" he asked the officer irritably as they followed her to her cruiser.

CHAPTER TWELVE

Bridgewater Police Station
An hour later

Seth irritably snapped, "Constable Manning, I've told you everything that happened, six times. Hearing me repeat the same thing for the seventh time isn't going to help your investigation!"

The blonde-haired and blue-eyed officer sighed. "I am sorry, Mr. Mitchell, but we want to be sure there are no variations in your story. If there are, Brett Galloway could get away with yet another round of harassment toward Miss Graves."

Seth stopped his pacing and stared at the wall. *Shit. Alexis shouldn't have to look over her shoulder, wondering if that prick is going to show up again.*

"You don't want that, do you?" she asked.

Fury fueled his bellow. "I want that bastard out of my woman's life!" Enough was enough. He was sick of his girlfriend being stalked and harassed.

Constable Manning nodded and pointed to the chair across the table from her. "Let's go over it one last time. You were loading a suitcase into the back of your truck when the accused arrived?"

"Yes. He was carrying a baseball bat and was swinging it around when he was yelling for Alexis." Seth couldn't hold back the shudder as he thought about what might have happened if he hadn't been there.

"Then what happened?"

He sat down and calmly repeated his version of events again to the police officer.

Twenty minutes later, she nodded. "I think we have enough to charge him with not only stalking but assault on both you and Miss Graves."

"You sure the jerk won't get off this time?" *He'd better not.*

She smirked. "If he does, it'll be a miracle. One of the tenants filmed it on their phone and turned it in."

He grinned evilly. "Good."

After taking a few more notes, she glanced at him and asked, "Are you sure you're okay and don't require medical attention? You have a large bruise on your forearm. It's really starting to swell. I suggest you get it looked at."

Seth realized he was unconsciously rubbing the area in question. What had started out as numbness and a dull ache was starting to become sharper, more pronounced. "I'm okay."

"Mr. Mitchell, you were hit hard with a baseball bat. It's possible you broke a bone."

He shook his head. "I'm fine. If I get any worse, I'll go to the ER. Thanks."

Constable Manning stared at him. Seth guessed she didn't believe him. "May I check it? I have first aid training."

"I guess, but you're not going to find anything." *Bullshit.* It was really painful and felt like someone was grinding glass in his arm.

The young constable rolled her eyes and gently poked at the edge of the large, almost black bruise. It wasn't painful, more annoying than anything. She poked around a few more times. No pain. She slid a hand under his arm. That hurt a little, but Seth didn't allow her to see it.

"Move your fingers for me, please."

He tried doing as instructed. No, go. *Shit.*

"Uh-huh. Does this hurt?" She gently used a finger and her thumb to apply pressure to both sides of his arm.

White-hot agony shot through his body and stars exploded in his vision. Seth tried not to yelp in pain.

"Mm-hmm. I hate to say it, but you're going to require medical attention. That arm feels broken."

Aw, fucking Christ. Concern for his girlfriend overrode his pain. "Did Alexis get checked out yet?"

"I looked at her before she went into interrogation. So far, she's fine, but like you, is refusing a checkup."

"I'll only go if she goes," Seth said stubbornly.

Constable Manning rolled her eyes skyward. "That's what she said about you. Is there anyone you want to meet you at the hospital?"

"My partner and best friend." He rattled off Blaine's cell number.

Alexis let the ice pack drop to her lap.

"Put that back. The doctor said to hold the ice pack on there for another ten minutes," Mirabelle scolded.

"He also said it's just a bruise, and I don't have a concussion." *Bug off, Mirrie. If I didn't need you and Blaine to drive Seth and me home, I'd tell you to take a flying fuck.*

An icy softness was pressed against her cheek. She tried pushing it away, but Mirabelle held it still. "Honey, you don't want your eye swelling shut, do you? You won't be able to see out of it."

"What the hell is the difference? I can't see now that my glasses are broken." Even close up, Mirabelle was blurry. Anything beyond her was a haze of colours and shapes. With a sigh, Alexis hoped her old glasses, tucked in a box in her apartment, were still wearable. They'd been weak for her a year ago. She made a mental note to order a new pair with her current prescription the next morning from her favourite online site. She wouldn't be able to drive until her new glasses arrived in a week's time, but it would be better than not seeing anything.

"Surely you want to be able to see Seth a little when he's finally released, don't you?" her boss asked.

Alexis sighed. Mirabelle had been prattling on about her and Seth's no longer secret affair for the five hours they had been waiting for him in the ER waiting room at a Halifax hospital. He had a broken forearm. Alexis felt sick every time that hit her, even though she knew it could have been worse. *A lot worse.* Another wave of nausea bubbled in her throat, held back only by sheer determination. It was too close for her, the first time anyone had been hurt by Brett. He was escalating and getting more dangerous in each new city or town. *He hurt Seth, dammit. What will he do next? Kill someone?*

Someone tucked a tendril of hair behind her ear, a gesture meant to soothe, but Alexis didn't feel comforted. She felt like the entire world had crashed down around her. Seth loved her and would die to protect her. She couldn't live with herself if anything else happened to him at Brett's hands. She hugged her aching stomach, hard, and a tear slid along the bruise on her cheek. *I have to leave now, before he hurts Seth again, or goes after someone else. Tomorrow.* Seth needed her to help him that night, or so she told herself.

Something blurry appeared in front of her, and a calloused hand gently touched her chin. "Oh, god. Seth," she whimpered as she leapt up and threw her arms around his neck. She felt his good arm slide around her waist as he stood up, lifting her feet off the floor as he hugged her tightly.

"How long will you be in that cast?" Mirabelle asked.

"A few weeks." Seth kept his arm around Alexis after her feet hit the floor. He cricked his neck, and she saw the sling supporting his left arm.

Automatically her arm went around his waist, supporting him, even if he didn't need to lean on her. His arm tightened around her shoulders briefly before they started walking toward the exit.

"Well, it's a good thing you're right-handed. You can still do a few things while that heals," Blaine said.

"Like what? Doodle? I can't carve worth spit like this, and you know it," Seth grumbled.

"I can do the carving," Alexis told him.

All eyes turned to her.

"Why not? It's not like I wasn't doing a little here and there with Seth's help," she mumbled.

"Get new glasses, and you have a deal. I don't want you slicing your hand open because you can't see shit, sweetheart," Seth ordered.

"Don't go there, or I may start waving my arms around. Since I'm so blind, as you put it, I may hit something vital." Alexis let the threat hang in the air.

He paled a little.

"Get a room, will you?" Blaine muttered.

Seth and Alexis flipped him the finger at the same time.

In Seth's bedroom that night, Alexis stared down at Seth, who was lying in bed, and asked, "Are you sure you want me to sleep here? What about your arm?"

He shook his head. "It won't bother me. They had to numb it to set the bone."

"But still—" Hesitant, she was terrified of hurting him. A broken bone was agonizing. She had cracked her femur in school in a sledding accident, and it still ached during the worst nor'easters in the wintertime.

"I'll be fine. Come to bed." Seth held out his good arm and beckoned to her.

Reluctantly, she crawled under the covers but stayed close to the edge of the bed.

"Get over here." Seth's order was a low growl.

Nice try, Mitchell. If you think I'm going to allow myself to hurt you, you're wrong. "I'm not going anywhere, go to sleep." She snuggled under the blankets and sighed.

"I sleep a lot better with you against my side. Now get your ass over here, woman."

The order was clear. Either let him touch her or else. With a long sigh, she scooted over just enough for her arm to brush his good one. She yelped in surprise when he wrapped the arm around her waist and rolled her on top of him. "Seth Mitchell, what the hell are you doing?"

He thrust his hips upward, hard, his erect cock pressing against her mound. "I need to fuck you." His hand slid up her hip, under her t-shirt, and cupped a breast.

Tingles of pleasure rippled downwards into her core. It was tough not to grind her hips into his rigid length. "I don't think you're in any shape for that." He shifted again, this time thumbing her nipple. Tingles of delight sparked along her nerve pathways. She couldn't stop a moan from sliding out of her throat. "This isn't a good idea," she panted.

"You're soaked, aren't you? Bet you'd come if I touched you." His fingers slid downward, slid the lace of her panties aside, and worked their way between her lower lips.

Alexis bit back the scream that was building in her chest. Involuntarily, her hips thrust against his hand in a silent demand for his touch. *Shit, it feels amazing.* Lust overrode her worry and flooded her senses. "Damn you. I can't control myself when you're touching me like that." She moaned loudly and leaned forward to grip the headboard so she wouldn't squash him.

"Don't fight it. Let me make you come," he whispered huskily.

He stroked her clitoris once, twice, three times. Pleasure tingled along her cunt. "Oh god, yes!"

"Come for me. Show me how much you love my fingers inside of you." He slid a finger up her sheath and drew a circle around the walls.

"Seth, please, stop teasing me!" she pleaded and ground her pussy against his fingers.

He rubbed the pad of his finger along the front of her sheath several times, applying more pressure each time. Her pussy started convulsing as she came with a loud cry of release, her nectar soaking his fingers. She was vaguely aware of him lifting her slightly before he roughly pulled her downwards.

"My turn." He thrust his hips upward to impale her with his rigid cock.

Oh god, it feels so fucking good. She squeezed his length with her pussy muscles and ground her hips downward.

"Ride me, Alexis. Show me how much you love it when I fuck you," Seth ordered hoarsely.

Too far gone in her lust to listen to reason, she did as he said. She slid up and down, rocking her hips and squeezing his dick with her pussy. Her nectar coated him. She could feel it soaking the inside of her thighs. The feel of his pubic hair and balls rubbing her slit sent her over the edge. She screamed as her pussy pulled his cock deeper into her. It elicited a long growling shout of pleasure from Seth just as his spasms started, and a heat invaded her lower regions.

Shaking from the most intense orgasm she'd ever experienced, Alexis gasped for breath and almost fell upon Seth's chest. She eased herself down to lie on top of him, the scent of their combined sweat and lust for one another blanketing the room. His chest hair was soft against her cheek as she listened to the pitter-patter of his heart. He groaned between pants, and a shiver of alarm went through her. *Shit, I should have said no. I hope I didn't hurt him.* "Seth?"

His hand fisted in her hair a moment before he angled her face to his and gave her a long, tender and love laden kiss.

God help me, I can't leave him, now or ever. What am I going to do?

Seth gasped for air and tried to regain his senses. "That was fucking amazing."

Alexis let out a long sigh. "Says the man who probably won't remember it once the drugs wear off."

He blinked at her. "What drugs? I only had a shot while getting the bone set."

"What?" She shot to a vertical position, still straddling him.

He yanked her downwards, so she was lying on his chest again, using his good arm. "I don't like being doped up, and after that asshole ex of yours, I didn't think you'd like it either."

She growled. "Medical reasons are one thing, what he was doing was another. Cripes, I could have hurt you."

"I'm okay. I was careful. It doesn't hurt too badly, no worse than it did before we started playing around." It was true. The local anesthesia still dulled the sharp jabs, but he knew that would change in a few hours after the shot wore off. He'd wanted to have sex with his woman — the love of his life — before it was too painful for him to think.

"Don't do that to me again. I thought you were so fucking doped up that nothing would have stopped you from jerking off if I hadn't let you touch me."

"I was still horny enough to do that, but I was hoping I wouldn't have to." He gently brushed her bangs out of her eyes and placed a soft kiss on top of her head.

She eased off of him and snuggled up to his side. A few minutes later, he could feel her starting to relax into slumber, her body slowly becoming languid.

We should really talk about what happened, while we have a chance. After tonight, who knows how crazy things will be between court dates and everything else, while we're dodging Mirrie's questions about a wedding — Fuck it, why avoid it? His arm tightened around her, and Alexis sighed softly. *Why not allow Mirrie to go nuts for once? I'm in love with this woman, and it's time to let the world know.* "Alexis?"

"Mm?" Her voice was dreamy. He could tell she was almost out.

Hell with it, it's not like it can't wait a few more hours. "Go to sleep."

"Um, okay." She cuddled closer to his side and looped her arm around his waist.

"I love you, sweet girl," he whispered against her hair.

He only got a soft sigh in reply.

Monday Morning
Mirabelle's Shop

"Seth Mitchell, what in the hell do you think you're doing?" Mirabelle demanded from below him, to his left.

Without taking his focus from the half-painted mural in front of him, he shot back, "What does it look like?" He dabbed a little blue paint inside the outline of a tulip. Two more colours would be added to it later, to give it depth and make it look more realistic.

"You're not supposed to be on a ladder until that cast comes off!" she scolded and came into his line of vision.

Seth shrugged. "I want this done before the grand opening."

"Alexis said she'll work on it. Get down. Now." Mirabelle glared up at him.

"I'm in the middle of something." He stared at the flower intently before moving on to another one. He dipped a fresh detailing brush into the can of violet paint in front of him and slowly started filling in the finely outlined flower.

"Seth Mitchell, get down before I call Alexis and tell her what you're up to." Mirabelle tugged on the hem of his jeans, and there was a warning note in her voice.

His brush went wide on the can. "Hey, don't shake me! I

don't want to mess this up."

"It's my store. I'll fucking shake you if I damn well please," she replied angrily.

With an annoyed sigh, he glanced down at his best friend's wife. "I can't finish this if you don't let me do my job."

Mirabelle's blue eyes were narrowed to thin slits, and her face was bright pink. She looked pissed. "Your job is to help Alexis. Period. Not to be doing stupid things like climbing even a short step ladder when you can't hang on to it!"

"I got bored of sitting down and doing nothing. You know I hate being idle."

Her gaze softened a little. "I know, and I understand, but I'd still feel better if you kept your feet on the floor, not on a ladder's rung."

"Mirrie—" He let out a long sigh.

"Besides, what if Alexis sees you up there? She'll freak."

He glared at her for a long moment to show his disgust at her using his woman to provoke him into doing what she wanted. With a long sigh, he slowly started gathering his supplies. "All right, you win. Jesus."

She gave him a triumphant smile and started putting the covers on the cans of paint.

He had just hit the floor when Alexis found them.

She squinted up at the mural and shoved her older glasses upwards on her nose. "Was someone working on that?"

Seth shot Mirabelle a filthy look.

"Yes, I was," Mirabelle replied.

Alexis blinked. "I thought you didn't know how to paint."

Mirabelle grinned. "Seth was telling me what to do. It was fun even with him grumbling at me."

"If you're the one doing it, why aren't you on the ladder?" Her gaze turned to him and narrowed a little.

Shit, she knows.

"I wanted a break?" This time Mirabelle looked guilty.

"Uh-huh, and I don't need glasses," Alexis shot back, her

voice full of sarcasm.

Seth rolled his eyes.

Her gaze latched on to him. "I'm letting it go, this time. However, if I find out you're doing stuff against doctor's orders after this, there will be trouble."

"You'll do what?"

Alexis glanced at Mirabelle. "We'll discuss that later."

Mirabelle held up her hands and started backing away. "I think I heard a customer." She disappeared.

Alexis stared up at him with her arms folded across her chest and started tapping her foot.

"Sweetheart." He gave her a coy smile and trailed a finger down her arm.

Her eyes narrowed. "Don't sweetheart me, Seth. You know it's not safe for you to be on a ladder yet."

"I know that, love, but I hate not being able to do my work."

She smiled a little. "You can afford to take a few weeks off while your arm is healing."

Ugh. Please. I'm so fucking sick of not being able to work after two days of this shit. How am I going to keep busy for three weeks while my arm heals enough for me to use it a little? "I'm bored. Do you really want me idle?"

She sighed. "You don't want to do anything I suggested, like design some woodwork for the Wile's renovations, or just draw for fun?"

He took a step toward her. "I don't like leaving this job unfinished."

"Then let me help you finish it. Supervise me and pass me stuff. Don't risk breaking your neck doing something unsafe." There was a soft, worried plea in her voice, one that Seth couldn't ignore.

He slid his good arm around her waist and pulled her close. "On one condition."

She snuggled up to him. "What's that?"

"You know those scarves you picked up the other day?" A naughty vision of her tying him to his bed caressed his mind. Damn, he loved it when she let herself go and became ultra-commanding in the bedroom.

"Mm, hmm. What about them?" She sounded interested.

"I want to use them in a very specific way." His voice lowered in timbre, just loud enough for her ears, and he flicked his tongue along her earlobe to emphasize his point. A soft kiss on her mouth and a forehead nuzzle had her snuggling deeper into his arms.

Her eyes widened a little as she got it. "That sounds interesting."

He loved the spark that lit up her gaze. "Smile for me, Alexis."

She complied. "Why?"

"Seeing you smile makes me happy."

She grinned.

Without thinking, he clamped his mouth over hers, not caring if Mirabelle or a customer saw it. *Alexis is my girl, and dammit, I'm going to let the world know it.*

Two days later
Seth's House – On the back deck

Seth's arm snaked around Alexis's waist and pulled her backwards.

With a giggle, she eased down to sit on Seth's lap, careful not to brush the arm encased in a cast, held in place by a sling. A moment later, his mouth claimed hers, and his tongue slid between her teeth. Automatically, she reached around to tangle her fingers in the short hair at the nape of his neck. The arm around her tightened for a moment, the strong fingers digging into her hip.

Disappointment shouldered its way in when Seth pulled

back a little. It disappeared when he started gently placing kisses along her forehead, eyebrows, nose, cheeks, and finally back to her mouth. Feeling cherished was something Alexis wasn't familiar with, but she loved it.

"More," she murmured when he pulled back a second time.

"After a bit. I think we need to talk." His voice was low, husky, and intimate. It sent a shiver of pleasure through her body, but something else was lining his words.

Alexis guessed what it was. They hadn't talked about the incident that had Brett facing multiple charges of aggravated assault, stalking, public intoxication, and other crimes Alexis hadn't known about. Brett's slimy lawyer wasn't going to get him off this time, not with the videos from Alexis's neighbours and the witness accounts. Constable Manning suggested Brett was going away for at least ten years.

It would be a decade of peace for Alexis. Hopefully by then, he would have gotten the message to leave her alone and move on with his life. She shifted enough to stare at Seth over the top of her new glasses. "It's about Brett, isn't it?"

Seth brushed her bangs out of her eyes. "No, but it sprang from what he did."

Deflated, her shoulders drooped.

Seth patted her bottom. "I'm not dumping you if that's what you're afraid of."

Whew. She had been worried he'd break up with her after things quieted down. Alexis immediately relaxed and let him pull her closer. "I thought you would, after what he did."

Seth's brow furrowed. "Didn't you hear what I said right before the police herded us into their cars?"

"Yes, but I thought it was—"

"The heat of the moment? No." He shifted and touched her chin.

Nervous, Alexis lifted her gaze to his. In his deep blue

depths, she saw so many things—protectiveness, honesty, kindness, and something that made a thrill journey up her spine.

Love. Seth loved her, just like she loved him.

She reached up to touch his lips with her fingers. *Tell him the truth. He needs to know why you stayed here after Brett found you the first time.* "I love you, Seth," she whispered.

Silence.

She closed her eyes. *Shit. Now I've done it.*

A moment later, Seth cleared his throat. "I love you, too, Alexis."

Whew! She relaxed against him and snuggled deeper into his lopsided embrace.

"That wasn't so hard, was it?" he asked.

"Finding the courage to say it was the roughest part of it," she admitted.

He kissed her. Tingles of pleasure tickled her heart, her lips, her arms, everywhere. She adored this man. He was her entire world.

After a few minutes, Seth pulled back and murmured, "Marry me, sweet Alexis."

She froze. *He didn't ask me that question. Did he? Oh shit.* "What?" she exclaimed, shocked.

"I asked you to marry me." He chuckled and kissed her again.

His fingers slid up her back to rest on the nape of her neck, and his thumb started making a slow, soothing circle just below her hairline. Normally the action would have had her whimpering and languid, but the shock of his quiet statement erased it.

Her eyes bolted wide open. She suddenly felt like a deer caught in headlights. *No. Don't ask me that, Seth. What if Brett gets out and starts causing trouble again? You don't want that. You deserve a better life and a better woman than me. Fuck. Why now?*

"No," she replied, her voice shaky.

At first, Seth wasn't sure if he had heard Alexis right. "What?"

She stiffened, even when he tried massaging her neck and back.

"We don't have to do it right away. We can wait a while and see how things go." His hand dropped to her waist, and he tried caressing her hip. Hurt slammed him between the eyes when she pushed herself away, off of his lap, and she strode to the edge of the deck with her back facing him. Her breathing was erratic and shallow like she was prey and was cornered. *What is she so afraid of?* He stood up.

"I'm not ready," she whispered when he came up behind her.

He slid his arm around her waist and kissed her shoulder. "It's okay. It takes time to adjust to things."

She started trembling. He tightened the arm and nuzzled his face into her hair.

"Seth—"

"We can live here, and we'll slowly start getting things together. We don't have to set a date, not for a while."

"Seth, please—"

"You can go to the shelter and get a cat if you want." He loved cats and had considered adopting one a few months ago. Having Alexis move in would be the perfect time to get one, or two, depending on if they could get a pair that got along.

Fear started travelling through his gut when she turned and touched his cheek. "Please listen to me," she whispered.

It turned into a knot of despair, but he kept rambling, to keep up the illusion everything was still perfect. "Do whatever you want to make my house into yours—"

"Seth, I love you, but I'm not ready for a huge step like

that," she pleaded.

He froze.

"I'm finally free of Brett for the first time since I was eighteen. I need time to think, to breathe, and to stop looking over my shoulder. I want time to enjoy being me without the burden of Brett, or him causing trouble."

His arm dropped to his side. Hurt burned its way through every nerve in his body, which made his jaw clench, and his eyes snap closed.

Her fingers caressed his shoulder through his t-shirt. "If we get married now, I'll feel like I'm chained up again, and I'm scared I'll start resenting you after a while."

Time morphed backwards, to the same spot on the deck.

"You won't let me have access to your money because you like keeping me chained up like a dog!" Janie screamed.

"What money? You've already gone through what little I had, and you've driven me into debt so far, it'll be years before I can dig my way out!"

"Liar! You have more, and you don't want me to have it! You don't want a wife. You want a pet!"

Cool fingers touched his jawline. "Seth?" The female voice echoed in his head for a second before it mutated to something higher pitched and with hate behind it.

Chained up. Like a pet.

His hand fisted as the pain along his nerve endings flipped to blue-hot rage.

"Get out!" he bellowed.

Disbelief slammed into Alexis like a truck. "What?"

"Get the fuck off of my property. Now!" Agony burned his voice, making it hoarse and deeper.

"Why?" Shock zinged through her a second time.

"You want to be free? Fine, you have it. I won't chain you up." He took a step toward her.

Fear travelled up her throat. She could see the veins in his good arm pop out as his muscles bulged a little. "I didn't mean it that way."

"Then how did you mean it?" he demanded hotly.

"I need some time to figure out what I want without looking over my shoulder," she replied. Damn it, her voice shook. Hearing and seeing him in so much pain was killing her inside.

"I said we could wait a while," he muttered.

"What if it takes more than a few months for me to settle down?" Alexis still felt jumpy, like Brett was going to appear any second. She hadn't felt this bad since the first time she took off on him. Ten years of hell, thanks to Brett, and it would take a long time to get over the paranoia.

"If you really love me, it wouldn't even be an issue." He took another step forward.

Automatically, she backed up. *Don't aggravate him anymore. Get him calm so he can think rationally.* One, two, three more steps, and she was trapped against the railing. Terror made her visibly shake, her eyes wide, face pale, and a cold sweat broke out on her neck. Agony's heavy fire burned into her as she watched his glower darken, and his hand lifted. *He wouldn't, not after knowing what Brett did to me.* She couldn't move. The pain in his eyes trapped her.

Abruptly, he turned and stomped away. Fear kept her frozen in place.

Glass shattering had her jump a clear foot in the air. When she dared to move her gaze, she saw the small, glass-topped table between the chairs was shattered. Blood dripped from Seth's knuckles onto the shards and the varnished wood beneath them. Had he hurt himself so he wouldn't hurt her? "Oh my god, Seth!" she whimpered and took a shaky step toward him.

He whipped around, and the hate blazing in his eyes

stopped her. "Get out of here."

The snarl sent a shudder of dread through her.

"I'm taking you to the hospital." She moved another step closer and was rewarded with a louder snarl.

"Get your things, and get the fuck out!" he bellowed and pointed to the driveway with blood dripping from his hand. There were at least several lacerations, one that needed stitches.

The sight of the blood made a knot of queasiness rise in her throat. "Why?"

His body was shaking violently, with rage or hurt, Alexis wasn't sure. She took a chance on another step, and he bent over to scoop up a fallen, now empty beer bottle. He lifted it menacingly above the cast on his left arm, as if he was going to smash it.

Her feet moved her body backwards without consciously thinking about it.

"You don't like being chained up, as you put it, so leave." Hate flew from his lips.

"Seth, I'm not leaving." She wasn't. Not until they cleared the air between them.

"You are if I say so. I'll fucking call the cops if you don't get out of here now. Mirrie will give you your stuff after I pack it." He dropped the bottle and lifted his hand to point to the stairs leading down to the driveway. Blood dripped from between his fingers.

Vomit bubbled in her throat. "No," she whimpered in disbelief.

"Goodbye, Alexis." His voice was icy, strangled, and venomous.

She stared at his cold, unwavering glare for a long moment.

He had made up his mind. They were done. Agony ripped through her, tearing her heart, and turning it into shreds. With a sob, Alexis turned, and without looking back, she ran down the stairs to her car. One last, lingering glance at the house was all she allowed herself before she shakily put her car in reverse and tore off, the tires spitting rocks like misshapen bullets.

CHAPTER THIRTEEN

Three Days Later
Alexis's apartment

"Alexis Graves, open the damn door!" Mirabelle's voice carried a threatening note. Several loud knocks followed her bellow.

Alexis cringed and kept pulling breakable items out of the cupboards. One thing about living simply, you could pack in a hurry when the time came. She hadn't really unpacked more than the bare essentials, just in case Brett found her again.

"Alexis!" Mirabelle's voice rang through the wood again.

Fuck off, Mirrie. I can't keep working for you now that Seth and I broke up. Agony made her throat close, and a tear slid down her cheek. She wiped it away, annoyed her grief was rising to the surface again.

A few more bangs rang through the door. "I know you're in there!"

A loud crash had Alexis cringing again. *She's not going to leave until she sees me.* With a long sigh, she gave in and whipped open the door.

"It's about time!" Mirabelle exclaimed with a huff and her hands on her hips. Her eyes were narrowed, and her lips were pursed.

"What do you want?" Alexis asked with a sigh.

"An explanation." Mirabelle started tapping her foot.

"About what?" Alexis knew what Mirabelle was in a tizzy over. It was the damn letter stating she was moving.

"Quitting on the spot isn't like you," Mirabelle snapped, a little too loudly.

Across the hallway, a door cracked open. *Fucking nosy neighbours.* With a low grumble, Alexis yanked Mirabelle inside of her apartment and slammed the door.

"And what's with you looking for a job in Ingonish? That's a bit of a drive, isn't it?" Mirabelle demanded.

Alexis didn't reply as she brushed past Mirabelle and went back to the box on the counter, half-filled with breakables. *Who says I'm going to drive there from Bridgewater every day? It's not like I'm wanted here.*

Mirabelle followed her but stopped at the threshold to the kitchen. "Why are you packing?"

Alexis winced at the confusion in Mirabelle's voice. She wrapped a glass in newspaper and gently set it into a box. "I can't stay here." She tried to keep her voice level, and not let Mirabelle know how heavy the agony of losing Seth was in her chest.

Mirabelle stared at her. "Is it because of your ex-boyfriend? I thought he was going to stay in jail for a long time."

Alexis shook her head. Well, maybe it was a little. That was what had prompted Seth's question and her refusal.

Mirabelle was silent for a long moment. "Did you and Seth have a fight?"

Hearing his name sent a harpoon of pain into Alexis's heart. She shrugged, unable to reply around the large lump in her throat.

"Oh, sweetie, it'll get better."

Alexis stiffened when she felt Mirabelle's hand on her shoulder and heard the soothing tones. The tears were hot irons in her chest. It hurt to breathe. She trembled as she tried to contain it.

"Do you want to talk about it?" Mirabelle asked softly.

A gentle hand tucked a loose tendril of hair behind her ear, and a soft pat on her back was Alexis's undoing. With a sob, she crumpled against Mirabelle's side and clung to her boss. "He asked me to marry him," she choked out between loud wails.

"Oh, sweetheart, that's wonderful." Mirabelle sounded so happy.

Shit. She's not going to like this. "No, it's not," Alexis whimpered between sobs.

"Yes, it is. He really loves you."

"Then why did he break up with me?"

The hand patting her back suddenly stilled. "What?"

"I can't marry him, Mirrie. I can't." The burning agony in her heart became heavier and felt like lava. Seth's reluctance to let her have some space had ripped her soul to shreds.

"Why not?" Mirabelle demanded.

"Seth deserves better than someone like me."

Mirabelle framed Alexis's face in her hands and stared at her intently. "Says who?" she asked with narrowed eyes and compressed lips.

"Dammit, look at me. My entire life is a fucking mess. I have an ex-boyfriend on crack who follows me wherever I go. He tried killing Seth, for fuck's sake. I need time to breathe before I can think about getting married," Alexis replied with a sob. Her throat hurt, and she felt like she was going to barf on Mirabelle's suede heels.

"Did you tell Seth all of this?" One of the heels started tapping, a gesture that always sent Alexis into red alert.

"I tried, but he wouldn't listen." Her head drooped, and her chin bounced to her chest.

"Did he say he could wait for a while until you were feeling more confident about marrying him?" Mirabelle asked, her eyes becoming thin slits.

"Yeah, he did," Alexis admitted.

"Uh-huh," Mirabelle muttered, disbelief thick in her tone.

What the hell? "What's that supposed to mean?"

Mirabelle's hands dropped to her hips, and she glared at Alexis. "It means I think you're a stupid, fucking chicken."

Alexis blinked at her former boss, taken aback. "Why?"

"Any woman in her right mind would jump at the chance to marry a man like Seth."

"I'm not denying that, Mirrie, but—"

Mirabelle shook her finger in Alexis's face. "Oh no, you don't. No buts, young lady. You just screwed up a great thing because you don't think you're good enough for Seth? I don't blame him for getting upset if you're going to take that attitude," she scolded.

"Mirrie—" Alexis pleaded. *Oh shit.*

Mirabelle held up a hand and snarled, "Be quiet! I'm not listening to any more excuses. If you love Seth, you'll march your ass over to his workshop and talk to him."

"I can't. He'll kick me out." Like he did the other day after their argument.

"He's not unreasonable once he calms down," Mirabelle shot back.

"How do you know he's not angry now?" Disbelief ran from her head to her toes.

Mirabelle stared at her blankly.

Right. I should have known she had her nose up his ass, too. "How upset is he?"

Mirabelle's expression softened a tad. "He refuses to go into the store. He said he'd rather drink turpentine than go near anything that reminds him of you."

"Shit." Tears prickled Alexis's eyes. *Damn.* She had done a number on him. It sounded like he was hurting as much as she was.

"I'm sure he'll be better if someone drops by with an apology and tells them they are in love with him," Mirabelle said and gave Alexis a pointed look.

"Positive?" Hope rose in Alexis's heart.

"I sure am. See you on Monday morning at the store. Your

resignation letter is null and void, for the record," Mirabelle said with a wink.

Alexis nodded. She'd return to the store on Monday, come hell or high water. It was only Thursday, so she had the weekend off to straighten things out with Seth. *Thanks, Mirrie.* "Okay," she replied, teary-eyed.

"Think about what I said." Mirabelle patted Alexis's arm.

"I will." *I already have, and I know what I'm doing. Mirrie, you are the best.*

The instant the door clicked shut behind Mirabelle, Alexis ran into her bedroom. Thank heavens her clothing wasn't packed yet. She quickly pulled out a short blue denim skirt, sandals, and a pink blouse that showed off her cleavage, one that Seth had admired several times. Determination and love for Seth fueled her actions.

He wouldn't know what hit him.

Seth's workshop, behind his house

Country music blared out of the overhead speakers, the mournful songs a testament to Seth's despair and confusion. He sat in the corner of the dark workshop, his head against the wall, his face contoured in agony, and his hand fisted around a bottle of scotch as more of the sorrowful lyrics swirled around him. *Why did I tell her to leave? I should have let her have more space than demand we get married right away.*

He lifted the bottle to take a swig, but it fell lax to his side. *Drinking never solved my problems with Janie, so why the fuck am I doing it with Alexis?* With a loud curse, he chucked the full bottle across the room. It hit the inverted horseshoe above the door and shattered — the strong odour of booze mixed with the scents of sawdust, glue, and fresh paint. "Fuck her," he muttered, his voice half slurred from exhaustion and being half drunk.

The lights came on, and he felt exposed. "Fuck who?" a feminine voice asked from his left as the music abruptly stopped.

He glanced up and saw Alexis standing by the stereo system. White-hot agony tore through his chest. "Get out!" He picked up a hacksaw and heaved it. It clattered to the floor and missed her by several feet.

"Oh my god. What the hell were you doing?" Alexis demanded.

"Rearranging the shop. Don't you like it?" he snarled and gestured with his left arm, still encased in the cast. The entire shop was in disarray. Tools were strewn across the floor, the workbenches, his stools and every other flat surface. Shattered planks and shards of wood littered the floor. Paint coated several areas, from the tables to the tools, and up the walls.

She sighed and picked up a screwdriver. "Why did you do it?"

"Why the fuck not? It's all mine." He clumsily wiped a hand across his mouth.

"You're ruining your livelihood." She picked up another tool and set it on a paint-free spot on one bench.

She looks so fucking delectable in that short, tight skirt, and that fucking blouse that always sends my libido screaming for her pussy in my face.

He forced his half-erect cock and desire for her to calm down. *Fuck. I'm not drunk enough to be numb. Not yet. Why did I throw away the bottle?* "That's my fucking problem. Mind your own business, Alexis."

She didn't glance at him and slowly started picking up the mess, one tool at a time.

Seth watched her with guarded eyes. He wanted to jab a screwdriver between his ribs to stop the agony of seeing her. He felt something by his hand and fisted it. A sharp twinge reminded him of his encounter with the glass table three days before. The stitches were healing nicely, but still hurt and itched a lot. *Better to feel it there than in my heart.* He lifted his hand to his thigh and felt the weight of a hammer. His eyes closed, and his jaw clenched, uncontrollably, as he lifted his arm to heave it.

A whiff of flowers preceded a firm but soft hand on his wrist. "Don't do it."

He opened his eyes to glare at her. Her face was barely six inches from his, her luscious lips almost begging for his kiss. He inhaled sharply and ground out, "I don't have to listen to you."

"No, but aren't you afraid of hurting yourself? What if Blaine walked in just as you threw it? Wouldn't you feel bad if you hit him?" Her fingers touched his cheek.

Her soft touch sent zaps of pain through his heart. "Blaine won't show up. I told him to leave me alone."

"What if it was Mirrie? She won't listen to you."

His arm started going lax. *Fuck.* Alexis was right. Mirabelle wasn't one to give in. "Tough on her," he muttered.

"More like tough on you if you wound up hitting her. She'd never let it go." She gently rubbed her thumb up and down the side of his wrist.

More tension eased out of his arm. "Why are you here?" he asked wearily.

Tears formed in her eyes. "I've been thinking."

"About how fast you can blow this town, right?" His words were heavy with pain. His entire body felt leaden like he was turning to stone.

She shook her head. "No. I can't leave, not this time."

Lava poured through his veins, and it hurt so much. "So, you get some kind of perverse pleasure in torturing me, huh?"

She touched his cheek. "Seeing you hurting makes me sick."

He let it erupt and tried pushing her away. "Then leave me

alone!" he bellowed in her face.

"I can't leave you, Seth. I love you, and I want to marry you," she whispered.

He froze and stared at her.

A tear slid down her cheek, and she wiped it away.

He stiffened when she started to crawl onto his lap. Pain and love mixed together in a torturous cocktail as she straddled his legs and cradled his head in her hands.

"Please, don't throw away a great thing because of my fears. Help me work them out, and help me become the woman you deserve," she murmured, placing a kiss on his lips.

His eyes closed as her mouth covered his again. It was so hard to resist her.

"Help me find myself, Seth." Her lips were so soft, and her taste was making him sick with wanting her. "I love you, Seth. Don't kick me out again. Please. Let me stay."

I'm not sure if she's trembling violently from cold or nerves, but dammit, it feels so good to have her in my arms again.

Her lips brushed his jaw, his cheek, and finally, his neck. She sniffled loudly, the mournful sound tearing away his last means of defence.

With a low groan, the hammer fell to the floor, and his arm clamped around her. "Baby, you don't have to change. You're perfect now," he whispered.

She lifted her head, tears shimmering on her cheeks, and stared down at him. "How can I be perfect when my entire life is a fucking mess?"

He brushed the hair out of her face and stared up into her deep brown gaze. "You just are." It was all he could get out before she kissed him again.

The pain evaporated like morning dew, and Seth relaxed as her tongue slid into his mouth. Alexis snuggled closer to him on his lap and rested her head on his shoulder. Seth obliged her, needing the contact with her for comfort as much as she needed him.

"Are you really in love with me?" she finally asked after a while.

"More than you know, my love." He nudged her cheek with his hand.

She lifted her head enough for him to kiss her.

"Seth?"

"Hmm?"

"How anxious are you to have kids?" She blushed.

"I'd love to have one, but we can wait if you want." He wanted to be a dad, but it wasn't necessary for a while. Alexis needed to adjust to living in one spot and being adored instead of abused. In time, they would talk about it.

"I'd like that. I feel too greedy to share you with anyone else for a while." She smiled slyly.

He snickered. "I'd like to get rid of the condoms, though. That night we didn't use them was amazing."

"The best sex ever." She nuzzled her mouth against his.

"We'll top it sometime." He didn't know how they would, but with time, he knew all of their best loving was in the days and years to come.

"We always do, each time it happens. I hope it stays like this."

"If we work on it, it will, Alexis." He stared deep into her eyes, relieved and joyful she was there, and willing to work on their relationship.

She gave him a watery smile. "I love you."

He kissed her. "I love you, sweet girl."

"When do you want to set a date for the wedding?" she asked and stroked his arm above the cast.

"When you're ready. I won't push it this time." He wouldn't. If they were together, that was all he cared about.

She grinned sheepishly. "I don't have a place to live at the end of the month."

Damn, how much do you want to bet she is already packing?

"You gave your notice. Fuck, what were you thinking?"

"I was going to move out of Bridgewater, but I don't want to now." She played with the collar of his t-shirt and blushed.

His next question came so damn easy. It was what he had hoped for all along until she was ready for another, bigger step. "Move in with me."

Her brow furrowed. "I thought it was all or nothing."

"Not this time. We'll stay here and take each day as it comes."

She kissed him, her tongue sliding between his lips. Desire licked at every nerve ending, zooming into his soul. His cock went from flaccid to fully erect in no time, burning with the need to fuck her until he couldn't breathe. He shifted his hips to press his erection against her mound and slid his hand under her blouse. His fingers found a bare, engorged nipple, and he flicked it with his thumb.

Alexis moaned low in her throat. "Your hand and arm," she whispered in protest.

"Fuck them," he muttered. "I need you, sweet Alexis." He moved his hand down to her skirt. He shoved it up, loving the feel of her bare skin against his fingers. So silky. Her pussy was bare, wet, and ready for him—god, how he needed to get into her now. "Help me with my pants. I can't wait much longer, sweetheart."

"You have me, Seth. Now and forever," she murmured and started unbuckling his belt. He let out a loud groan as her fingers found him.

She was his.

Just like he was hers forever, scars and all.

The End

YOU MAY ALSO ENJOY THE FOLLOWING FROM EXTASY BOOKS INC:

Stricken
V.J. Allison

Excerpt

Marti Marlowe Lewis groaned inwardly and resisted the urge to bang her head on the desk as Kara breezed into her office with an armload of files, her travel mug, and a smug smile.

Damn it, she's early! She must have figured out I've been avoiding her!

Kara plopped the files on the desk and flopped down in a chair.

Marti rolled her eyes skyward. "What's on your mind, Kara?"

"Oh, not much, but I'm betting there's a lot on yours."

"If you mean Leslie, you're right. She's still on suicide watch at the hospital." It was a reference to their most recent emergency case, a fourteen-year-old girl who had been raped.

Leslie hadn't been fully suicidal until the test showed she was carrying her rapist's child.

"I wasn't talking about her, but damn it if she still feels that dying is her only option," Kara said sadly.

"Yeah." Marti played with her pen. "Lucy asked me to be

Leslie's counsellor."

"Why won't you?"

"You know why."

"Martine, that in itself is exactly why you're the best one to help her."

"I can't. I won't be able to stay detached and professional if I go near her. I did offer insight to what Leslie may be thinking and feeling, just in case Lucy needed it."

Kara stared at her and, with a sad smile, nodded in understanding.

Talk revolved around the teenager and a few other clients.

Marti was starting to think she had distracted her friend long enough to escape, and growled in resignation when Kara leaned back in her chair and narrowed her brown eyes.

"So, do you feel like telling me why you practically dragged me out of the agency on Monday, and why you didn't say shit about Dennis working for your cousin's company?"

A headache started forming along Marti's temples and forehead. "Sorry, I wasn't thinking straight after seeing Sheryl."

"So she knows your cousin. Are you sure she'll tell Miranda she saw you?"

"Yeah."

"Damn those memories, huh?" Kara knew the rift between Miranda and Marti started about seven years ago, and why it had happened.

"Uh-huh." Without seeing anything, Marti turned her gaze to the windows that faced the Citadel and sighed.

No way was she admitting it wasn't really Sheryl that made the past rear its unwanted head. Kara knew she had been engaged to someone in Miranda's employ, but not his name, only her former betrothed was from a rich family, and a real estate agent.

Miranda's business sense is still razor sharp. He's who I would have picked to run the Halifax branch.

"I understand why you don't want to talk to Sheryl. What I don't get is why you were so cold to Ewan. You're a lot nicer than that."

Obviously, ignoring him had the opposite effect of what I hoped. Damn it.

"He knew my ex-fiancé."

"And since he knew your ex, I suppose he's also bringing back some stuff you'd rather not think about, huh?"

Marti nodded.

"If you knew him before, you also know how nice he is."

Nice? He's one of the sweetest, kindest guys in the world, a true gentleman.

Until you get on his bad side . . .

"Yeah, I guess."

"Ewan knows how great you are. Your name came up when we were discussing some of our friends, and he seemed to be open to meeting you. I can't see how you two could stand there and glare at each other if you were friends."

"We weren't exactly friends," Marti replied, a little too defensively. "He worked for Miranda. With my ex. Can we please drop it?" She grabbed a file and flipped it open, determined to distract Kara and change the subject.

She felt Kara staring at her. "What?"

"Do you still love him?"

Marti blinked. "Do I still love who?"

"Your ex-fiancé."

"Kara, that's one of the stupidest questions you've asked me."

"Martine, think about it. You were pretty damn rude to Ewan the other day, and I can tell you're squirming now by thinking about your ex. That tells me there's still a little something left in your heart for him."

"There hasn't been anything left for him, not since I met Gabriel," she whispered with a shake of her head, and felt a weird clench in her stomach as she remembered the look on Ewan's face when their eyes met for the first time in over six years.

"I can understand why you may not feel comfortable around any of Dennis' coworkers because it's your cousin's company, and how you're not talking to Miranda, but keep in mind you're going to be seeing them from time to time, if we have a party or something."

Marti shot her friend a filthy look. "Kara—"

"Are you really that scared of two people who know your ex-fiancé that you'd stop hanging out with your friends? That sounds pretty damn selfish to me."

Marti's headache went from a dull roar in her ears to a jack-hammer between her eyes. Her first instinct had been to run after seeing Ewan's name listed as branch manager in the lobby.

Seeing him standing at Sheryl's desk made a rush of un-welcome memories from their time in Bridgewater flood her system.

Watching his face turn to stone and his gaze fade from its characteristic warmth to an unnerving frost had hurt. There had been a time when she only saw it aimed at others, mostly her cousin, in the nine months she and Ewan had been a cou-ple.

It ended over seven years ago. We're both adults. It's not like Bridgewater, it's a much bigger place. Kara and Dennis are not my only friends here. I can still avoid him most of the time. If we do run into each other, we can be polite.

Or I can.

Whether he is or not is up to him. Knowing Ewan, he'll pretend I don't exist unless we're alone . . . Then he'll bawl me out again, and I won't blame him if he does.

With me, he was all hot air, which is a sign he cared. It's when he gets cold it can get nasty, and he starts cutting people down with words. I always hoped he'd never get that way with me . . .

"You're right, Kara, it is pretty damn selfish. I won't do it, on the condition you let me help you in the kitchen for a while, until I'm more comfortable being around them."

"You got it. Sorry I had to corner you like this, but you've been hiding from me all week. It was the only way I could grab you and torture you enough to talk."

Marti nodded and smiled as her mental burden lightened a little. "I forgive you."

Kara grinned evilly.

As her friend turned her attention to the files between them, a long shudder went up Marti's spine as another image of Ewan's frigid stare rose in her memory.

Please let him have the sense to let things go this time . . .

ABOUT THE AUTHOR

V.J. Allison was born and raised in southern Nova Scotia, Canada, and her work reflects her strong Maritime roots. She is a stay at home mother to a son on the autism spectrum, married to the love of her life, and "mama" to a rescued Maine Coon cat named Marnie.

She has been writing various stories of novel length and short stories since her school days, and sees writing as a vital component to her life.

When she isn't writing, she loves to read romance and science fiction novels (notably Star Wars); listen to music (heavy metal, rock, alternative); watch various crime and forensic dramas; watch science fiction television shows and movies; and spend time with her large family and many friends.

This self-proclaimed geeky rocker chick is a warrior and advocate for various chronic illnesses including Occipital Neuralgia, Trigeminal Neuralgia, Diabetes, Migraines, and Glossopharyngeal Neuralgia. She is also an advocate for the prevention of animal cruelty and is a voice for Autism Awareness.

https://vjallison.com

www.ingramcontent.com/pod-product-compliance
Lightning Source LLC
Chambersburg PA
CBHW070623130626
46556CB00001B/450